"You do like walk

Before I could retort, he had me twisted around so my back was cradled against his chest, and he had my wrists pinned at my stomach with one hand. The other was at my throat, his thumb digging under my jaw to force me to tilt my head to the side and expose my jugular. His fangs scraped over my skin and a scream was dragged out of me as I struggled vainly against his hold.

"Ah, yes, I remember now. This is what you fear, is it not?"

My only answer was to increase my helpless squirming, a thin sound of panic and terror dying in my throat.

"Well, then, pet, since you're not much impressed by pain, perhaps this will deter you." His cool lips trailed upward, rubbing against my skin like melting ice until they brushed against my earlobe to whisper his threat. "Every time you disobey me, I will bite you. Make no mistake, the last time I did was in haste. From now on I will make every effort to make it last. Each . . . and every . . . time."

As those last words trailed off, he struck, his fangs piercing my skin so quickly and cleanly that all I felt was pressure, not pain. Then, whatever the hell it is in vampire saliva that makes it feel good kicked in— and this time I was writhing against his hold for a totally different, far more shameful reason. . . .

Books by Jess Haines

HUNTED BY THE OTHERS

TAKEN BY THE OTHERS

DECEIVED BY THE OTHERS

STALKING THE OTHERS

FORSAKEN BY THE OTHERS

ENSLAVED BY THE OTHERS

Collections

NOCTURNAL
(with Jacquelyn Frank,
Kate Douglas, and Clare Willis)

THE REAL WEREWIVES OF VAMPIRE COUNTY
(with Alexandra Ivy, Angie Fox,
and Tami Dane)

Published by Kensington Publishing Corporation

ENSLAVED
BY THE
OTHERS

JESS HAINES

ZEBRA BOOKS
KENSINGTON PUBLISHING CORP.
http://www.kensingtonbooks.com

ZEBRA BOOKS are published by

Kensington Publishing Corp.
119 West 40th Street
New York, NY 10018

All Kensington titles, imprints and distributed lines are
available at special quantity discounts for bulk purchases for
sales promotion, premiums, fund-raising, educational or
institutional use.

Special book excerpts or customized printings can also be
created to fit specific needs. For details, write or phone the
office of the Kensington Special Sales Manager. Attn.: Special
Sales Department. Kensington Publishing Corp., 119 West
40th Street, New York, NY 10018. Phone: 1-800-221-2647.

Zebra and the Z logo Reg. U.S. Pat. & TM Off.

First Printing: July 2014
ISBN-13: 978-1-4201-2404-0
ISBN-10: 1-4201-2404-8

First Electronic Edition: July 2014
eISBN-13: 978-1-4201-3516-9
eISBN-10: 1-4201-3516-3

10 9 8 7 6 5 4 3 2 1

Printed in the United States of America

Acknowledgments

As always, I must thank my beta readers for their tireless efforts to set me straight.

Kristin, thank you for helping me finish this puppy on time and with minimal psychological damage. You are my favorite architect.

Tori B., you make me laugh and gave me encouragement I didn't know I needed.

Tori N., you're bloody brilliant. Thank you for helping make this a better book in ways you may never know.

J.C., you are the best cheerleader, and don't let anyone ever tell you otherwise.

Brooklyn Ann, you helped me figure out how to fit in a touch of romance in the darkest of moments. How the hell did you manage that?

Kate, I'm sorry that I'm not sorry, but the socks had to stay.

To those who had a hand in the research that went into this book, whether they knew it or not, thank you. A special word of thanks to Captain Awkward and the rest of the Awkward Army for introducing this lurker to terms like "pantsfeelings" and concepts that gave more depth to parts of this story than I thought I was capable of capturing in words. To the people of YouTube, Twitter, and the blog-o-sphere I follow, there are too many of you to list, but I love you fiercely for the education and entertainment you provide. A huge thank you to MacAllister Stone and the gang at the Absolute Write Water Cooler for providing invaluable resources and the kind of camaraderie one could only expect from other writers who have been there and done that.

I want to acknowledge the Polaris Project (www.polarisproject.org) for the education they provided on the current state of human trafficking in the United States and abroad. Their website was an invaluable resource for me when doing research for this book. I hope you'll consider showing your support of the Polaris Project, and other organizations like it, to help put an end to human trafficking.

Thank you to my agent, Ellen Pepus, and to the team at Kensington who have worked so hard to make these stories shine and get them into the hands of readers. John, Peter, Vida, Ross, Alex, Justine, and everyone else who had a hand in getting the H&W Investigations off the ground, you guys are the best.

Last but certainly not least, thank you to all you fans out there.

You all rock my socks. Thank you for all you do.

*He who fights with monsters should look to it
that he himself does not become a monster.
And when you gaze long into an abyss,
the abyss also gazes into you.*

—FRIEDRICH NIETZSCHE

Chapter One

My mind was a fragmented haze, but I found the glue necessary to pull it back together as soon as a voice I hadn't heard in years—except in my nightmares—rang out.

"I know you're awake. Open your eyes."

Panic drove me to move before I was fully conscious of the decision to do so. Hurling myself off the floor and in the opposite direction of his voice, I hadn't made it two steps before cold, strong fingers wrapped around my wrist, jerking me back and into his arms. Cloth brushed against skin that hadn't been bare before I lost consciousness, heightening my terror. I quickly closed my eyes, not wanting to meet his gaze. Despite knowing it was useless to fight, I squirmed as much as I could against that iron grip.

"Calm yourself," he said, not unkindly. I made a small, helpless sound, squeezed out of me when his hold tightened. "I only wish to speak with you. I don't mean you harm."

"Liar," I wheezed, redoubling my efforts to escape. "Let go! Murderer!"

"It's cute when you say it."

I made a sound, half laugh, half sob. Oh, yeah, that was funny all right. Memories of a room full of dead kids on a dance floor, of slick gore gleaming under a strobe, of dead eyes and a woman in a blue shirt being drained of every drop of blood, assaulted me.

Hilarious.

His grip tightened, choking off my panicked, nonsense noises. Once I quieted down, the vampire held me to him with one arm. His free hand grasped my chin and forced my head up and to one side, then the other. Inspecting. No doubt spotting the telling scars on my neck, tiny and faded as they were.

"Your fear of me is understandable but unnecessary. I need answers, Shiarra. That's all."

I didn't open my eyes, but I stopped struggling. My heart was still racing, and panic was still urging me to fight like a wildcat. It was the wash of helplessness that led me to weaken, stilling in hopes of finding some later opportunity to escape.

Captive. Kidnapped by a murderous monster who had every reason to want me dead. Oh, God. If I didn't figure out a way to get out of here, *now,* I was going to die. There was no maybe about it—this time there was no one around to stop him, and even with the Other-taint in my blood, I had no hope of overpowering or outrunning him. He had proximity. Eye contact might strengthen his hold on me, but when we were this close to each other he could exert some control over my will and body and there would be nothing I could do to stop it.

"You know very well what I can do to you. I'm too pressed for time to wring answers out of you right now. If I release you, will you sit and speak reasonably with me?"

When he put it that way, it was hard to think of him as a bad guy. He sounded accommodating, almost sensible.

Except he was the furthest thing from rational. Max Carlyle was crazy; a mass-murdering sociopath. Not only had he abducted me—was this the third time, now?—but this time he'd learned from his prior mistakes and taken away everything familiar, right down to my clothes. I had no idea if Sara or Devon were dead or alive. No clue if Royce knew what had happened to us or if any of my friends knew where to find me. Dragging things out might be the only way to get through this intact. If I gave Max what he needed, he might kill me. If I didn't, he might bind me to him by blood again and *then* kill me. At least cooperating—to some extent— meant keeping my sanity.

My voice came out in a dry croak. "After—will . . . are you going to let me go after I answer you?"

He laughed, the sound a soft rumble in his chest that vibrated through my bones. "You should know better by now. I will go easier on you than originally intended. Fair enough?"

I couldn't answer—I was too busy shaking from

the icy chill in the air and terror at the images those words conjured.

He loosened his grip on me, but only to slide his arm around my waist as he urged me to walk. Though I hadn't the faintest clue where he was taking me, I still didn't dare open my eyes in case I might inadvertently look into his own and be spelled into a mind-warping black enchant. Redundant, perhaps, since I'd forever be obligated to answer his call when in close proximity—like now—but I couldn't stand the idea of losing what scraps of free will I had left.

We stopped, his hands shifting, guiding my shaking frame like one might a broken marionette. He helped me into the seat, and I sensed him crouch down before me. A cold void where something warm and living should have been. I gripped the chair arms, my nails cutting into the fabric and a faint cry escaping me at the chill of his hand placed so familiarly upon my bare knee.

"Now, then. Do tell me how you came to be among Clyde Seabreeze's retinue. I was under the impression that you sought sanctuary with Alec."

My voice shook, teeth chattering as I forced out a few words. "Vacation," I lied. With Max it was a reflex to keep anyone connected to me safe from his wrath. "Just a vacation. He heard I was coming."

"A vacation." His tone was incredulous. "Alec allowed this?"

"Not his choice," I said, perhaps a little more forcefully than necessary. "I don't belong to him."

"No. Not anymore."

I didn't know what to say to that.

"Did Alec give you a taste of his blood?"

"Yes." The words were bitter on my tongue, made more so by the copper taste of fear.

"More than once?"

"No."

"Excellent," he said, and my skin broke out in fresh goose bumps from the slight stirring of air as he rose. "Lucky you, little love. You get to live to see another day."

I couldn't help myself; some of the tension that had drawn me so tight eased.

"You're doing very well. Just a few more questions, pet."

"I'm not your pet."

He chuckled. "Quite the contrary. You haven't been permanently bound by Alec, so I just may keep you for myself. It might take a bit longer to break you in since you've gone through withdrawal, but I can assure you we've got nothing but time."

I couldn't help it. I surged to my feet, hoping against hope that I could outrun him, needing more than anything in that moment to escape.

His fingers scraped over my back, his laughter echoing through the room as I made a hectic, panicked dash forward. I finally opened my eyes, daring the risk to search for some way, any way, to get out of there.

There was a single door, which I made a beeline for. The handle wouldn't turn no matter how hard I twisted it, and my cry of frustration warbled into a scream of fear as his hand settled on my shoulder, shoving me around until my back was pressed against the door. Stunned, I stared up into his patrician features, forgetting momentarily to close my eyes as I met his pale gray gaze.

He looked exactly the same as he had the last time I had seen him. His dark brown hair was cut short, but not so much that I couldn't see the curls threatening to escape their gelled prison. Dusky skin was too dark for him to be taken as a vampire by a casual glance—not unless you already knew what he was. His tailored business suit didn't hide the solid, muscular build of his frame, or the shadow of a rabid, murderous predator lurking behind the mask of civility.

There was no pull of his mind overtaking mine. All he did was smirk and lift a hand to dangle a set of keys between us—unmistakably mocking me.

"Not yet, pet. I'm not done with you."

Gone were any thoughts of cooperating. Mindless terror drove me to shove and kick and scratch at him, screaming as I fought to get him off of me. He pulled me away from the door, only to let me go again—and I am not ashamed to admit that I ran like my ass was on fire, putting as much distance between us as possible. I didn't stop until I hit the far corner of the room, shivering as I watched him out of the corner of my eye as he stood there, contemplating me. I wasn't entirely naked, but I felt stripped bare.

He flicked through the keys, found the one he was looking for, and unlocked the door. Hand resting on the knob, he looked back over his shoulder.

"I'll give you some time to calm down. Come to terms with the fact that you're mine now."

I shook my head, denying it, arms wrapped around my stomach to keep the bile in. His voice softened, became almost kindly, making his next words even harder to bear.

"No knight in shining armor is going to save you. There is no escape from this place, or from me, unless I release you. The more cooperative you are, the better you will be treated. If you continue to fight me, I'll either bind you to me or gift you to one of my number like . . . what was the name of my progeny you destroyed?"

He honestly didn't seem to recall Peter's name. The first vampire who had bitten me. The first vampire I had killed with my own two hands. I was too frightened to raise my voice to tell him. It didn't take him long to shrug it off as inconsequential and continue.

"No matter. I'm sure you remember what that was like. There are others like him who would be pleased to have the opportunity to break you. Choose wisely."

With that, he walked out, the door latching shut behind him.

Chapter Two

I scoured the room for tools to use for escape. Max must have learned his lesson from the last time he'd thought he had me under his thumb. My purse, like my clothes—save for a bra, panties, and socks—was gone.

Fucking hell, my anti-Other mind mojo charm was gone, too.

Like the last place he'd imprisoned me, the damp, musty smell to the air told me I was underground. The room was small; four plain, white walls, with no openings other than the door that had locked behind him. Maybe six long paces from one end to the other, leaving little room to move around. Cold. Not freezing. Not so terrible that I couldn't stand it, but I was grateful for my socks. Even still, I rubbed my hands over my arms and legs periodically to warm them up. As for furniture, aside from a neatly made bed, the chair, and a chamber pot in the corner (ugh), there was nothing.

No closet, no bathroom, no clothes—just the barest of essentials.

Thoughts of confinement and torture à la Christian Bale's plight in *Rescue Dawn* danced in my head as I examined the furniture for small nails or staples. The thought of being stuck in this room for whatever remained of my life made me sick. There had to be a way out. I didn't have any bobby pins in my hair and the contents of my purse weren't available, so my options for picking the lock were limited.

It took quite awhile, but I managed to pry off a couple of staples holding the fabric to the bottom of the chair. They were big staples, but the metal was thin enough to serve for a makeshift lock pick. I tore off most of my nails in my frantic efforts to dislodge the metal bits from the wooden frame.

I took a moment to feel gratitude toward my brothers for teaching me something useful when we were hell-raising kids—and that I had thought to keep those skills honed in case of emergencies like this.

Bending the metal into shape earned me a couple nicks that were made worse by the way my hands were shaking. I had to hold my wrist steady with the other hand while I worked on the first part of the lock, which left me unable to do much about the few drops of blood trickling from my torn fingernails or to wipe away the panic-induced sweat dripping into my eyes.

What normally would've taken me thirty seconds

to accomplish stretched out into ten or fifteen minutes. It didn't help that the first staple broke and the second disappeared, flying away to land somewhere on the carpet.

When the lock finally turned over, I closed my eyes and said a brief prayer of thanks under my breath, along with a request to anyone listening that luck would stay with me long enough to see me safely out of this hell. Then I stuck my stinging, bleeding fingers in my mouth, because *ow.*

I hoped my work had gone unheard. Not knowing what might be on the other side, I slowly opened the door a crack and peered through, checking for any sign of Max or his cronies.

The small slice of the hallway I could see was empty. Emboldened, I edged out the door, taking in my surroundings.

Like the house in upstate New York where Max had once kept me trapped, the floors were a highly polished hardwood, this time accented with a gold design that glowed by the light of intricate gas lamps. I was unnerved to see that there were numbered doorways spaced evenly up and down the hall. Many were shut, but based on the uniformity and the outer locks on most of the doors I had no doubt these were all prisons identical to the one I had just escaped. There was a carpeted staircase at one end leading up, but I couldn't see what lay at the top. At the opposite end of the hall was a set of double doors, one open a crack, light shining through the thin gap. Both options were a long way off from where I currently stood. There were faint sounds of conversation coming from behind one or more of the doors—hard to tell which—but no one was in sight.

Since the damp chill and stale taste to the air made me pretty certain I was underground, I headed for the stairs, hoping no one else was trapped down here. I wasn't sure yet that I could save myself, let alone other victims Max might be exploiting.

The staircase was curved, so I couldn't tell how far up it went. I trod as quietly as I could, peeking around each corner before working my way up the next set of steps. Still, every whisper of my socks on the carpet, every gasped breath, sounded too loud to my own ears. I prayed no one was around to hear me.

I approached a landing at the top of the stairs but I couldn't see where it led. I waited, keeping quiet and still while I strained to listen for any company. It seemed clear, so I crept quietly up those last steps—and stopped.

There was another door all right, but this one didn't come with a lock I could pick. Next to the thick, handle-less security door was a numbered keypad. The pad had two small lights: a red one, which was blinking, and a green one, which was off. Cracking security codes has never been my forte, and I wasn't about to risk setting off any alarms.

The security camera staring down at me from the corner might have made my worry about alarms moot, though.

Fuck.

I had no way to know if I'd been spotted but, considering my luck, I was reasonably certain I was in for a world of trouble. The best I could do at this point was delay the inevitable.

I rushed back down the stairs, taking them two at a time. The door at the other end of the hall was still open, so maybe there was another way out.

Taking no care to be stealthy, I booked it, forcing deep, even breaths so I wouldn't develop a stitch in my side. The doors blurred by on either side, and I could have sworn I heard crying coming from behind one of them.

Bursting through that door was a bad, bad idea. I came to a screeching halt, nearly falling on my ass as I skidded in my socks on the smooth hardwood.

Max and several other vampires were lounging in an expansive room full of soft pillows, Greek statuary that depicted more sexual acts than a XXX-rated movie, and a few naked men and women chained between the figures who had the glassy-eyed gazes of people drugged or too apathetic to know or care where they were. No—not just men and women. There was a golden-skinned creature vaguely similar in form to a human that hung limp, unconscious in chains, right next to a doe-eyed wood nymph. That poor creature's leaves and bark were browning at the edges, all the flowers in its hair shuttered up tight or wilting. Dying.

It was like a surreal art show. The people—and otherwise—were on display as much as the statues, lit by tiny, soft spotlights that highlighted every asset they had.

One of the vampires turned to Max, a smirk curving his lips as he swirled his wineglass, the red liquid inside looking a bit too thick to be wine. His accent was a genteel Cajun drawl, somehow fitting perfectly with the unusual burgundy suit and thick dreadlocks. "You didn't mention anything about a redhead for sale."

"Have you been holding out on us, Euphron?" another chimed in, rising slowly to his feet. "This one seems more lively than the others."

If I hadn't already been so stunned by the contents of the room, I quite possibly would've been shocked immobile by the palpable interest of over a dozen—old—no, *ancient*—vampires locked on me. This included Max, whose steely gray eyes had widened as he sat up in the oxblood leather chair he had been lounging upon, clearly taken aback by my spectacular entrance. The weight of age in this tiny room was crushing; a football stadium would be too small to contain the power they were unconsciously radiating. It only took a few seconds for me to figure out that, whatever the hell they were doing here, obviously they now considered me part of the menu. I hastily backed up, using my arms to cover as much of myself as I could, while Max schooled his own features into a passably blank expression.

"Of course," Max said, his smooth voice carrying only the tiniest hint of irritation as he eased back in his seat and nodded in my direction, "I had not intended to showcase her so soon, though I don't suppose there's any harm in it. She is newly arrived, and has not been groomed properly for servitude yet. I doubt you would be interested in one so fresh, Kyle."

I skittered back, but a guard who had been standing to one side of the door barred my escape and I backed right into him. He laughed at how I jumped at the unexpected contact before giving me a little shove in Max's direction. I pivoted and darted to the side so I could press against the wall instead.

No weapons, no way out, and surrounded by vampires. I was on the verge of hyperventilating, and Max didn't seem keen on stopping the guy he'd addressed as Kyle from approaching me.

This new vampire was well dressed in a tailored I-make-a-thousand-dollar-suit-look-like-cheap-trash way. He set aside a cane with a freaky demon-looking thing crouching on top with what I would swear were real diamonds for eyes before approaching me. The power of his mien paled to the invasive metaphysical touch that brushed over my skin, tasting some intangible part of me and making me want a piece of sandpaper, a pumice stone, and the world's hottest shower to scrub the feel of it off of me. His manicured nails were blunt, shining as brightly as that whiter-than-white smile when he ran a smooth fingertip over my cheek, the other hand lifting to toy with one of my bra straps. I flinched and batted his hands away before twisting aside and putting some much-needed distance between us.

"Mm, perhaps you're right. Aside from being fresh, she's got facial scars. I do hope you weren't intending on offering damaged goods."

Though I wasn't often hung up about my looks, his comment sent my hand flying to my lower lip in

reflex. I often did my best to forget about the scar
left behind when Peter bit me, nearly tearing my lip
in half in the process of assaulting me.

Another vampire spoke up, his tone dripping
disdain. "Look how scrawny she is. No meat on
her where there should be. And that skin of hers
is a wreck—the mark on her face is not the only one
I see."

And another. "This one is disappointing, Euphron.
Very disappointing."

Scowling, I dropped my hand away and balled my
fingers into tight fists of rage at my side, finding the
condescending laughter of the others in the room
too much to bear. Max started speaking but I cut
him off, shouting loudly enough for most everyone
to flinch.

"I'm not a fucking pet, I'm not your fucking play-
thing, and who gives a flying fuck if I'm scarred? Ask
Max how it happened. I got it while I was busy
killing one of your own, you fucking *leeches*."

Stunned silence followed my pronouncement,
and I took advantage of the moment to dive for
the door again, shoving the surprised guard out of
my way.

"Stop."

The word was quiet but forceful. Every muscle
in my body went rigid and I found I couldn't move.

"Come here."

The other vampires watched with interest as I
turned around, breaking out in a cold sweat as
I fought the command. I managed to hold out until
I made the mistake of meeting Max's eyes. Though

I didn't want to do it, one foot lifted, then the other, bringing me closer to him. After three steps, I was back in the room—and found at that point that I *could* stop, though I couldn't withstand the power of his spell enough to run again.

"Extraordinary," commented another vampire that had been quiet up until now, his fangs glinting as he favored me with a wolfish grin. "I do believe this one doesn't care for you, Euphron."

A few of the others seemed to find this funny, smirking or making wry comments of their own. Catty bastards. Max frowned, but didn't push for me to come any closer. The other vampires had their attention locked on me, but my world had narrowed down to shoring up my steadily eroding will, and maintaining the precious few yards that separated us. Every muscle in my body was twitching with the strain of being locked in place so I wouldn't move any closer to him; it was painful to stay where I was, but I fought the urge to close the distance between us with every last shred of self-control I had left.

"As I said," Max addressed Kyle, though he kept his gaze locked on mine, "she is newly arrived. She may not be a pretty showpiece, but her looks are not what makes her desirable."

Despite myself, a hot flush of embarrassment warmed my skin, no doubt reddening my cheeks. He might as well have called me an ugly cow—and no woman, no matter who says it or how true a statement it might be, likes to hear that she's unattractive.

"This is Rhathos's little pet hunter."

The vampires gave a collective intake of hissing

breaths. Max's satisfaction with the statement was undeniable, as was the sudden, intense flare of interest from the rest of his guests.

"Better yet," he added, "she has not been permanently bound."

The man in the burgundy suit came close enough to press a calloused fingertip under my chin, tilting my head up so he could peer into my eyes. His own flashed a dull red that matched his suit, burning deep down in those sloe eyes, but they held no draw for me. I would've pulled away if I could have, but I was still locked in paralysis from Max's command.

"Fascinating," he said, brows lowering as he regarded me with a curious, puzzled expression. "I do wonder how you managed to get your hands on such a prize piece. Better, how you intend to capitalize upon such a windfall."

"Name a price," said Kyle, withdrawing a cell phone that looked like it might double as a tiny laptop. It didn't take me long to figure out he was using it to pull up a banking program to transfer funds. Great.

Max shook his head, holding his hand out to me. I couldn't help stiffly edging over to his side, taking his hand, and letting him pull me into his lap. Not content to have me on the edge of his knee, he snaked his arm around my waist and tugged until my back was pressed against his chest, his other hand lightly twined with mine. A clear message for the others: I was his possession for the time being. I would've gladly disproven any assumptions that I was anybody's property, but my body wasn't in a co-operative mood.

"No sale. I'm not prepared to release her to an-other yet."

Oh, wasn't that just darling. I wondered when he would be "prepared" and just what made me so valu-able in the eyes of these vampires. Worse, what Max thought he could wring out of me before he turned me over to someone else.

"Pity, Euphron," said the one who had earlier been busy toying with his wineglass. "I wouldn't mind getting a taste of that one. I don't suppose you'd be willing to part with her for a night?"

My stomach plummeted. Max waited so long to answer I nearly passed out from holding my breath.

"I'll consider it," was the dismissive reply.

Talk turned to how he had gotten his hands on me, and his estimate as to how long it would take to make me tractable. It wasn't a question of if, or how, but *when*.

Something about his hold had left me unable to speak. It didn't stop the helpless tears or the sick feeling twisting my stomach in knots as they calmly discussed my fate. Max assured the others that he would "personally" see to my "education," whatever the hell that meant, and that he had no intention of wasting this opportunity.

If I had to go down I'd do my best to take him with me. That was the only consolation I had to keep from going utterly mad in his arms while they talked about destroying everything that made me . . . *me*.

After awhile, the talk turned back to the people

chained between the statues. My fear and impotent fury grew when I realized they were here to be auctioned off to the highest bidder and that Max was selling them for hundreds of thousands of dollars apiece—and the ones with Other blood for even more. Some of the "assets" that prompted the vampires to drop more money included quirks of lineage, artistic skill, and, in one case, a gift with languages. All of my fellow humans, I was irritated to note, were smarter, more talented, *and* better-looking than me. Though I wasn't sure I should be so thrilled about that, considering Max had alluded to putting me up on the auction block at some point.

It felt like a long time before the vampires were done. Max's fingers occasionally shifted, making my muscles seize up in renewed terror, though I couldn't withdraw from his touch. He never strayed toward inappropriate territory, but the constant reminders that I was trapped and helpless was doing plenty to fray my nerves to the breaking point. I figured out before long that he was doing it on purpose to rattle me. A silent reprimand that no doubt would be followed by something worse once he was done dealing with his guests.

Their chatter shifted to talk of politics and investments. I made mental notes of incriminating mentions of their names and businesses on the off-chance I might get out of there someday. Never mind the lack of a retainer fee. Hunting down each and every one of these sick fucks pro bono, as a favor to the rest of humanity, would be my pleasure.

Focusing on a future that might never come was better than pondering what Max might be planning to do to me as soon as this meeting was over.

While they discussed their business, one by one, the people were freed from their chains. Half a dozen men entered to usher them back to the rooms in the hall. The newcomers were all dressed in suits much like the ones Max's men wore the day I was kidnapped off the street, back when I had met him the first time. The rapid, efficient way his people moved gave me the sneaking suspicion that this human trafficking business was something they did often.

Worse, none of the captives spoke a word or did a thing to struggle for their freedom. They moved where they were bid, but slowly, further cementing my suspicions that they were drugged. Please, God, don't let them be so broken that they couldn't fight for their freedom anymore.

Don't let that be me someday.

Chapter Three

Some time later, Max pushed me off his lap so he could stand to see the other vampires out. Once they were gone, escorted by the security guards to their rooms or to pick up their "purchases," he turned to me. I still couldn't move. Though I strained every muscle to back away, I couldn't retreat or even cry out as he closed the distance between us. Instead of touching, he circled me, shark-like, considering before speaking. All I could do was stand there and tremble, following him with my eyes.

"How did you get out?"

The words spilled out before I could stop myself. "Picked the lock."

A casual, backhanded slap sent me tumbling to my hands and knees on the floor, blood dribbling between my lips. Max absently licked his knuckles, tasting my blood. He paused, glancing at the smear on his hand with a frown before narrowed eyes refocused on me.

"You disobeyed me, pet. I told you to calm yourself and consider your options. Are you so eager to be given to another?"

Something inside my head loosened; I recognized that feeling. It was him retracting his mental claws long enough to allow me to answer him without forced compulsion.

"Fuck you." I spat, getting blood on his gold-tasseled loafers. He tsked.

"I suppose I should be glad of your interruption. I do believe Kyle has taken a new interest in my stock. Thank whatever gods you pray to, girl. Your punishment will be easier for it."

I closed my eyes and rested my brow on the floor, unable to reply. His fingers knotted in my hair, dragging me up to my feet. At the last possible moment, I straightened my legs and threw everything I had into punching him in the jaw.

It was like striking iron. My knuckles and wrist ached from the impact. For his part, Max flinched—which was satisfying—but that was all.

Well, not all. His eyes narrowed, and a hint of red came to his pupils, his fangs peeking out between his lips as he spoke. "My. You do like walking the hard road, don't you?"

Before I could retort, he had me twisted around so my back was cradled against his chest, and he had my wrists pinned at my stomach with one hand. The other was at my throat, his thumb digging under my jaw to force me to tilt my head to the side and expose my jugular. His fangs scraped over my skin, and a scream was dragged out of me as I struggled vainly against his hold.

"Ah, yes, I remember now. This is what you fear, is it not?"

My only answer was to increase my helpless squirming, a thin sound of pain and terror dying in my throat.

"Well then, pet, since you're not much impressed by pain, perhaps this will deter you." His cool lips trailed upward, rubbing against my skin like melting ice until they brushed against my earlobe to whisper his threat. "Every time you disobey me, I will bite you. Make no mistake, the last time I did so was in haste. From now on I will make every effort to make it last. Each . . . and every . . . time."

As those last words trailed off, he struck, his fangs piercing my skin so quickly and cleanly that all I felt was pressure, not pain. Then, whatever the hell it is in vampire saliva that makes it feel good kicked in— and this time I was writhing against his hold for a totally different, far more shameful reason.

Unlike last time, he didn't suck greedily at the wounds, drawing my blood as rapidly as possible. Instead, it was something infinitely worse; he used his lips and tongue to do things that had taken previous lovers both hands and a map. Every twitch of his lips sent new pulses of pleasure shooting like lightning down my spine, making me shudder in ecstasy. He took his time about it, too, never sucking hard enough to steal more than a few drops of blood at a pull.

By the time he withdrew, I was desperately

aroused and so caught up in his arms that there wasn't a thing I could do about it.

Copper-scented breath washed over my cheek as he pressed a kiss there, even that small touch enough to set my now hypersensitive skin aflame. "Remember, pet. This. Every time."

Oh, I remembered. Despite the danger, despite a tiny part of me knowing exactly where I was and whom I was with, all I could think about was being pinned under Royce's weight, the feel of him inside me, the pressure of his mouth on my throat. Max's bite made it feel like I was there again, in that moment, enthralled by the pain and pleasure that made every cell in my body burn with need. With an intense longing to do anything—*anything*—to feel it again.

Max unceremoniously dragged me over to where the statues stood in silent judgment, pressing my wrists to the wall and then shackling them over my head. He followed with my ankles, cuffed roughly two feet apart with only inches of slack. Dismally, the first thought that occurred to me was that he was doing it so that there wasn't even the slightest chance I might rub my legs together to find some relief.

I dangled in the chains, gasping for breath, watching him with heavily lidded eyes. I couldn't move just yet, and the shock and need had not worn away enough for me to think of anything outside the blaze of desire.

"Now, I will give you one more opportunity to do as I told you. Consider your options."

With that, he left me hanging there—in every sense of the word.

It didn't take me long to figure out that being stuck in chains sucks.

The inability to scratch or rub at an itch because your arms are up over your head and you can't shift your weight is torture. Particularly when you feel like there's a fire burning between your legs. The knowledge that you can't do anything about it only heightens the sensation, makes it worse, in my opinion.

The horrible thing was coming to the conclusion that I very well would have given myself to Max if he'd made any sort of move to get me in bed. Therein lay the terrifying truth about vampires, the thing that haunted my nightmares and why I had been so very afraid of Royce. If they wanted you—*really* wanted you—you had no control over your body and no choice about how you felt about what they were doing.

Once I got my breath and a semblance of strength back, I fought against the chains for a while. They didn't give, and I was no closer to finding either freedom or relief than I'd been in Max's arms. Twisting my wrists didn't loosen the cuffs, and there wasn't enough room for me to slip a hand through.

It took a long, long time, but eventually the burning heat between my legs faded, and I was left with a fresh surge of terror as good sense returned.

Good *God*. To consider—even if only for a moment—sleeping with Max Carlyle . . . !

Shame liberally dosed with the sick feeling of

being trapped resulted in the unsteady but oh-so-familiar sensation of bile churning in my stomach. Crying hadn't done me any good so far but, to be perfectly honest, it was all I was capable of doing once the hopelessness of my situation sank in.

Not to mention the loathing and disgust I felt for myself, for my weakness, for feeling even the smallest margin of desire even when I knew I couldn't help myself. It wasn't my fault. I knew it wasn't.

That didn't make me feel any less sick and violated.

Max was right about one thing: more than pain, holding the threat of biting me over my head if I should step out of line would keep me in a cooperative mind-set. I'd continue to hunt for means of escape, of course, but I couldn't handle the thought of putting myself in a position to be so vulnerable with him again. For the time being, when he was watching, I'd play along with whatever twisted plans he had.

The rest of the time, I'd be clawing at the walls hunting for a way out.

Coming to that conclusion was great and all, but it didn't get me out of the chains. There was no clock or view of the outside to give me any hint as to the passing of the time. Hunger and a growing pressure to use the commode brought around a new kind of panic. What if he forgot about me? How long was I going to be stuck in these chains?

I was practically dancing in place with the effort to hold my bladder by the time Max sent someone to release me. The guy ignored my pleas and repeated requests to be shown to a bathroom. Instead, he held my arm tight enough to hurt and marched me back to the room I'd been locked in earlier—sans chair this time.

He shoved me inside and slammed the door shut behind me, leaving me alone. Though it was humiliating, I rushed straight to the chamber pot in the corner and made use of it, praying that neither Max nor any of his henchmen would barge in at an awkward moment.

When I was done, I noted that there was a tray set to one side of the door that held a bottle of water, some pills, and a bowl of thick soup—but no utensils. Despite feeling ill at being confined and the possibility the food might have something unsavory in it, I was ravenous, and rapidly devoured it. It was bland but filling, lacking any taint of poison or drugs that I could detect. The water was sealed so I knew it hadn't been tampered with, but I wasn't about to touch the pills, whatever they were.

After a few minutes spent fruitlessly scouring the carpet in search of the staples I'd dropped, I resigned myself to waiting for Max or one of his people to return. With nothing else to do, I settled down on the bed, lying back to stare at the ceiling.

Did Royce know Max had taken me? Before I woke up in this nuthouse, I was in California, hiding from the police and the werewolves in New York who were out for my blood. The master vampire of Los Angeles, Clyde Seabreeze, had been betrayed by his lover Fabian. It turned out Fabian was using Clyde, working with the necromancer whose zombies had been killing the vampires who looked to Clyde for protection. After conquering and assuming control of Clyde's empire, Fabian's first gift to his sire, Max, was—you guessed it—me.

I missed Royce with a fierce, desperate ache. It might have taken a hell of a wake-up call for me to realize it, but even though he was a vampire, Royce was no monster. I'd heard those words, even said and thought them before, but it wasn't until I saw what depths of corruption and betrayal Max and Fabian were capable of that I truly believed it. Compared to those two, Royce was a saint—and despite all the reasons I may have given him to be furious with me, he had remained patient and understanding in the face of my doubts.

It had taken me a hell of a long time to face facts, but being a vampire wasn't what made someone villainous. Like humans, they could use their power and influence for good, evil, and everything in between. It was too bad this hadn't sunk in until I was in a situation where the knowledge didn't do me any good, and I had no way of telling Royce how sorry I was for ever thinking he was capable of the same evils as Max Carlyle.

Max's men must have left me alone for a long time. I hadn't even noticed when I dropped off. The sound of a key rattling in the door startled me awake, a brief fright at not remembering where I was morphing into full-fledged panic as the memories of Max and my predicament came back to me. Jerking up to my feet and rubbing the sleep and dried remnants of tears out of my eyes, I stumbled back to the far corner of the room as the door opened.

This time two unfamiliar men entered, and neither looked friendly. One had a patch covering an eye bisected by a scar that ran from his eyebrow to his jawbone. The other was built like a truck and had the look of one who would joyfully kick puppies and other small, helpless animals. The way he was eyeing me made me wonder if he slotted me into that category.

"C'mere," said the one with the scar, beckoning for me to come to him while the other picked up the tray.

"No."

"Master says you been bit. Take yer damn vitamins, girl, and let's go."

The other guy extended his thick palm, now holding the pills from the tray. I didn't want to take them, but thoughts of Max's potential retribution if I should disobey his henchmen had me inching closer to take them. They watched impassively while I dry-swallowed the pills, grimacing at the bitter taste. Once I'd done as ordered, the big guy went off toward the stairs with the tray while the one with the scar led me down the hall to an unlocked door. He followed me inside, standing at the door with his arms folded while I took in the strange scene before me.

There were men and women being herded through an assembly-line process. First they were given some kind of wax treatment or had their eyebrows shaped. Then they entered a shower stall— open to the rest of the room, hoo boy—and washed up. Next they were toweled off and settled in front of a hairdresser. As their hair was trimmed, someone else gave them some kind of skin treatment; various oils or creams were rubbed onto any body part that didn't pass inspection. That was followed by a manicure, pedicure, and some attention from a young girl wielding a tackle box full of cosmetics.

It was like the world's creepiest spa. What the hell was this operation?

Once they were done, they were led out a door on the other side of the room by a guy in a suit, much like the one shoving me in the direction of the shower.

"Stop staring and get on with it. Haven't got all day."

The demand was clear—but there was no way I was getting naked in a room full of strangers. I edged away from him, shaking my head. He muttered under his breath and then reached out to grab my arm again.

I reacted without thought. As he tugged me forward, I used the momentum to slam my heel into his instep, followed by smashing my elbow into his face. As blood spurted from his nose he cursed and let me go. As he doubled over, I took the opportunity to knee him in the jaw, sending him stumbling back.

That earned a few curious looks from the workers and some of the people being attended to. The guards or handlers or whatever they were started moving in my direction, none looking too pleased. I didn't bother waiting around to see if anyone else

was going to try their luck at stopping me. I dashed
out the door, sprinting for the stairs.

Just my luck, as Scar-face stumbled into the hallway behind me, still clutching his spurting nose and
followed by a few other men in matching suits, Max
Carlyle was coming down the stairs, flanked by the
dark-skinned Cajun and a handful of bodyguards.
The vampire stopped in his tracks, once more
clearly as surprised to see me as I was to see him. I
twisted around, ran right smack into the chest of
Scar-face, and suddenly found myself on my back,
blood in my mouth and stars in my eyes as I blinked
up at the ceiling.

Max and the Cajun knelt down on either side of
me. Max touched my lip with his thumb, then
brought it to his mouth, sucking the blood off it.
Throbbing pain radiated from my mouth, warm
wetness sliding over my tongue and down my jaw
to drip into my hair. Though rattled and woozy, all
I could think about was escape. He put a hand to my
stomach to keep me from rising as he addressed the
other man.

"I'm quite at a loss, Francisco. She's infected and
clearly too violent to leave with the others. I need
her wits intact if she's to be of any use. What do you
suggest?"

Francisco also touched my bloodied lip, studying
me much as Max had done, though he didn't taste
what he got on his fingers.

"A puzzling quandary, to be sure. Remarkable
that she's been shrugging off commands." Had I?
That was news to me. "Rhathos had some success,

did he not? Perhaps you should explore his methods of taming her. He must have done something differently to merit her bowing to his will where she refuses to submit to yours."

"Shiarra." Max stroked my cheek with his free hand, and the bottom fell out of my world when I met his eyes. "Tell me what Alec has done differently with you. Why do you obey him?"

His voice rang so sweetly I couldn't help but answer him, though a few times I choked on my own blood. ". . . cares about me . . . doesn't hurt . . ."

Max's gaze flicked up to meet Francisco's, and the two shared a look I couldn't read. Reality came crashing back, along with the awareness that I was completely fucked. Francisco jerked back when I flailed, struggling to get out from under Max's hand. The ancient vampire hissed at me to be still. Though I hated him for it, I had to obey, going rigid.

Max gestured ahead to the room where Scar-face had earlier taken me. "The facilities, as I mentioned, are excellent. Take advantage as you please, and do let me know if you need anything else. I'll join you when I have a moment."

Francisco inclined his head and smiled genially. "Take your time, Euphron. I am in no rush."

Max scooped me up in his arms and, leaving Francisco and his guards behind, took the stairs. When he reached the security door at the top, he made me close my eyes before he worked the keypad. Only after the door was open, sliding on oiled rollers into a recessed alcove in the wall, was I allowed to look around.

The place was huge. The white marble floors veined with gold reflected the lights of half a dozen chandeliers above our heads, shining with rich opulence on the museum-quality furniture and artwork hanging on the walls. The brief glimpse I got of the prison I was leaving behind was of a section of the wall that slid back into place, silent and seamless, behind us. I couldn't even tell where the mechanism was to get inside, but did my best to take note of the details of the room so I could find it again. He'd designed the perfect camouflage to hide his stash of human captives.

Max's footsteps echoed softly as he carried me through the place, each room bigger and more magnificent than the last. It was like a weird cross between a swanky hotel and a museum. We passed an indoor pool, sparkling fountains, statuary, exotic birds in gilded cages, and uniformed maids and butlers who bowed and turned their eyes away when we passed.

Good to know wealth could buy blind eyes and silence about human trafficking to match the furniture.

Only when we reached a wide marble staircase leading upward did I think to shut my mouth. Judging by my stay thus far and all the carefully averted eyes, I didn't think calling for help to any of the people working here was going to do me much good.

We passed a few closed doors before we reached

the end of the hallway. The double doors swung open to reveal a room far more magnificent than the others. The place practically glowed with all the gilding. Intricate designs were inlaid into every surface and along the edges of the white lacquered furniture. The bed was the centerpiece; large enough for an army platoon, with gauzy white curtains that concealed the pillows and blankets that looked soft and fluffy enough to shame the clouds. Despite the color scheme, there was nothing feminine about it. The artwork was too dark, and the way everything came together was cold and somber; no amount of ornamentation could cover that up. Which made this Max's bedroom, I presumed.

The vampire carried me past the bed, glancing down as a shudder passed through me. He soon turned his attention back to the task at hand, taking me to a small painting at the far end of the room. I vaguely recognized the piece of bathing and lounging women as something by Sir Lawrence Alma-Tadema, though I didn't know the name of the painting off the top of my head. I had seen a print of it somewhere before—maybe at one of those funky galleries Sara liked to drag me to.

Max swung it away from the wall to reveal a hidden panel, keyed in a code, then pressed his palm to a scanner; a more high-tech security device than the one used to keep the people downstairs locked away.

Great. My plans for never getting out of here were coming together swimmingly.

A whole section of the wall slid away to reveal a secret passage. I would never have guessed the damned thing was there if Max hadn't revealed it. He lugged me inside, and I was not surprised to see a room similar to—but smaller than—his own on the other side. Instead of one giant bed, there were several smaller ones.

Unlike the rooms downstairs, this place opened up off a few others, including a large bathroom, a library, and—unbelievable—*outside*. Weak sunlight was visible through the far door, and I was bordering on desperate to break the chains of his will to make my way out there.

"Here, now," he said, his voice low and soothing in a way far too reminiscent of Royce's for my peace of mind, "perhaps you'll do better here. If you behave, you may stay. If you don't, back downstairs you go. Understand?"

All I could manage was a feeble nod. He smiled, the hint of fang in it sending my heart rate skyrocketing.

"Good. Go wash up and get some rest. I'll check on you later. We're going to have a talk tonight, you and I."

He set me down on the edge of a sofa. It was even softer than it looked, and I sank down into the cushions, unable to rise immediately. Max left the room, and a low murmur of chatter started up.

Startled by the voices, I reflexively yanked a pillow over myself to cover my near nakedness.

No one approached me, and whoever was locked

in here with me didn't seem to think they needed to show themselves yet. After a moment, I tossed the pillow aside and struggled to get to my feet. Dizziness would've sent me to my knees if I hadn't grabbed for the arm of the couch when I stood up. Rather than go to the bathroom to clean up, the first thing I did was make a beeline to the double doors that led outside.

I should've known better than to get my hopes up. Though this cage was prettier than the one downstairs, I was still trapped.

The courtyard sunroom was lovely and spacious, containing all the amenities you might find in a five-star hotel—including a pool with a cabana serving drinks, wonder of wonders—but it was completely enclosed by a series of iron latticework and thick glass. Probably bulletproof, from the looks of it.

That didn't stop me from shuffling over, hoping to find some crack in the defenses, some hint of a means of escape. Of course there wasn't any secret door waiting for me—but I was shocked to see that, beyond this lovely and obviously temperature-controlled prison, the ground a couple of floors below was covered in a blanket of snow. In the distance, a tall stone fence surrounded the property and, beyond that, thickets of pine trees dotted the snow-capped hills, with no sign of other buildings or roads that I could see.

Max had taken me far away from Los Angeles. It didn't look anything like this in Southern California. Though it had been chilly enough for light jackets at night in LA, it certainly hadn't been cold enough to herald snow before Fabian's pet necromancer put me under. The type of greenery visible under the layer of snow on the distant hills spoke of something much farther north.

I sank down onto a poolside chair, pressing a hand to my forehead. I was far away from home, God knew where. Trapped. Even if I managed to make it outside by some miracle, I wouldn't last long in that cold without more suitable clothing. Max probably had a long coat or something I could steal out of his wardrobe, but the idea of running barefoot through the snow and woods with nothing more than my undies and bra . . . ouch. If I couldn't find shelter, frostbite and exposure would kill me, assuming Max didn't find me and snap my neck first.

A panic attack wouldn't help anything, but it sure felt like a good time to give in to one.

"You should do as he told you," said a clear, ringing voice from behind me. I glanced over, not particularly interested, but soon found myself unable to look away.

A gorgeous woman stood there, draped in diaphanous silks that did nothing to hide the perfection of skin that somehow managed to be paler than mine and yet appeared to glow in the sunlight. Hair like spun gold trailed nearly to her waist, and her eyes glittered with an unnatural greenish hue, brighter than emeralds and shining with some inner fae light. The only thing marring that perfect beauty was the slight discoloration of the skin around the edges of a golden collar locked around her throat.

"Please," she said. "He makes it harder on all of us when one disobeys."

I decided not to antagonize my new roommate. She looked fit and toned and, considering those glowing eyes and skin, was clearly Other. Likely she had the strength to snap me in two if I ticked her off.

"Sure," I replied, resigned. "Give me a sec to get my wind back."

She watched, curious and unblinking, as I slowly levered to my feet. My ribs still ached from Max's unwanted bear hug. The dizziness passed after a moment, and I followed her back inside. Once in the bathroom, she stepped in when she saw I was having trouble peeling off my clothes. As much as it would have bothered me at any other time, by that point I was far too tired to care.

The shower helped wake me up, but the lady had left with my underthings while I was washing. A towel and a short satin robe had been left on the marble sink for me. After drying off, I wrapped the robe around myself and edged back into the room with the chaises and beds, a little afraid of what I might find waiting for me.

The woman with the green eyes beckoned me to one of the beds, where I settled in silent misery, curling up into a ball as she drew a blanket over me. I hated that this place was so opulent, that it felt so good to sink into the plush softness of that bed and find comfort in the heady lavender scent of a familiar fabric softener wafting up from the sheets. No matter how good it felt, this place wasn't safe, and all the luxuries in the world wouldn't change the fact that I was imprisoned against my will.

Words in a language I didn't know spilled from the Other's lips, singing me into a deep, dreamless sleep.

But before I went to that dark place, I could have sworn I heard the rustle of wings.

Chapter Four

I woke up to the sound of screaming. I rolled, falling off the bed in my haste and landing painfully on my hands and knees.

A few other people were huddled back against the walls or hiding behind furniture. I peered over the edge of the bed, gaping at the sight of Max pressing the green-eyed woman against the wall. Her skin reddened wherever his bare skin touched her, and she was crying out in pain.

He pulled her wrist up to his lips, holding her fast as she writhed in agony. When his fangs broke through, some of her blood escaped in a thin, golden trickle down his chin, and a sick-sweet scent like overripe peaches wafted from her skin. Somehow, I knew the source was that weird liquid in her veins, though it didn't smell anything like the normal copper-tainted human, vampire, or Were blood.

As he had with me, he took his time, though he had to know he was causing her an excruciating amount of pain. When he withdrew, he let his hands linger, his fingers leaving a trail of ugly red welts behind. As he loosened his grip, she slumped to her knees at his feet, panting and sobbing, eyes squeezed tightly shut as she cradled her bitten wrist against her chest, tucking the fist under her chin.

"The next time you disobey me, I will take you to my bed again. Understood?"

She nodded, her hair falling in a shining curtain to obscure her features—but not so much that I couldn't see the mixed burning hatred and horror glittering in her gaze as her eyes opened to slits.

He turned to me, his eyes blazing red. I struggled to my feet as he approached, but dizziness and a touch of nausea would've sent me tumbling back on my ass if he hadn't grabbed my wrist before I fell, yanking me against his chest.

I scrabbled for something—anything—to use to defend myself. He drew me to him as my fingers closed around the neck of a nearby table lamp. There wasn't a lot I could do against his strength, but I did swing the lamp I'd grabbed at his head. The bulb shattered and the metal stand bent against the arm he threw up to block it. He wrenched the makeshift weapon out of my hand and tossed it aside, then pulled me closer.

I focused intently on his chin so I wouldn't meet his eyes, panting as I struggled to get out of his grip. An odd scent, mixed vampire musk and the sickly sweet blood of the woman, had my eyes tearing up. Not enough for me to miss the light film of liquid gold

at the corner of his lips, more of it staining his teeth—
which I saw all too well when he snarled at me.

Pure, unadulterated terror shot through me, but
his hand tangling in my hair and forcing my head
back made it impossible for me to do anything
about it. I squeezed my eyes shut before he could
bespell me again.

"You are *mine*," he snapped, grip tightening to
the point where I was straining to breathe. "You do
not obey or answer to that creature or her dead,
false god! Do you understand me?"

Not really.

I felt the distinct bite of claws against my scalp
when I hesitated.

"Yes," I gasped.

"You do not," he said. "You say so out of fear, not
understanding."

Couldn't argue with that, even if I had the breath
for it.

He stiffened, then abruptly shifted his grip,
loosening his hold on me so that he was support-
ing instead of asphyxiating me. The claws retracted,
replaced by the gentle stroke of his fingertips. If I
didn't know any better, I'd have called his touch an
attempt at being soothing. All he accomplished was
creeping me the fuck out.

"Tell me, Shiarra, what was Alec Royce's plan for
you? Do you know?"

Unable to stop shivering, I shook my head. With
our bodies crushed together like this, I was learning
far more about the hard, muscled frame beneath
the immaculate suit than I wanted to. Not to mention

I was really, *really* hoping that his clear excitement pressed against my thigh didn't have anything to do with me.

"Pity," he said. "Who is his second now that John is gone?"

I shook my head again, too afraid to speak. His gentle stroking of my hair became a shade more forceful, hinting at his displeasure.

"I don't know," I said, stammering. Why was he asking me something he must already know? Considering how Max had turned Royce's former second-in-command against him, I found it hard to believe he didn't have other spies in place to tell him these things. Maybe confirming his suspicions? Testing the depths of my knowledge or just how willing I was to betray my lover? "He doesn't talk to me about his business."

"Little liar," he breathed, whispering in my ear as he tangled his fingers in my hair again and drew my head back. "Someone had to take his place, and Rhathos does not let his new pets stray. You were there. You know something. Stop trying my patience and tell me."

Panting, I clutched at his shoulders, trying to push him away as he leaned in. My voice broke on a scream as his fangs scraped over my jugular. I was dimly aware of other voices rising in terror, people rushing around us to hide in the other rooms.

"Please, I'm not lying! I don't know, I don't, I swear!"

He growled—a soft, dangerous sound I might not have heard if I hadn't been pressed so close against him. I was glad I didn't know anything about Royce's business, because I knew I wasn't strong enough to withstand whatever Max might do to drag information out of me. He was quiet save for that low rumbling, and with his fingers tightening on my hair, I was afraid that he was contemplating either snapping my neck or draining me dry.

"He must have fortified his defenses since I attacked. Who were the replacements for the guards who were killed?"

I wracked my brains for something to tell Max. I didn't want to betray Royce, but I didn't want to die for him, either. When Max's fangs pricked my throat, threatening to puncture my skin, I stammered out a response.

"M-m-mouse is s-s-still there, and Angus, Clarisse, Wesley, Reece, and Ken. I don't know the other vampires by name—"

"How many are there? Describe them."

I did. He made the occasional thoughtful sound when I described the handful of other vampires I had met in Royce's apartment building, but he didn't interrupt. When I was done, he said nothing for a time. His grip on me gradually loosened, but he didn't let me go. I stayed still and quiet, hoping against hope that he was losing interest in interrogating me and would leave me alone.

Instead, he blindsided me with a question I wasn't expecting.

"The werewolves he keeps—do they have any relation to the pack you are allied with? The Sunstrikers? Who fought with him when I was in New York?"

He interpreted my astonishment as deliberate hesitation. The silky way he spoke told me better than words that I was in deep shit.

"Choose your words wisely, pet. Lie to me one more time, and I will bind you to me again, offers for you be damned. Taste my blood again and you'll tell me everything, and worship me while you do it."

Oh, fuck that noise. I squirmed desperately. For a crazy second, I wished I had the hunter's belt with its stakes and the enhancements it might give me, even if it meant risking losing my body in the process to the dead mage whose spirit fueled the magic.

Max shook me until I subsided, then removed his hand from my hair long enough to run one of his nails over his throat. While I was busy gaping at the self-inflicted wound, he shifted his hand back behind my head to pull me closer. The slice was sluggishly dripping what looked like tar with gold flakes in it. I shrieked my response, shoving my arm up under his jaw to keep from being forced to drink. Cold liquid slid along and clung to my skin like an oil slick when my bare arm touched his neck. Eww.

"I don't know! I didn't even know he was working with Weres! Please, I don't know anything about it!"

He shook me again until I was grabbing at his shirt to stay steady. That conveniently made it easier for him to draw my head to his shoulder, that much closer to the seeping wound. He tilted his head, his lips brushing against my ear as he spoke in those low, silken tones, the promise of my death in his voice.

"Listen to me, little girl, and listen well. I have limited time, and even less patience. You will obey me, and you will tell me everything that you know. Binding you to me means that, after I wring information from you, you will become useless to me. If I cannot sell you to another and must resort to force to get what I ask, I will keep you by my side until time ends. I will make every day you live a waking nightmare. I will sire you if only to have the eternal pleasure of making you experience exquisite agony from dusk till dawn."

Tears sprang into my eyes as he yanked my head back again. I wished I knew what to say to make him stop, to leave me alone, but no words could escape past my fear-closed throat.

"The only way you will ever be free of me is to submit, and once you do, you will be sold to someone who will most likely bind you to them for what remains of your pathetic, insignificant life. Choose your path, my pet—the hard road of servitude or eternal pain. Your choice."

Though I wish I could say I was brave in the face of danger, this was like nothing I'd ever faced before. Royce wasn't here to protect me. I was too far away for him to "feel" my location, so no one knew where I was. I didn't have the chance of a fart in a windstorm of finding a way out of here. Max cutting himself removed any doubts of my coming out of this predicament intact. Before, I might have been able to pray and hope and lie to myself that everything would be okay. I'd outwit Max and escape somehow, or Royce would figure out where I was and save me. That I was so close to being turned into a mindless puppet again drove home just how unutterably screwed I was.

"Tick-tock, pet. Make your choice before I must choose for you."

A life of indentured slavery with the unknown looked a shade better than an unlife devoted to torture. Heart heavy, I choked out a few words, my stomach twisted with sickness and a bitter taste on my tongue at my own weakness.

"No, the werewolves with him aren't Sunstrikers. I don't know of any alliance between the Sunstrikers and any vampires. The ones who helped in the battle against you were there because my ex-boyfriend was their leader, and he asked them to come. They were there for my sake, not for Royce."

He stilled, and I discovered I had a whole new reason to be afraid. Something about what I'd said was important. Important enough that he flung me aside—with enough care that I landed on a nearby couch, thankfully not breaking anything in the process—and stormed off without another word.

What the hell had I just done?

Chapter Five

Max left me alone for a while. Long enough for the other donors or prisoners or whatever they were to creep back into the room, though they all avoided me like the plague. There were just shy of a dozen of them, all trapped in here with me.

Well, all of them except for the Other with glowing green eyes, so like the Los Angeles necromancer's that the sudden reminder of that backstabbing little shit made me shiver.

She sat down next to me on the couch, that borderline-rotting peaches scent wafting from her like perfume. Her skin showed no sign of the damage that Max's touch had done to her earlier, save for two tiny puncture wounds that were wreathed with red rings of what probably passed on her for infection. Her blood had dried into twin lines of pale golden film, staining the collar of her robe. She didn't appear to care about that, or that the thin material was gaping open.

"One day," she said, voice low and oddly calm, "I will kill him."

"If you have any ideas how to go about it, I'm all ears."

Her eyes glowed—literally glowed—when she turned to me, one hand curled around her collar. "If I had an answer to that, I would have done it by now."

I scooted away, putting more space between us.

The glow dimmed, her features twisting into a rueful, far more human smile. "My apologies. The others have no heart to defend themselves. I thought you . . ."

The way she trailed off made me worry about hearing her complete the thought. Whatever she might think, I wasn't crazy enough to attack Max Carlyle without a hell of a weapon and an army at my back. Hell, if I had the option, I'd nuke him from orbit. Just to be sure.

"Your name is Shiarra?"

At my nod, she removed the hand from her collar to place over her heart. I couldn't help but notice as she shifted her hand that her palm and fingers looked burned, like she'd left it on a hot stove. "I prefer the name Iana."

I nodded again, not feeling particularly chatty.

"Is it true? Did he successfully depose Clyde Seabreeze?"

Frowning down at my fists clenched in my lap, I thought about not answering. It probably wasn't in my best interests to alienate this woman, but this wasn't a safe topic for casual conversation. Tone curt, I hoped she got the hint that I wasn't going to give any details. "Yes, I guess he did. Fabian is running Los Angeles now."

Her tone became urgent, demanding. "You must not tell him how to reach your wolves. He will use them to speed his plans to take New York away from Rhathos of Thessaly. Ian Taft barely clings to Boston. Too many bow to his whims, or turn a blind eye to his machinations. New York cannot fall. There will be no one left on this continent to keep him in check if that happens."

"I'm doing my best," I muttered, embarrassed for no reason I could readily put my finger on. "What do you mean, anyway? Who is Ian Taft?"

"The Master of Boston. The one who replaced Euphron of Sicyon as commander of the northern colonies after Rhathos drove him out. Euphron will take this land. All of it, if he's not stopped. If I could only get rid of this"—she tugged at the collar again, grimacing—"I could lay waste to this gods'-forsaken place."

"Don't start that again," one of the others hissed from across the room. "If he finds out, he'll get mad and hurt the rest of us. You know he will."

Iana quieted, hands clenching into fists. Though I wasn't totally comfortable making direct contact, I liked the idea of her being able to do something to destroy this place. Whatever she was, it must have been something powerful if Max kept her in a collar that suppressed magic or shapeshifting. If he couldn't face her as she was, maybe finding a way to free her could be my ticket out of this hellhole. Light, careful, I touched her shoulder, flinching a little from the intensity of the gaze she leveled on me.

"Why can't you take it off?"

Her expression turned sardonic. Heat bloomed in my cheeks. "Sorry, just asking. I'm not exactly familiar with mage-work like that."

Even as I said it, I realized that wasn't true. Maybe the collar she was wearing was something like the collars on Christoph and Ashi, Royce's unwilling "guests" back in New York. They were werewolves, but because they had attacked him on his own turf, Royce had chosen to hire a mage to find a way to prevent them from using their supernatural strength or shapeshifting powers. Thanks to the collars they wore, they were, for all intents and purposes, human.

Better than being dead, I supposed, though Ashi might have disagreed with me.

"I require a mage to remove it," Iana said. "Max will never do it of his own accord."

Arnold might not like the idea, but if I could get this woman to help me escape I would do anything to help her. Even without knowing what kind of Other she was, whatever she was capable of without that collar, it couldn't possibly be worse than what Max was doing to me and the rest of these people now. I was willing to bet that, like Royce, now that she had known captivity she was unlikely to hurt anyone without serious forethought once she was freed. She would probably need shelter. Friends. Someone who understood.

Even if Arnold wouldn't help her, I wouldn't stop until I found someone who could. She had to believe it—and so did I—if I was going to get her on my side.

"If we can get out of here, I know someone. He'd help you."

She didn't reply, her gaze going distant as she gave another tug at the metal band around her neck.

I tried again, a little more forceful this time. "I promise. If we can find a way out, I know a mage. He can probably do something about it for you."

"What makes you think you can? I've been that monster's prisoner since he was driven out of Boston during the police strike. A century, mortal. What makes you think you can find a way out of here when I am so much more than you and I've been trying for a hundred years?"

"Hey," I said, tone sharp to cut through the despair she was radiating before it could infect me, too. "Don't give up before we've even tried. You didn't have me here before. We'll find a way."

The flat look she gave me wasn't encouraging. I mustered up a glare, hiding creeping doubts behind a not-so-false anger that she wasn't even willing to give me a chance.

"Are you going to help me or not? If you prefer to stay here, by all means—"

Her voice was soft, raw, but I still shut up when that haunted gaze met mine. "Please. I can't remember what I looked like. I can't be like this forever. Stuck in this body. This weak. I can't."

She probably didn't realize her nails were digging into her skin, thin rivulets of golden liquid trickling down her forearms, accompanied by that sick-sweet smell of her strange blood. I grabbed her wrist, pulling until she noticed and stopped hurting herself. Glowing eyes narrowed and focused intently on me.

"Listen," I said, "we'll figure out a way out of this. Help me, and I'll figure out a way." Somehow.

Another voice from behind startled me. "You promise? You'll get us out of here?"

If I hadn't known better, I would have thought I was looking at Mouse's twin. The mute vampiress had been turned by Max, and he'd been very intent on getting her back when he invaded Royce's home, so maybe I shouldn't have been so surprised to see someone who looked so much like her. This girl was shakier, maybe, human and still talking, but otherwise a dead ringer.

Startled by that thought, I glanced around the room at the others peeking in warily from behind furniture or just beyond the doorways in the other rooms. Max was keeping a bunch of humans on hand for I-*really*-didn't-want-to-think-about-what. At first I thought they were all women, but then I spotted a single man in the back, hollow-eyed, slender and swarthy. Even though his skin was naturally a darker hue, he looked too sallow to be healthy. As soon as he noticed I was looking at him, he averted his gaze.

Now that I was paying more attention, it looked

like most of the women here—save for myself and Iana—were short, curvy brunettes. Most had pale skin and a fragility about them that made them all look like china dolls. They looked delicate and easily breakable, and, in some cases, already broken. The lost and hopeless or empty expressions were more prevalent than those with hope.

Knowing Max had a type was enough to set my skin crawling all over again.

The woman who had spoken to me was biting her lower lip, doe-eyed and clearly frightened. Whether she was scared of me or Iana or maybe of Max overhearing our plans was up for debate. Still, there was a sliver of trust in her gaze that made me ache for her. I only hoped I was worthy of whatever confidence she and the others trapped here might put in me.

"If I find a way out of here, I'll come back for you. All of you. I won't leave you here."

Couldn't leave them, more like. The thought of what Max must have been doing to these people sickened me to consider. No wonder they were so frightened. Mouse had failed to obey him once and was rewarded with decades of torture and the loss of her voice. What it must have taken to make a vampire as old as she was, who should have been able to heal most any wound instantly, lose her voice was too horrific to consider for long. What might he do to these girls if I found a way out of here and he thought they had helped or supported me somehow?

Not to mention that he might have Sara and Devon in his clutches. I had no idea what he or

Fabian or Gideon might have done to the two after capturing us and knocking me unconscious. Devon was a White Hat—a human who was part of the Kill All the Supernaturals Because They're Scary and Different club. He was probably still alive, if a bit emotionally scarred, since Gideon had taken a shine to his good looks. Of course I was worried about him, but I considered Devon to be smart and capable enough to find a way out of the mess. On the other hand, Sara, my best friend and business partner, should never have come with me to California. She didn't have the experience with vampires that I did, and it was my fault she was taken. Maybe even dead. She shouldn't have had anything to do with the Others, and had only come to Los Angeles because she had unwittingly been dragged into messes of my making.

The more I thought about what had happened to us and what Max might be planning, the angrier I became. I had to take a few deep, slow, measured breaths to keep my vision from turning hazy with whatever Other-ness was infecting me. I clenched my fists and focused grimly on the need to plan over the desire to dissolve into a helpless, hysterical wreck. Max frightened me, yes, but he had to be stopped. If I got out of here and he couldn't get his hands on me, I had no doubt he'd take out his frustrations on anyone he thought might have done something to aid me. I couldn't let that happen. Not to these girls, not to anyone.

This was about more than just me. This was more than just my personal safety and liberty at stake. Not only these victims surrounding me with their cautious, fragile hope, but whoever else might be stuck in the lower levels, and any men, women, and Others who might be taken in the future for Max's slave auctions.

Not to mention any Others Max was planning to kill or enslave as he carried out his plots to take control of more territory. Clyde Seabreeze might only have been the first—or maybe only the first vampire whose territory was taken in Max's name that I knew about. After all, I had witnessed his failed attempt at wresting control of New York from Royce. Who was to say it had been the first time he'd done something like that? And it had been clear from his tactics that he did intend to take control of the area and the weaker vampires in it, not destroy them. Even if he wasn't a nice person, the former Master of Los Angeles could still be alive, captive somewhere. If this Ian Taft person was next on Max's to-do list, he had to be warned. They all needed to be saved.

There had to be a way to stop this operation. As scared as I might be, I had a purpose now. No matter what might happen to me, I had to find a way to destroy Max's empire, stop his plots to take more power and land, and free these people. No matter how tempted I might be to give in to fear or weakness, I couldn't afford it anymore. There was too much at stake.

I started pacing, needing to work off some of my jittery energy so I could focus. Alternately flexing and clenching my fingers, I ignored the others as they scattered. Their fear of me wasn't helping my concentration.

Max obviously wanted something from me, but how he intended to make me an obedient little puppet and what he thought I might be able to do for him or give him was anyone's guess. Chances were, he was either going to use me as bait or to hurt Royce again. Or, seeing as he had taken so much interest in the Sunstrikers, he might think my connection to the werewolves would give him a way to make another attempt at taking control of New York.

If I was going to get out of this mess, I had to be smart about it and come up with a way to fool Max into thinking I was beaten and cowed.

The trick would be maintaining what was left of my sanity and not falling into the trap of being beaten into submission. Somehow I would have to fool him into thinking he was exerting his will over me while holding on to my plans of escape and revenge. If he managed to break me down enough to truly control me, or lost his temper and gave me another taste of his blood to bind me to him permanently, I might as well already be dead.

Chapter Six

Max came back for me a few hours later, though he took a different approach. He entered the room, scanning the stricken faces of his captives until he spotted me. The smile that curved his lips could have been considered charming if it wasn't so devious.

Instead of making a grab for me or using his mind-mojo to order me around, he stayed by the door and held his hand out to me.

"Shiarra, come with me. I won't harm you."

I eyed the outstretched hand with open distrust. *Yeah, right. And I've got some beachfront property in Kansas to sell you.* Though I bit my lip to keep from saying the words out loud, I couldn't bring myself to move any closer to him. Pretending to be cowed wasn't that hard since he scared the shit out of me. Pretending to be obedient was something else entirely.

Irritation flashed over his features once it sank in

that I wasn't about to jump to obey. He started to move forward before thinking better of it, staying by the door and gesturing sharply for me to come closer.

"Would you like to be returned to that room in the basement? I'm not in the habit of rewarding insolence, girl."

As badly as I wanted to bristle at his tone, the last thing I wanted was to be trapped underground again. At least in here I could see daylight, and I wasn't completely alone.

Resigned, I trudged over, though I didn't take his outstretched hand. The vampire's fingers locked around my wrist. It wasn't just the chill of his touch that made me shiver, goose bumps breaking out over my skin.

He led me out of his bedroom and through a winding corridor, then downstairs to a large room with one door, two fold out chairs, and nothing else. The windowless walls were whitewashed, the chill from the floor tile nipping at my toes as we shuffled inside. The drain and slight dip in the floor didn't bode well for this place's purpose. Compared to the opulence of the rest of this palace, the austere surroundings were at once both striking and imposing. He let me go, seating himself in the nearer chair to watch me with cold detachment as I stood there like an idiot, nervously fidgeting with the hem of my robe, waiting for him to say something.

When it became obvious that no explanations were forthcoming, I inched over to the other chair and sat down. Slow, careful, just in case it wasn't here for me—but he didn't stop me, and still didn't say anything. I adjusted the robe as much as I could to keep it from gaping open.

The silence was unnerving the hell out of me. "Why am I here?"

"Patience. You'll see."

Well. That was helpful. I fished again, curious if he'd spill anything useful.

"Why did you take me?"

Max glanced at me, one brow arching as his expression turned quizzical. "Why would I not take you when the opportunity presented itself? You are valuable in the eyes of my enemy."

It made a twisted kind of sense, but it didn't give me any clues about why I was in this room or what his plans were for me. Not knowing with certainty why he kept threatening me with binding without following through was driving me around the bend. There had to be a reason for it. Like Royce had when I first met him, Max was manipulating my fears to make me do what he wanted. It didn't mean his threats were empty, but it did mean he was avoiding the easy way of controlling me— through a permanent bond of blood—for reasons he wasn't putting on the table.

Though I wasn't hopeful he would answer, I figured it couldn't hurt more than it already did to ask.

"So what am I here for? What are you going to do to me?"

He smirked, his tone droll. "I suppose you're afraid of being ill-used."

"Yeah, you know, this whole master-slave thing you've got going on has put some really unnerving mental images of chains and leather junk holders in my head. Can't imagine why."

His blank expression told me my admittedly twisted and inappropriate humor was lost on him.

"Look," I said, "I don't know what you want, and I don't really want to die."

Max shook his head, his brows knitting and mouth twisting into a frown. Bordering on irritated. "I believe I have already expressed that you are worth more to me alive than dead. For the moment, all I want is for you to obey when given an order."

"Come on, that's not what I mean. Chances are, if you don't tell me what's expected of me, I'll piss you off and bad things will happen. To me. A lot. I don't like that idea, and I'd like to avoid that scenario of me being a whipping post as much as possible. Can you give me some clues here? Please?"

"Your fear is understandable." He rose, stalking closer on light feet. There wasn't any point in running away, but I was too cowardly to hold my ground. I rose and scooched away until my back hit the wall.

I closed my eyes so I wouldn't meet his gaze. It took every ounce of self-control I had not to flail and scream when his hand closed over my throat. Not that I could have managed a sound once his fingers tightened. The pressure startled me enough to open my eyes, if only to slits, as my own hands came up to his wrist to try to pull him off of me.

"Don't fret, my dear," he said, breathing the

words in a low, menacing hiss. "It's not your place to worry about these things. You're still under the impression you have free will. Until you're convinced of your place, we'll take it one command at a time. Relax and be still. Just do as you are told and you'll find it is not so terrible to be mine."

Not so terrible. Says the mass-murdering, slave-trading, misogynistic sociopath. His total confidence that I would be "convinced of my place" made my muscles quiver and twitch, but if doing what he said would save me some pain, then I would make an effort to play along—for now. I stopped pulling at his wrist, loosening my grip. As I did, so did he, his hand withdrawing to rest against my cheek instead. Though I gasped for breath, I stayed where I was, not wanting to provoke him into doing something else to hurt me.

On the bright side, since I was both human and a girl, maybe at some point he would underestimate me in a way I could use to my advantage.

His fingers lingered on my chin, drifting up to run the pad of his thumb over my lower lip. Resolution to play along or no, I flinched and slapped his hand away, turning my head to the side and bracing for the inevitable retaliatory blow.

It never came. Instead, he laughed.

"Oh, I see now. You think your virtue is in danger of compromise, don't you? Is that why you shy from my touch?"

"It occurred to me," I muttered.

"Not to worry," he said, his tone gone light with mirth as he strolled back to reseat himself in the chair he'd earlier vacated. "I'm afraid you're not up to my standards, my sweet. In all practicality, you're hardly malleable enough for the purpose, and you will be no good to me if I break that fragile spirit of yours."

Thankful for the added distance between us, I peered at his features to see if I could detect any signs of a lie without opening myself up to being bespelled. I didn't see any facial tics. That coupled with the inflection of his voice and his eyes remaining steady on rather than sliding away from or seeing through me made me fairly certain he was telling the truth. He might feed on or even hit me again, but he didn't have pantsfeelings for me. Score one for the home team.

Marginal relief at having one of my most pressing worries put to rest eased some of the tension knotted between my shoulders. I was by no means in the clear yet, though, and the courage that I'd scraped up to grill him about his plans had deserted me.

There was nothing of interest in here but him, and considering he might try to pluck my eyeballs out if he caught me at it, staring at the guy wasn't an option worth exploring. I picked at the remains of one of my broken nails, attention fixed on my hands, though I watched from the corner of my eyes as he plucked imaginary lint from his tailored slacks.

It was probably only a few minutes, but it felt like hours later when the door opened, several figures outlined in the frame.

Sara, pushed from behind, stumbled inside and fell to her knees. I was across the room like a shot, kneeling to wrap my arms around her and glare up at whoever had pushed her.

Fabian, master vampire of San Francisco and conqueror of Los Angeles, grinned down at us, his pet necromancer Gideon following in his wake. A pair of zombies brought up the rear. I didn't recognize the first one, but a pang of loss and regret sliced through my heart when I saw that the other was Tiny.

The big man's eyes were sunken and filmed over, his mouth slack and dark skin turned a mottled gray in death. His head lolled unsteadily, probably due to how Fabian had snapped his neck when he killed him.

Once both zombies were inside, Gideon kicked the door shut and leaned against it to survey the room. Tall, slender, and dapper in a dark green suit that would have looked ridiculous on someone else, he smirked and gave me a little finger wave when he noted my attention was on him.

Fabian strode over to take the seat I had vacated, folding his hands over one knee. Death and decay, chokingly thick, drowned out every other scent in the room. The pair of vampires watched with interest as I crushed Sara's shaking frame against me, her fingers digging deep furrows in my skin as she gripped my arms. Neither of us dared speak, or even move, uncertain what the monsters had in store for us now.

The older vampire rose, sweeping his hands down his pants to clear off more imaginary dust. Sara and I both shrank back as he approached, though we were clinging to each other too tight to get very far. Once he was close enough, Max bent at the waist, reaching for Sara. That was enough to spur me to action.

Though he was undoubtedly faster and stronger than I was, and even though I had resolved not to give him a reason to hurt me, right then I didn't care. Rage and fear and frustration drove me to my feet, my fist arcing up in a smooth swing that bloodied his lip and split my knuckles. He brought his arm up to block the next hit, his bloodstained smile enraging me further. Something was off about my vision and his reaction, but it didn't matter. Nothing mattered but getting him away from Sara.

Snarling, I did everything I could think of to drive him back. Fingers curled into claws, I swiped at his face, arms, and chest, kicking at his shins, throwing punches at his solar plexus—and he shrugged off every attack, eyes narrowed, moving at about the same speed I was as he parried or took each strike. What game was he playing?

In a moment of clarity, I recalled his swordfight with Mouse, then the later one with Royce when he had made his bid to take control of New York. During both fights, he had moved in such a blur that my eyes hadn't been able to follow. He was barely moving a fraction of the speed I knew he was capable of, which meant this was some kind of test, not a fight. Like an adult dealing with a little kid's tantrum, letting them wear themselves out before stepping in to end the theatrics.

That thought was enough to make me hesitate,

which seemed impetus enough for him to move in and sweep my legs out from under me, sending me crashing on my back on the tile.

"I see," Max said, Fabian nodding sagely as if agreeing with some brilliant observation as I lay there, gasping back my breath and clutching at the back of my head. Nothing manages to make you feel like the greenest rookie quite like being dropped on your ass.

Sara scooted over, taking one of my hands, though her gaze stayed focused on Max as if she was afraid he was about to make another grab for her.

"Yes, you were quite right," Max continued. "I should have considered the option earlier. We'll have to do something about that infection."

"Yes, of course," Fabian replied. "Gideon?"

The necromancer moved into my line of sight, coming to a halt beside me and Sara. Fabian waved airily in my direction, still beaming at Max as though they had just shared in some wonderful, terrible secret.

"See what you can do about that, hmm?"

Gideon nodded, then turned to me, considering. He rubbed his chin, then knelt down next to Sara. She edged away, clinging to my hand, which he was attempting to pry out of her grip.

"Don't touch her!" My demand went ignored.

"Relax, Sara." Gideon lightly touched her shoulder, and to my surprise, she did as he said. She didn't let me go, but she did let Gideon reach for me without protest this time, which, come to think of it, didn't seem like such a good idea.

Though it made the ache in my skull momentarily blinding, I yanked my hand away from both of them and rolled into a crouch, putting some distance between us.

"Spry little thing," Fabian commented.

Max made a sound of irritation. Gideon pursed his lips, then held out his hand. The glint in the necromancer's eyes spoke of some kind of plan—something he was trying to convey—but I wasn't sure what the message was supposed to be.

"Come on, Copper-top. You want to stay that way forever?"

I glared at him, staying right where I was. "Like what?"

"An abomination. And I'm not just talking about your face."

That prompted a deep growl—too deep—not right. The desire to rip him to shreds with my bare hands was so strong, I had to clench my fists to keep from springing at him. Sara gasped, but I didn't spare her a glance just yet. All my attention and fury was focused on Gideon.

His taunting smirk didn't help. He gestured at my hands. "Look for yourself. Does that seem normal to you? I'm not your nail technician, so . . ."

Suspicious, I did—and couldn't tear my gaze away. My nails had formed into thick, curved talons and the back of my hands were covered with a webwork of spidery black veins, easily seen under my pale skin. It was enough to shake me out of my building rage.

"What the hell is happening to me?"

"You are not quite vampire, nor quite werewolf," Max said. "You've been infected by both, though it seems the vampire in you is more prominent. It is in your best interest to let the necromancer see to you, Shiarra. If not, you may die."

"And then he can't use you to infiltrate whatever wolf pack that infection is connected to. Too bad, so sad," Gideon said, throwing an arm dramatically over his eyes as Fabian and Max both glared at him. Clearly this was not something they had intended to make me privy to just yet—the key to how Max intended to use me.

As much as I didn't want to believe either of them, wanted to think it was just another ploy to mess with my head, I couldn't deny the evidence. Gideon had used the same tactic on me as he had with Sara; riled me up to bring my weaknesses to light so he could exploit them. What worried me more than the necromancer manipulating me or even the thought of dying because of whatever was in my blood was why Max cared enough to fix it— and what price he'd make me pay for my continued survival.

"Kneel."

I glared, remaining exactly where I was.

Max repeated the command, and I felt the pressure of his will behind it this time, forcing me to obey. "I told you to kneel. Get down and be still."

Both of my knees cracked on the tile, a jolt of pain driving through them, then up my wrists and forearms almost to the elbow as I caught myself before I fell in a sprawl. I stayed that way, panting, staring at the curved claws biting into the pale rose-colored ceramic.

The evidence of the taint in my blood was right before my eyes. Undeniable.

I was Other.

And Max still had the power to control me.

Worse. He had Sara. He had everything he needed to make me a cooperative little puppet, and it didn't take binding or turning me to do it.

Gideon crouched down in front of me. "Look up." I did, staring at but not really seeing those magnificent, glowing green eyes of his. I flinched when his palm settled over my heart, but couldn't break away from his gaze or touch. He didn't say anything, but I felt . . . different. Cold spread in my veins, making me shiver. All the hairs on my arms rose, and the scent of something rich and sweet sparked a sudden, fierce hunger, made stronger with every thud of what sounded like muted drums beating in my ears.

The hunger grew sharper as a dull throb of pain in my gums was followed by the taste of copper on my tongue. I turned away, clapping a hand over my mouth, a combination of disgust warring with the hunger that grew so strong at the hint of blood rolling over my taste buds that it was turning into hurt.

Unsatisfying. My own.

'Don't let them see the fangs. Work with me and I'll get you two out of here.'

An intrusion into my head, complete with a range

of foreign emotions and nebulous desires. Fear for someone else. Calculation. Deception. Like the belt—but not. I almost gaped at Gideon before I remembered to keep my mouth shut, though my eyes were wide as he put on a look of disgust that was so convincing I might have bought it if he hadn't just been in my thoughts.

"There isn't enough vamp blood in there for me to work with. Or she's stronger than you thought," Gideon declared, rising again and rocking back on his heels, arms akimbo. He was lying through his teeth to his lover and his lover's sire—and I had no idea why. What game was he playing? "My, my. You did mess this one up, didn't you?"

Fabian gave the necromancer a look of warning as Max made a soft hissing sound.

"Thank Rhathos for this mess," was Max's reply. "He never did know how to care for his toys."

"And you do?" I muttered, scrubbing the back of my hand over my mouth. It came away smeared with black and red, and I wondered exactly what part of my freakish nature had put that fresh look of terror in Sara's eyes as she scooted away from me. Better to focus on that than the desire to pounce, drag her closer, sink my teeth into—

No. Not her. Never her.

Gideon dangled something green at me, drawing my eye. A handkerchief that stank of chloroform and, under that, rotting meat. Blanching, I waved off his offer, moving over to stay as close as Sara would have me without flinching away.

"Well," Max said, "I suppose there's only one way to guarantee cooperation, then."

Fabian nodded, that high-wattage smile slipping just a tad. "Of course. You may have her, sire. All that is mine is yours to command."

Gideon said nothing, but there was a new scent under the herbs and chemicals clinging to his skin and clothes—something that told me he didn't like what Fabian's statement implied. For a second, I thought Fabian meant me, but then Max moved and removed all doubt.

Max did not bother to acknowledge Fabian's offer, but he did move closer to us, once again reaching for Sara. Whether it was done to deliberately provoke me or not, I didn't have the self-control to keep from swiping at him, a growl rumbling in my throat.

He backhanded me so hard, I think I might have blacked out for a minute.

As soon as awareness trickled back, I reached for Sara, hoping to shield her before Max could lay a hand on her—but she wasn't there. Blinking hard, I looked around, fighting the woozy unreality that made everything seem so hazy in my vision. The blobs of color a few feet away soon reformed into the figure of Sara, seated in one of the chairs, her head hanging and blond hair a shining curtain in front of her face. The zombies were holding her arms, keeping her pinned, while Max waited next to them and Gideon leaned against the far wall, pointedly looking away.

"Shiarra, we're going to try something new." Max

snapped his fingers, then pointed at a spot by his feet. "Come. Kneel here."

I spat a bit of blood in his general direction and gave him a one-fingered salute instead, keeping my ass planted right where I was. Gideon's smirk made me feel better about my little act of defiance, even though I was sure I would pay for it later.

Max didn't appear too troubled by this. He reached out to Sara, one hand tangling in her hair and jerking her head up. She grimaced, obviously in pain, but didn't make a sound. His other hand swiped down her cheek, leaving behind a thin line of red that soon trickled in a sheet of blood down her pale skin. Fabian's look of boredom as he watched all this from against the wall next to Gideon somehow made it even worse.

Eyes widening, I struggled to get to my feet, but Max must have struck me too hard. I couldn't get my balance, earning more bruises as I stumbled and fell.

"Kneel as I told you, or I'll do the same to the other side of her face. You wouldn't want that on your conscience, now, would you?"

"You heartless fuck," I said, tongue thick in my mouth, something sharp biting into my lip as I spoke. "Touch her again and I'll kill you."

The threat might have held more weight if I'd been able to stand while I delivered it. His nail swiped in a matching line down the other side of Sara's face, soon followed by silent tears, her pleading gaze driving a spike of dread deep into my chest. I had to stop this.

Desperation got me to my feet, anger drove me forward, and fear for Sara had me throwing myself on Max in a frantic attempt to force him away from her. He grabbed my forearms and used my own momentum to send me hurtling past and sliding across the tile until my back thumped into the wall at the other end of the room.

Slow, taking his time, he pulled one of Sara's wrists from Tiny's grip and yanked her arm up, ignoring her struggles as he watched me catch my breath and drag myself back to my feet.

"Are you ready to obey?"

I ignored Max's question, my own voice warbling with uncertainty. "Sara?"

Her reply was hushed, strained, laced with fury and pain. "Fuck him."

I didn't need further invitation. Growling, I pushed off the wall and rushed him again, fingers hooked to claws to tear him off of her.

He caught me by the throat as soon as I was close enough, ignoring the bite of my nails as I shredded his long-sleeved button-down and clawed the arm that held her. He shook me a little, but I wasn't deterred in the least.

That is, I wasn't until he shoved me down to my knees, then yanked Sara's arm so hard I heard something pop, dragging her wrist to his mouth. His pale gray eyes stared into mine, cold, empty as he bit her, ignoring every effort I made to pull her arm out of his grasp even as my vision blurred from lack of air from his fingers crushing my windpipe.

Distantly, I heard her scream, noted her kicking and thrashing as she fought to get free, but the worst thing was being so close and yet so very helpless to stop it. There was nothing in his gaze that said he was sorry. Nothing that hinted at compassion or understanding. All he was looking for was acceptance from me. Acceptance and submission.

Every instinct I had was screaming to keep fighting, but he would kill her if I didn't relent. I'd seen him do it before, and that wasn't when he had anything personal at stake. Terrified that he might not stop, I grabbed at his shirt front instead, tugging, pleading the only way I could, desperate to find a way to get him to let her go.

As soon as I stopped fighting, he withdrew from her wrist, licking the faint sheen of red off his fangs before speaking down to me.

"Get on your feet and kneel where I instructed."

He gave me a little shove as he let me go, and though I rubbed at the sore spots that would undoubtedly become bruises on my throat later, all I could focus on were the twin trickles of crimson on Sara's wrist and the tiny sounds of hurt she was making. Her eyelids were half-mast with a languorous mix of exhaustion and terror I was all too familiar with. Gasping like a landed fish, I got shakily to my feet. Once I found my balance, I moved to the spot Max indicated and knelt, just as he'd wanted. Gideon was shifting from foot to foot. The necromancer was obviously uncomfortable but made no move to step in or help either of us.

Max was all too pleased. "Very good. It seems she can be taught after all."

Sara was crying again. My own eyes stung with unshed tears as I stared up at the sly, pleased smile of my captor.

As soon as I got my hands on a weapon, I was going to kill that son of a bitch.

He let go of Sara's arm, which fell limply to dangle at her side. The agonized sound she made and the boneless way her arm moved hinted at dislocation. As much as I wanted to get up to help her, Max might hurt her again if I tried. I glared up at him, wishing I could somehow hate him to death.

Fabian was looking at Sara with naked hunger glimmering in his eyes. I had the sudden, horrible thought that she might only be alive right now because Max had told him she might be useful to use against me. Had that changed?

"Sire," Fabian said, "we have a plane to catch."

"You may go. I'll call if I have need of you. I'll see you both the week of the full moon."

Fabian nodded at Max's dismissal and put his arm around Gideon's shoulder, urging him toward the door. The necromancer looked back, his gaze locked on Sara with an expression that was somewhere between calculation and concern. He surprised me by halting in the door, shrugging off Fabian's touch and addressing Max directly.

"If it's not too much trouble, I'd like to stay."

Fabian was clearly annoyed by his lover's temerity. His dark complexion became more so, his brown eyes glinting with a hint of red embers in the irises. "Gideon. Now is not the time."

Gideon didn't give an inch. There wasn't a bit of fear in him for angering Fabian, surprisingly enough. Even more unexpected was his gesturing at Sara, impassioned in a way I didn't fully understand.

"She's my responsibility. Let me take care of her injuries." Then he looked right at me, something in his tone telling me there was more to what he was saying, though I wasn't sure what. "I'll help with her, too. Let me do this."

Max's gaze narrowed, thoughtful as he took in Fabian's reaction. "What do you have to gain from this, little spark?"

If Gideon was annoyed by the slur, he gave no sign. "A familiar. She's already been marked once. When you don't need her anymore, alive or dead, I can still use her."

That sent a fresh bolt of panic up my spine. Marked. A familiar. Had he and Fabian lied to me back in Los Angeles? Were those blood runes he had supposedly removed, the ones that let magi use Sara like a living battery to power their spells, still there, unseen under her skin, maybe not as dormant as we thought? Had his ritual keyed those runes to him alone, rather than leaving her open to assault by any passing mage?

Gideon glanced at me as he stressed his next words, though there was no mental message to go with it this time. "Though I'd prefer her *alive*."

Holy shit. The necromancer really *was* planning on busting us out of here. I had no idea how or why—something must have changed between him knocking us out for Max's benefit back in California and whenever he arrived here with Fabian to deliver Sara like some twisted housewarming present—but I was grateful for that change of heart, nonetheless.

"So be it," Max said.

Gideon's smile contained a world of mischief, though he did a passable job at making it look sincere and pleased as he bowed his head. Only I caught his wink—and Fabian's fists clenching at his sides.

"Sire, I must protest—"

Max cut Fabian off. "The necromancer made his choice. You know the rules."

"Yes, sire," came the sullen response. "I'll be in touch."

Gideon blew Fabian a kiss. "Don't worry. I'll be home before you know it."

Fabian's discontented growl was low, but clearly audible. He turned on a heel and stalked out of the room, not bothering to shut the door behind him. I had to wonder what those "rules" were that Max mentioned. Was Gideon considered a power unto himself? Was it possible Fabian couldn't force him to do anything he didn't want to? Maybe that had something to do with why Gideon chose to stay behind.

My gaze flicked to Sara, slumped in the chair, her cheeks wet with blood and tears. I would do anything to keep her safe. If Gideon couldn't get me out of here, I'd be content with helping her escape this hell. After all, it was me Max wanted to break.

For her sake, I would bend and bow and scrape. But knowing that Gideon might get us both out alive was the first sign of hope I'd been given since I stumbled into Max's clutches.

I only hoped I could stomach being as obedient as he wanted until then. Judging by the sinister smile he turned on me, it wasn't going to be easy.

Chapter Seven

I paced beside the pool, flexing my hands. It wasn't just because I was incredibly nervous and worried about Sara, though that played a huge part in my jittery energy. The movement helped my concentration as I practiced making my nails grow into bone-white talons, then back to normal.

That might come in handy later.

The other captives, even Iana, avoided me. Sara had been taken elsewhere by Gideon. Max brought me back to my prison and then left to parts unknown. He either had better things to do than deal with my combined panic and rage, now that he knew how to make me do what he wanted, or he wanted me to stew for a while. Maybe both.

If I could have, I would have torn the place apart to find Sara and get the hell out, but even my new-found Other side didn't have the strength to break down the door. After I tried a couple of times, bruising my shoulder, a voice over an intercom relayed that Max said if I kept it up, I would be sent back downstairs.

After that I flipped off the security camera above the door and stalked outside. Now all I had to keep me company was a vast sense of helplessness and a desire to control or unleash whatever was making my blood turn black. After refusing to acknowledge what I might be turning into for so long, it was strangely easy to accept my new abilities now that I wanted to use them. If I could summon those heightened senses and make that increased strength appear at will instead of only when I was angry, maybe I could use them to escape this mess.

So far, making the claws come out was pretty easy. If I concentrated on the thought of danger, they formed with little more than a tingle, growing out of the nail bed. Making them go away was harder, and they almost hurt as they slipped back under the skin.

Aside from the claws, I had no way of knowing for sure if concentrating was making anything else happen. I didn't want to break any furniture testing my strength and I wasn't about to ask Iana to be a sparring partner. Even with whatever edge the Other side might have given me, collar or no, I was sure she could wipe the floor with me.

She appeared, as if summoned by my thoughts, inches away the next time I turned around. Smothering a startled gasp, I suppressed the urge to hit her for scaring me. I ran at the mouth instead.

"First thing we do when we get out of here is buy a bell for that collar."

She smiled, though there was little humor in it, then gestured at my hands. "I wouldn't do that. If he catches you, he may declaw you."

She wasn't kidding. I raised a hand to eye level, staring at my fingertips. A massive shudder rolled down my spine. "Well, this place keeps getting better and better."

She inclined her head, a subtle glow building in the depths of her eyes. "You have a better chance of escape than I do, and my freedom hinges on yours. If you compromise that, I will be very displeased."

Awesome. Like I said, better and better.

Rather than risk pissing off her or Max or anyone else, I stalked over to the nearest empty pool chair and rested my elbows on my knees, cupping my chin in my hands. The sparkle of sunlight on the pristine carpet of snow outside our prison felt like a taunt, reminding me of the freedom I'd lost.

Iana pressed a hand to my shoulder, sending a jolt of heat through the thin silk of my robe to seep into my skin. I did my best not to flinch away, turning my head to look at her out of the corner of my eye.

"There is . . . something new. Something dark in you. What did they do while you were gone?"

Oh, that was a pleasant thought. Just what did Gideon do to me when he touched me? "I don't know. There was a necromancer—"

Iana made a sharp, hissing sound, her hand moving in a gesture that looked something like what I'd seen Arnold do when casting freehand spells. As I stumbled away from her, putting distance between us, she cried out in pain as nothing but a few fizzling blue-white sparks trickled from her fingertips just before she clutched at her collar. The skin around her throat and on her palms and fingertips where she grabbed at the metal was reddening.

When I reached for her, her hand shot out, slapping my own away. The sting was nothing compared to the mixed fear and loathing on her face. I wasn't totally sure if it was directed at me or at my mention of Gideon, but it wasn't pleasant to have that fierce, glowing gaze focused on me. Never mind if that collar protected me from her magic—there was nothing to say she might not use her supernatural strength to snap my neck if she wanted.

"A necromancer," she said, staring into nothing. "I thought they . . . never mind. If you've garnered that thing's attention, there is nothing I can do to help you. Not like this."

"What's wrong with me? What do you mean, 'not like this'?"

"It's in you. In your blood. In your head. You're cursed. Without the collar I might be able to get it out, but this . . ." She tugged at the creepy fashion accessory, a low growl of frustration telling me better than words what she meant. She couldn't cast a damned thing with that circle of metal cutting her off from wherever her power came from. It was still there. The sparks, even if they signaled the spell fizzling, told me as much. She just couldn't do whatever it was she needed to in order to complete casting.

If only I could be sure she intended to help me, not destroy me, when she was trying to cast that spell on me.

I had already committed to finding a way of freeing her from Max if I managed to do the same. Now it looked like I'd be putting myself back in danger if I did find a way to free her. If I could have, I would have throttled Gideon for messing with my head and complicating this mess. Even if he was my best shot at finding a way out, who was to say he wasn't doing it to find a way to have me under his thumb himself?

"Look, Iana, I'm sorry it scares you. Gideon saved my best friend's life. He hinted he wants to get us out of here. He's not a good guy—okay, he really *is* a bad guy—but I'm not sure his motives for being here are evil."

She gave me a look that told me clearer than words she thought I was being hopelessly naïve.

Okay. Maybe I was. I sometimes had a hard time believing the worst about people, and never mind that I was a private investigator who regularly saw the ugly underbelly of "polite" society. Gideon had already proven more than once that he was two-faced. He was good at sneaking under defenses and manipulating people. He'd managed to get close enough to Sara to nearly kill her, sucking her energy or her soul or who knew what out through the blood runes carved into her arm by the long-dead sorcerer, David Borowsky. We'd trusted Gideon to keep his word when he promised to get rid of the runes. I wondered what he'd really done. They weren't visible on her skin anymore, but if what he'd said was true, he might have done something to key the runes to himself instead of leaving her open to any mage who wanted to steal a bit of her.

If Sara's mage boyfriend, Arnold, ever found out, he'd probably kill Gideon with his bare hands.

I wondered if Arnold had any idea we were in trouble. He hadn't answered my last message, left when I was still with the White Hats—humans who fancied themselves vigilante supernatural hunters—in Los Angeles. Maybe he'd team up with Royce and ride in to save the day once they figured out where we were.

And maybe I'd win the lottery, too.

Iana stared at me, intent, like she was peeling away the layers of whatever she saw on my face to read the truths hiding in the dark corners of my mind. Maybe she was assessing whatever Gideon had done to me in some way I couldn't see or understand. Either way, the two of them gave me the heebie-jeebies.

"You do realize how foolish that makes you sound, do you not? You should be afraid of it. Necromancers are things of darkness and corruption. Everything they come into contact with dies, quick or slow."

I snorted. "Tell me something I don't know."

That probably wasn't the right thing to say, judging by the murderous look she gave me. I held my hands up in surrender. "Okay, okay. Sorry. I know he isn't all sweetness and light, and he's definitely got something up his sleeve, but right now nothing scares me more than Max and what he might do to my friend Sara. They have her. He's using her to make me do what he wants."

"That doesn't mean you need to play along. It's probably using your feelings for her to goad you into doing what it wants. That's how their tricks work."

"No kidding. You think I don't know that?" Scowling, I folded my arms. "I wish you wouldn't call him an it. He might not be human, but I don't think he merits an 'it.'"

The glimmer in her eye took on a sardonic sheen when she cocked a brow at me. "You're changing the subject. Whatever the gender, it is irrelevant. That thing isn't here to help you. It's here to help itself. You're just letting yourself be used, and in a far more insidious way than Max Carlyle ever intended."

"I can't watch them hurt her. I just can't. I have to get out of here, and if that means letting a necromancer help me, so be it."

Iana shook her head and turned away, the curl of her lip telling me she was still disgusted with my life choices. Neither of us was ever going to get out if she wasn't open to using whatever options were available to us, no matter how distasteful they might be.

Gideon might have thought Sara and I were both pawns to be shuffled around at his whim, a means to who knew what end, but I could play that game, too. Who said Others were the only ones who could be manipulative?

Then I remembered that I wasn't exactly human anymore, and had to swallow down a sick feeling of inevitability. I didn't want to turn into the kind of monster I'd always been afraid of, but if that's what it took to escape, I couldn't afford to be squeamish. I would be as careful as I could be, bearing in mind what Gideon was and what he'd done. He wasn't just a manipulative asshole. He was a cold-blooded murderer. Letting him help me was a risk I was willing to accept if it meant escaping this place.

"We'll get out of here," I said, not sure if I was trying to convince Iana or myself. "Whatever it takes."

She didn't answer, padding away on quiet feet to leave me alone with my thoughts of curses, death, and whether I might not be letting circumstances bring out an evil in me that maybe had been there long before I started turning Other.

Chapter Eight

After the initial meeting with Fabian, Gideon, and Sara (I didn't think zombie-Tiny or the other zombie guy counted), Max didn't return for days. I kept waiting for the other shoe to drop, but by the third night, it was getting hard to stay on the razor's edge of readiness to face whatever evil might be waiting for night to fall.

There were a couple of touch-and-go moments where I nearly flipped out. One was when a trio of suited guards came in. I rolled off the bed I was lounging on and put it between us, looking for something to use as a weapon. They just stood by the door and smirked at me, sharing amused looks at my confusion and panic. A minute or two later, a couple of women in leather collars and, incongruously, neatly pressed maid's outfits, came in with a cart of supplies to clean the rooms and change the bedding. Apparently this was something they did every two or three days.

Talk about awkward misunderstandings.

The constant, fearful jitters faded by the end of the week. Instead of jumping at every unexpected sound and intrusion of Max's security team and cleaning crew, it became too commonplace to worry about. Aside from telling us to get off the furniture they needed to clean or to lift our feet so they could vacuum a patch of carpet, they left me and the rest of Max's captives alone.

It was so odd to see how he had set up his private harem. We were treated relatively well, given pretty much anything we wanted, and left alone by Max's minions. We weren't starved, by any means. The cabana I'd noticed on my first tour of the place provided meals as well as drinks. Lots of iron-rich foods, like vegetables, nuts, shellfish, and steak, along with daily vitamin supplements, most likely to combat the frequent blood loss the others suffered from Max's attentions.

We were supposed to return our dishes through the same slot they were provided through. It was too small to squeeze through and escape, but big enough for plates, bowls, and small glasses to be passed back and forth. I couldn't see much of the kitchen through the slot, but it looked like the people who ran it were all collared and uniformed. Trapped like the rest of us. The forks and spoons they passed us were plastic, and all our food was already cut up, so we didn't need knives. The design was clever but chilling in its efficiency.

My presence didn't change the routine a bit. The other captives might have been a tad nervous around me, but even they didn't treat my arrival as unusual for long. For the most part, the others avoided me the way they avoided Iana; not making eye contact, scooting away or getting up to move to another room if one of us got too close, keeping responses monosyllabic and hushed, like they were afraid of being punished for talking to us.

Maybe that wasn't so far from the truth, since they figured from my conversations with Iana that I might be the one to save them. Or maybe they thought that getting too close might make Max furious with them for helping me. Whatever it was, it meant I was left alone a great deal of the time.

Basically, it was boring and claustrophobic as fuck, and never mind that my shoe box of an apartment back in New York could have fit into our prison ten times over. With no human interaction, TV, or Internet, and nothing much but a collection of books to keep myself busy, it was a wonder I didn't go nutty from all the time I had to spend twisting myself in mental knots coming up with and discarding useless escape plans.

Being bored was infinitely preferable to being tortured, but I was also worried for Sara's safety. The one time I got brave enough to ask one of the security guards if he knew anything, he told me to sit back down and shut up. I didn't want to invite trouble or give Max or his people a reason to send me back to my prison in the basement, so I did as I was told.

It might have saved me some pain, but it still left me in the dark. Where had Gideon taken Sara? What else had they done to her? It wasn't like I could do anything about it, or about my own predicament, but I couldn't stop worrying about her.

I was also worried about Devon, my hunter friend who was probably still in Fabian's hands, but Sara was like the sister I never had. The woman had more money than God, and yet she had taught me that it didn't take money to live a rich life. She was the one who took me on adventures to see plays and improv shows I never would have gone to alone, to view artwork in galleries I wouldn't have known existed, to attend readings by authors I never would have thought to look up, and to see bands I'd never heard of in dives I wouldn't have set foot in if I didn't trust her so much.

That was what killed me the most about her being taken. Devon chose this life of tangling with vampires. He knew the dangers involved and had decided to take the risk. Sara was only in trouble because she was my friend.

Not knowing if she was badly hurt, or if she was even still alive, gnawed at me like a dog worrying a bone. Worse, I was afraid Royce was unaware that I had fallen into Max's hands. The last time we spoke, he knew about Clyde's trouble, and that a necromancer was involved. I hadn't a clue, at that time, that Max might have had anything to do with it.

Though I also had a thread of a blood bond remaining to Royce, just as I did to Max, I didn't think he could still feel what I was feeling like he had when I was in New York. He'd mentioned once that proximity strengthened the bond. It was a one way street for vampires—they could feel and exert some control over their bonded human servants, but for the most part it wasn't supposed to go the other way around. I couldn't be sure what he knew or felt about me or my predicament. Considering I must be at least a few hundred miles away, he might not even be able to tell if I was alive. Did he feel my fear? Did he know how scared I was, not just for myself, but for Sara? Did he know how much I missed him? I couldn't let it go even though I knew it wasn't helping to linger on questions no one would answer.

After a week of sitting and stewing in mystery, I could almost believe Max had forgotten I existed. A couple of the girls had loosened up enough to say more than two or three words at a time to me, and I knew all of their names now, but not much else. We weren't buddies by a long shot and, while they might have been comfortable with each other, I was clearly still too much of an outsider—too Other— for them to want to get chummy.

A good portion of my time was spent working out nervous energy in the pool or reading books. The library had a fairly extensive collection of classics and some recent literary fiction, though I couldn't help but wonder if he had books like *Memoirs of a Geisha,* Stoker's *Dracula* and *The Handmaid's Tale* stocked for his captives because he had a sick sense of humor or if the irony went right over his head. Whatever the reason, the reading material was about the only thing that kept me from going completely bonkers. This was like some weird vacation, except I wasn't staying in a hotel I could check out of whenever I wanted, and I was more worried about vampire infestation than bedbugs.

When Max did show up, I nearly had a heart attack. With my nose buried in a book, and after getting so used to the comings and goings of his security and maintenance people, I didn't even notice his entrance. It was his voice that made my heart seize up in terror, except he wasn't talking to me, or paying me much attention at all.

"Did you miss me, sweet?"

My fingers tightened abruptly around the paperback copy of *The Count of Monte Cristo*, tearing a page in the process. I peered over the top of the book, otherwise going still. Sick relief that he was talking to someone else didn't unravel the knots in my stomach. I didn't want to give him a reason to look my way or to notice me.

Halfway across the room, Max was sitting on a divan beside Vivian, one of the girls who made it a point to avoid talking to me. It was late, dark, with only a few lamps casting pools of light to hold back the shadows. Everyone else had cleared out when I wasn't looking.

Vivian was staring down at her hands clenched together in her lap, nodding a little too emphatically in response to Max's question. He smiled and held out a hand, palm up. Though hers shook, she untangled her fingers and placed a hand in his. He lifted her wrist to his mouth and bit down, his gaze flicking in my direction. Too awkward to leave the room, too late to hide behind the book—I focused on Vivian's face instead, heat burning my cheeks.

Though she didn't make a sound, her breathing had sped up, her mouth slack, her eyes closed.

It felt like walking in on people having sex who were a little too involved to bother stopping on their voyeur's account. The reminder of why the other girls were here was enough to turn the blood to ice water in my veins.

The reminder that this might be why I was here as well paralyzed me with fear.

Max pulled away from Vivian before long, his tongue scraping over the place he'd bitten. Even from this distance, I could see the slick coat of red staining his fangs and tongue, like he'd been sucking on a cheap, too red lollipop. Her trembling increased marginally, but she didn't pull away or do anything to fight as Max licked at the punctures. I had to wonder if he was making such a point of it for my benefit or hers.

He pressed a light kiss to the bite, set her hand back down in her lap, then reached over to tilt her head so he could press another to her brow. It might have been sweet if she hadn't so obviously been making an effort to keep from bolting in terror at his touch. Considering how cavalier he was with human life, it was no wonder she was afraid. Any bite from him could be her last.

His gaze briefly slid back to me before he rose and stalked back to the exit on quiet feet. He glanced at me once more over his shoulder, then to the book in my hands.

"You might find something like *The Picture of Dorian Gray* more enlightening."

I nodded mutely, staring back at him as he slid out of the room like a shadow, the door lock engaging with a click. Just before the door shut, I almost called after him to ask if Sara was still here and alive, but the thought of having his attention on me again for any reason filled me with sick dread. What if he decided to feed on me next?

And exactly what kind of object lesson did he think I might learn from *Dorian Gray*? It wasn't like I was about to sell my soul to Max for the sake of beauty or wealth. Unless he wanted me to read and reflect on my relationship with Royce, which was already borderline Faustian. Or had been, before he sent me away from what might have been a very long and decadent life together. He had stashed me in Los Angeles while he dealt with whatever troubles were threatening me in New York. Royce never had been quite clear on what I was hiding from, aside from the police, though I trusted his judgment enough to accept it was serious business.

Whatever the reason, I had to keep in mind it was Max Carlyle making the suggestion. Who knew what he might be thinking? The guy was crazier than a shithouse rat.

Once I was sure he was gone, I put my book down, clearing my throat. Vivian didn't look up, her attention fixed on her hands, once again clenched in her lap. I moved to her side. She shrank away when I sat down next to her, like she thought I might hurt her, too. I held out a hand in offering as a lump formed in my throat, too big to talk around. She tilted her head to look, biting her lip, I supposed either too afraid to move or speak. Knowing what that felt like, I kept my mouth shut, leaving my hand where it was.

After a very long moment, she slipped her hand into mine. I gave her cold fingers a light, and what I hoped was reassuring, squeeze. Her trembling didn't let up in the slightest but her bunched shoulders did come down a bit. Long, wavy strands of dark brown hair clung to the perspiration on her skin.

She didn't say anything. She didn't have to.

Every tear that slid down her pale cheek was like another knife in my heart. Once again, all I had done was sit back and watch as Max assaulted someone. Some part of me was too cowardly to interfere. All I could offer her was a bit of empty comfort, a human touch to remind her that she wasn't alone.

Chapter Nine

It was odd, but it stung my pride as the days passed to see Max come and go, drinking from the girls or from Na'man, the one guy he kept locked in here with us. He left the others shaking, emotional wrecks in his wake—while completely ignoring me.

He occasionally took one of them out with him, then returned them a few hours later as pale shadows of themselves. I did my best not to think too hard about what he might have done to them during those little excursions. I could guess by the trauma-tized looks and empty gazes, the way they shivered and cried once he was gone.

Those were the times I was thankful he seemed to have lost his interest in me. And hated myself more for being too afraid to try to stop him from hurting them, and for being grateful it wasn't me.

It was even worse when I finally worked up the courage to ask him—from safely across the room during a rare daytime visit—if Sara was okay. He looked at me with such a flat, emotionless expression, his gray eyes washed out to the point of appearing nearly colorless in the dim sunlight, that I couldn't find it in myself to say anything else. I had to turn my gaze away. He didn't stay long after that, taking blood from Iana and then leaving without a word. It was disheartening, to say the least.

His perfunctory appearance and manner made a little more sense a couple of hours later. The smell of rotting peaches from Iana's strange blood was still on the air when Vivian called out from the pool room, the urgency in her voice and frantic gestures bringing all of us to hurry and gather by the windows.

Red and blue flashes flickered across the snow, splashing against the stone wall to the southeast. We couldn't see them from this angle, but there were emergency vehicles of some kind on the property.

Tense, excited, we all pressed against the metal bars and craned our necks, trying to spot a uniform or a police car.

No one said anything for the longest time, all of us collectively holding our breath, watching for any sign of rescue. Then a couple of men in police uniforms, a tall, skinny guy in an FBI jacket, and one of Max's henchmen walked around the side of the mansion, coming into our view.

We screamed and hollered and banged on the metal keeping us from the glass, trying to get their attention, but they never once looked up. I didn't want to believe it, but I had the sinking feeling that our prison wasn't just soundproofed. The glass was probably tinted in a way to make it too reflective for anyone to see in from the outside. Max's man adjusted the collar of his coat and looked our way. His casual glance and smug smile told me he must have known we were screaming for the officers' attention but were never going to get it.

Being trapped in that room, seeing the police so close and not being able to do anything about it, was one of the most helpless, awful experiences I'd had since Max had taken me. They didn't look up. Not even once. Obviously they couldn't tell we were here, couldn't hear our cries for help. They might have been here searching for me, or they might have been here because word got out about Max's shadier activities. They knew *something* was wrong. Even from where I stood, even with the wrought iron bars in the way, I recognized the look of the warrant in the officer's hand as he gestured at Max's man.

They stood there talking for a few minutes, their lips moving, the occasional hand gesture taking in the house or the expanse of the property.

After awhile, Max's security guard walked back toward the flashing lights with one of the police officers. The FBI agent and the other officer stayed where they were, their hands moving in sharp, urgent gestures as they had some kind of disagreement. The agent kept pointing at the house. The officer kept pointing back toward the flashing lights. I had the sinking feeling the local cops might be in Max's pocket, and trying to dissuade the FBI, on his behalf, not to look too closely at what was hidden behind the curtain.

Even a vampire couldn't say no to a search warrant. I straightened a bit as the FBI agent moved through a door below us and out of sight, the officer shaking his head before following reluctantly in his wake.

Even though there wasn't anything more to see, we all stayed right where we were, glued to this one tiny hope that we might be found and rescued. A few minutes later, there was a bit of noise from the common room. I glanced back, as did most of the others, in time to see Max ushering Gideon and Sara before him.

She was leaning heavily on the necromancer for support, head hanging, her normally sparkling blue eyes gone dim from what looked like a nasty combination of exhaustion and blood loss. Sara usually had some color in her skin, but at the moment she was even paler than I was, and there were unhealed bite marks visible on her arms and throat. Quite a few more than had been there when I last saw her.

And she sported a brand-new collar, white leather to match the loose silk wrap and pants that washed out her already pale features.

Fighting back the urge to throw myself on Max and throttle the unlife out of him, I scooted around the gathered, gaping throng by the windows and headed straight for Gideon and Sara. Max barely paid me a glance before speaking in hushed, urgent tones to Gideon, clearly continuing some earlier thread of conversation.

"They won't find them. Stay here, and don't provoke them or I'll revoke my hospitality and you can find your own way back to Los Angeles."

Gideon scowled but didn't argue. After his tight nod, Max turned on a heel and stalked out, the door sliding into place and locking behind him.

The necromancer's attention turned to me as I approached. The muscles in his jaw and neck tensed, but he stayed put as I yanked Sara out of his arms and into a hug. She gave a startled yelp before returning the gesture. Disgustingly, she smelled like him, the odor of chloroform and dead things clinging to her like a revolting perfume.

"Jesus, don't scare me like that," she scolded, returning the hug once she saw it was just me.

"Scare *you?* Cripes, woman," I said, pulling back to look her over, "I've been worried sick about you. Are you okay? I mean, obviously not, but—"

"Relax! I'm fine. I'm alive. Gideon has been watching out for me."

I turned a murderous glare in his direction, a vein throbbing in my temple. He didn't seem terribly bothered by it, though he didn't meet my gaze for long. If the bite marks were his idea of "watching out" for Sara's health, I could give him a few puncture marks of his own to see how it felt.

Sara's hand on my chin forced me to look back at her instead. She gave it a little shake. "Stop that. He's done the best he could. What about you? Are you okay? How are you holding up?"

I took a breath and forced myself to relax. "I'm okay. As well as could be expected, I guess. Any idea what's going on? With the cops, the FBI?"

"Someone broke Mr. Carlyle's cover," Gideon said, but from the tone of his voice I wasn't sure how he felt about it. When I looked back at him, he was staring at the video camera above the door.

Much as I wanted to ask questions about his plans, I didn't dare. Not while we were being watched. I hated it, but I'd have to trust that he'd give me a signal when he was ready.

I gestured for Sara to follow me back outside. As I led the way, she looked around, one brow raised, otherwise not seeming very impressed with the surroundings. Maybe she was staying in an equally opulent prison. I had no idea if Max had stuck her in a closet or another big suite of rooms. I wasn't sure I wanted to know.

Gideon trailed after us, adjusting the cuffs of his long-sleeved shirt, which was a dark green that matched his eyes. Sara and I sat down and the necromancer leaned against the door frame, watching from afar with obvious interest. The others gave us a wide berth but kept an eye on Sara and me. Mostly on me. Except for Iana, whose golden eyes were glowing intently as she stared unblinking at Gideon, her hands hooked into twitching claws.

"There's got to be a way out of here. Some way of letting those cops know we're here."

Sara shook her head. "I don't see how. I heard you guys banging on the bars before we came in."

That gave me pause. I looked down at the seat, then back at the window. The wrought iron bars didn't have enough room between them to squeeze a hand through to bang on the glass, but they *did* leave enough room for one of the chair legs.

I rocketed to my feet, grabbing the chair and

scraping it across the inlaid tile. "God *damn,* Sara, this is why I love you. You're fucking brilliant."

Puzzled, she rose, following me at a slower pace. "Uh . . . thanks? What'd I say?"

"Grab a chair. Come on, the rest of you, too!" I hefted the one I'd dragged over to the iron bars, adjusting the legs to poke through the holes. As soon as the others saw what I was doing, they all went for chairs and stools, anything that might have legs long enough to reach the windows beyond the bars. We wouldn't be able to get out, but we might be able to attract some notice from the cops searching the grounds.

I shoved at the chair, braced for the impact against the glass. It shivered and chipped under the blow, but didn't crack.

The others started doing the same. Iana and I did the most damage. In addition to being sound-proofed and tinted, the damned windows must have been bulletproof or something. Hairline cracks were the best we could do, even with supernatural strength, but I was betting the noise might attract attention if we kept it up.

Gideon didn't try to stop us, but he did turn a newly appraising eye in my direction when I glanced at him over my shoulder.

The rest of us continued our assault on the windows, doing everything we could to make noise. That is, until someone smacked me on the back of the head hard enough that my forehead snapped forward to hit the chair, momentarily knocking me senseless. I fell to the floor and the chair landed on my chest hard enough that I was sure there would be a huge bruise on my ribs and stomach later.

Breathless and stunned, once I blinked the blurriness out of my vision and could do more than gasp air into my constricted lungs, I stared up at the angry guard looming over me. It was the guy with the eye patch and scar, whose bandage-covered nose I had probably broken when I busted out of my first holding cell. His face was reddened and twisted with fury as he glared down at me with his one good eye. A couple of other guards in their sharp suits were driving back the other women, yanking chairs out of their hands and shoving them away from the bars. Most of the ladies fled immediately, two or three screaming in terror, but Iana and Na'man stood their ground.

"You are one stupid girl," Scar-face said, giving me a kick in the ribs that knocked the little breath in my lungs right back out.

Sara flung herself at him, snarling, but was thrust stumbling back, landing on her ass with a smack loud enough for me to grimace in sympathy. She didn't have the benefit of my strength or reflexes, and was still dealing with blood loss to boot, but she didn't look too badly hurt. She winced a bit, struggling to get to her feet, but I hadn't recovered enough to help her.

"Move!"

I might have said something caustic to the guy if I had the breath for it. Instead, I stayed right where I was, flailing a bit as I tried to figure out how to make my everything stop hurting and get away from the asshole. He grabbed one of my arms and slid me closer, flipping me on my stomach to slap a pair of handcuffs around my wrists before yanking me up to my feet. I stumbled along with him as he pulled me by the arm. Gideon gave me a little finger wave and a smirk as Scar-face dragged me past him. I stuck my tongue out at the necromancer in return since I couldn't give him a one-finger salute.

The guy pulled me along with him, past a couple more guards keeping an eye on the door who watched with dull curiosity as we passed. He took me into Max's room, pulling me to one of the upholstered benches. Rather than let me sit on it, he put a foot on the back of one of my calves, sending me to my knees on the carpet, then sat down on the bench himself.

Rude, inconsiderate bastard.

I resettled myself as comfortably as I could under the circumstances, muttering under my breath the whole time. Scar-face didn't say anything, though he did look a bit too pleased with himself for me to think that whatever Max had in store for me was over yet.

A little while later, the other two guards brought the chairs and stools from the pool room into Max's room, leaving them next to the door. The flunkies glanced at me curiously once or twice, but for the most part concentrated on their task.

Once it looked like all of the chairs were out, the lot of them shuffled into Max's room. Two of them stayed on their feet while the rest sat in the chairs, playing with cell phones or staring with obvious boredom into space.

One of them called out to Scar-face. "How much longer?"

"Dunno. Top floor is done, but they've still got a lot of ground to cover before they'll 'ave searched the whole grounds. Pull out a pack of cards or something. We're going to be here for a while."

The other guardsmen grumbled a bit, but didn't argue. The one who had asked how much longer went back into my gilded prison only to return a couple of minutes later with a book in hand. *Catch-22*. Of course.

Time passed. It got dark outside. The men took turns grabbing dinner from inside. Though I got pretty hungry and thirsty during the wait, I didn't bother asking for anything and nobody offered to get me anything.

A crackle of static from a radio I hadn't seen was followed by a voice I didn't recognize. "We're clear. Move the chairs to the basement, then report in. Stokes, stay with the girl."

Everyone but Scar-face got up and cleared out, each of them carrying a couple of chairs. There were three chairs left behind, but I doubted any of them would come back to finish the job. Scar-face— Stokes—had eaten and resumed his seat on the bench, though he didn't seem very pleased to be left with babysitting detail. To be fair, I wasn't too pleased about it, either.

We waited in uncompanionable silence for what felt like hours but was probably only twenty minutes.

Max stalked in, moving with the liquid grace of a hunter on the prowl. His eyes gleamed with predatory intent, the tension in his shoulders and the thin lines around his mouth making his agitation obvious. One sharp gesture was all it took for Stokes to get up and hightail it out of the room.

I might have laughed at how nervous the guy got and the wide berth he gave Max as he nearly ran from us, but now I was alone with an angry, probably hungry, vampire.

Once the door shut behind Stokes, Max closed the distance between us. He didn't say a word, but the weight of his displeasure was palpable. The subtle gleam in his eyes turned into a fierce, red glow and the pressure of him digging into my mind to take control was so sudden and painful that I could barely breathe.

I was in such deep shit.

Chapter Ten

Max didn't have to touch me to make me hurt. I couldn't move as he used our locked gazes as a channel to bring memories to the surface. One, of his progeny pinning me to a bed in a cold, damp room, making sure it hurt as he sucked the life out of me. Another, of being held in Max's arms, of the disgust and revulsion that had wracked me once I realized how much I wanted him to keep biting me. And another, of just how good it felt to be bound, to bend to his will, the warm glow of basking in his praise—and the pain in my heart when he was disappointed with me, the aching burn of loss when Royce and his minions wouldn't let me go so I could return to his side.

It was like living it again. Re-experiencing those memories in all their Technicolor glory. Feeling it all over again.

And all the while I knew he was there, seeing and feeling it, too. Somehow I knew he was that deep inside, taking all my secret shame and making it his.

He let out an audible hiss before he turned away from me, breaking the mental connection between us. The loss of him was nearly as painful as the claws he'd hooked into my brain, leaving me gasping with shock. Wide-eyed and open-mouthed, I stared up at him from my knees, pulling back as much as I could.

The vampire turned his gaze heavenward in a gesture that looked more like something my parents did when they were annoyed with me than I cared to think about. He then hooked a chair with his foot, pulling it closer so he could take a seat across from me. This time I thought better of meeting his eyes and ducked my head, bracing for whatever he might do to me. Yell at me, send me to bed without dinner, take away my TV privileges . . . The facetious thoughts were the only thing I could cling to in an effort not to go mad with terror that Max might dig into my thoughts again.

"Shiarra," he said, drawing my name out like a paper cut—so sharp and quick that you don't feel the pain until you realize you're bleeding. "I've done my best to be temperate with you, but your reticence is wearing on my patience. I don't have the time to deal with you or your insolence. Wresting control of cities from other vampires to place my progeny in key locations is far more important to me than wasting my time trying to use your connection to your pack when we are still weeks off from the full moon. Why do you insist on acting out in ways that interrupt my work and draw my ire? Are you deliberately setting out to anger me?"

I wasn't quite sure how to answer him. Did he think I was acting like some headstrong teenager, lashing out at restrictive house rules? Or did he really not realize just how fucked up his operation was and that anyone with half a brain cell in my situation would be making every effort to escape?

I was starting to think it might be the latter because he was laying his cards on the table. Telling me he was actively working to take over other cities was a bad sign. Vampires were renowned for playing their cards close to their chest. Admitting what he was doing likely meant he intended me to play a part in it.

Knowing why he had ignored me for days at a time didn't improve my outlook on my situation one bit, either. The werewolf responsible for my infection was dead, and most of his pack hated me with a passion. Whatever Max thought of my connection to the pack of Sunstrikers, their pack leader—my ex-boyfriend Chaz—wouldn't let them do a thing for me anymore. Volunteering that information might lead Max to decide to cut his losses and kill me. If I kept it to myself, I would live longer and there was still a chance at escape or rescue.

Max shook his head when it became clear I wasn't going to respond. "This lack of acceptance of your new lot could have been the death of you if you were with someone else, but I don't think you've quite grasped what your place here means. You are mine. As I told you when you got here, there is no escape from me unless I choose to let you go."

I glared up at him, trying on a little anger to hide

the fear raging inside. "I'm a person, you asshole. You don't own me. You never will. You can lock me up, but I'm not yours and never will be."

Max stared down at me, one hand lightly rubbing his chin as little furrows appeared between those gray eyes. He didn't exactly look angry or frustrated. Considering. Like he thought I was being dense and was trying to decide how to explain the facts of life to me. After a while, he spoke again, this time with a tone of gentle scolding like a parent telling their wayward teenager not to stay out so late and to call next time. What a crock.

"I do believe your inability to accept your place is why this is so difficult for you. Rhathos was far too lenient with you."

"He doesn't own me, either."

He voiced a soft, mocking laugh. "Oh, yes he did. Long before you met him. The moment he acknowledged your existence, you were his. The only difference between us is that I do not lie about your place in my household." That felt far too uncomfortably like trains of thought I'd had myself. An unbidden memory of a low, husky voice promising just that made me shiver. "*Don't doubt for a moment that you're mine, my little hunter. You've been mine longer than you know.*" Max, who didn't seem to notice he'd hit a nerve, continued his little lecture. "Do you know what makes me the master here, and you the slave?"

I bit my tongue so I wouldn't say something that would land me in further trouble.

"You let fear rule your actions. You accept that I

am stronger than you, and capable of hurting you, so you do as I say when directly ordered to avoid punishment. While not ideal, it is acceptable. I don't stamp out that fire that makes you continue to hope and search for a way out because it would destroy the spirit that makes you attractive." He leaned forward, one finger pointed at my face as he growled out his next words. "However, that does not give you license to incite rebellion in the rest of my pets."

"Oh, please," I said, my cup runneth over, "are you even listening to yourself? We are *people*, Max, not animals. You can't keep us like . . . like pets. Are you honestly surprised we're trying to get out any way we can?"

"As I said, I expected it of you. Not from the others, who know their place. Or did, until you put those idiotic notions of rescue into their heads. Do you have any idea how much work you've undone?"

That made me bristle. It rankled to think that he had those girls so cowed that no one had thought to try to get the attention of outsiders before today. "Good! They should be trying to get out! I don't care what century you're from—you're in America. Don't you know what you're doing is illegal and wrong? Hasn't living so much history taught you anything? Don't tell me you've never heard of the Emancipation Proclamation. What you're doing has been illegal even longer in England. Since . . . since . . ."

"1102."

"1102, right." I said. Then exploded. "Come on!

You know it's not right, you know the history of it better than I do. Haven't you ever seen that Liam Neeson movie? This can't end well for you."

"Don't be foolish. Making something illegal rarely stops it from happening, it only sets guidelines in place to punish those who are caught," he said, his tone still pedantic and I-know-best-so-just-sit-back-and-shut-up. "Slavery is not a new concept. It was done long before my time, and is still more common today than you think. It's quite a lucrative business and has paid my dues to country and sire for centuries. You should be thankful you haven't been sold as a pleasure slave or assigned to menial tasks. Appreciate your value, girl. It's saved you more pain than you know."

"Are you kidding?" I asked, incredulous. "*Thankful?* For *this?* There's nothing right or fair about anything you're doing here!"

"Fairness matters in the minds of Americans who see it as a means to their ends. It does not matter here." He took an unneeded breath, frowning down at me in obvious disapproval. "I am going to tell you a little story. When I am done, I'm going to do something to remind you of your place and ensure you never forget the time you spend with me, however long you may live."

My lip curled. "You think I'm ever going to be able to forget what you've done to me? To Sara?"

"If you were to fall into another's hands, perhaps," he replied. "What I have in mind will prevent even the most powerful mage or vampire from wiping it from your memories."

That chilled me. Whatever he was thinking of doing was undoubtedly going to be unpleasant.

"You have met Mouse. You know she is my progeny, yes?" At my cautious nod, he smiled in a way that set my skin crawling. "Good. And I am sure you know she is mute. Did she ever relay to you the story of how she was made so?"

"You tortured her. She didn't do something you wanted, so you tortured her until she couldn't talk back to you anymore, you sick bastard."

"It is not so simple as you make it sound. Truly, did no one tell you how it really happened? What she did? Or, more specifically, exactly what I did to her?"

My stomach churned as I thought about it, scrounging for any recollection of Mouse or anyone else in Royce's apartment building speaking about her past. Most of my time spent there had passed in a fog of pain or fear or some other unpleasant emotion whenever I wasn't loopy from the mind-mojo Max had worked on me.

The first few days of my blood bond-induced haze, I had nearly clawed holes in the walls to escape and make my way to Max's side or clung to Royce as he fought to keep me from answering the call. Then I passed more time, bitter and listless, just wanting to go home. That was followed by some of the most intense pain I'd ever experienced in my life as I went through withdrawal pangs for vampire blood. Every other visit after that had been too brief to get to know anyone in Royce's home beyond a passing acquaintance.

No, I had no idea how Max had stolen Mouse's voice. He clearly gathered as much by my expression, because he leaned forward to tip my chin up to make sure I was looking into his cold, gray eyes as he told me.

"She had the voice of an angel, once. My angel. Her voice was why I made her mine. My little bird sang for me and did my bidding—until Rome, where she attempted to disobey me."

The blood on his breath as he leaned even closer made my eyes water, but I didn't dare blink or look away. "She grew a conscience. The opera she was performing called for the death of the male lead, but she refused to kill the boy. Not even for her art, she told me. Not even for me.

"When we returned to the Americas, I took my time with her. I'm sure you realize what a busy man I am, so you can imagine what dedication it took for me to set aside at least an hour every day to personally oversee her punishment and reprogramming. Sharp objects. Blunt ones. Silver. Cold iron. Blessed objects. Unholy relics. So many methods, so few that worked the way I desired. It took decades for me to discover a way to make the damage to her vocal chords permanent, seeing as she was already turned, but it's a technique I perfected on her."

Oh, *God.* I'd known Mouse was mute, and that Max had a hand in it, but I had no idea his sadistic streak went so deep. The guy had exhibited some unbelievably psychotic behavior when trying to wrest control of New York from Royce's hands back when I first met him, and I had seen some horrific things since I arrived in this Motel Hell, but I had no idea he had been so cruel to mute, gentle Mouse. No wonder she always got a look like she wished she could hate him to death whenever he was mentioned.

Max was looking at me expectantly, one brow raised, like he was waiting for a reply. My throat was so constricted and dry, I had a hard time speaking. After a couple of attempts, I choked out a few words. "How could you do that to her?"

"I told you why," he responded, voice cold as a winter night. "She is mine and she will never forget it. Not if she lives until the sun this forsaken rock circles burns out. Even when her voice returns—oh, yes, it may take another century or two, but it will come back in time—she will remember what comes of disobeying me. You're about to learn the same lesson, my little red-headed vixen. The question is, will you do as I wish without further motivation, or will you hold out to see what else I can strip from you? Or just how much pain you can endure?"

My voice was trapped in my throat, fluttering like a wounded bird. If it escaped, I had the feeling the screams might never stop.

The hard look on his face melted away, leaving a congenial smile that crinkled the corners of his eyes in a way that might have been attractive on someone less insane.

"Very well. Shall we begin?"

I shook my head, twisting away, pain shooting up my arms as I fought the bindings. Max snapped his fingers, and a pair of men sauntered in, both of them wearing slick plastic aprons over their jeans and T-shirts. A sick little voice in the back of my head reminded me it was the sort of thing a butcher might wear to keep the gore of the slaughter off their clothes.

They each took one of my arms and hefted me up between them, the tips of my toes dragging on the cold marble as Max led the way out of the room. Though I'd seen enough of the huge mansion that I was starting to get a feel for the twists and turns of the place, I didn't recognize the route we were taking. We went down a few flights of stairs until the unmistakable damp chill of a basement crept over my skin, the taste of wet earth and burning wood crawling over my tongue as I took a shaky breath.

This wasn't the same place as the rooms where he had initially kept me and entertained those other vampires during that auction. This felt more unfinished, like a subterranean cave. The ceiling was rough wooden beams mostly hidden in shadow high over our heads. Somewhere above us, a heavy door slammed and the darkness became a tangible thing.

There was light ahead. Flickering. A fireplace? The brick fixture was deep, but the warmth and light from the fire had a minimal impact on the grave-like chill of the underground space.

I did my best to dig my heels in when I spotted the table covered with an array of shining tools: knives, needles, saws, scissors, and every other instrument of torture you might expect in some psycho doctor wannabe's collection. There was a second stainless steel table next to it covered with Velcro straps. My breath was knocked out of me as I was picked up and bodily shoved facedown onto it, the cold biting into my skin through the thin robe and against my cheek.

"You know," Max said, strolling over to the fireplace as the two men strapped me down to the table, "I do enjoy reading science fiction. There are a number of authors who come up with the most outrageous ideas. For example, have you heard of a fellow by the name of John Norman?"

I grunted, out of breath and otherwise unable to reply. Out of the corner of my eye, I saw one of the guys who had dragged me down here make a face behind Max's back. The same guy who came over to shove a piece of leather between my teeth and strap it around my head.

It didn't take long to immobilize me. The short robe I was wearing was tugged up on the left side, a swipe of something cold and wet against my hip making me twitch. Judging by the sharp scent, it was rubbing alcohol. I was probably going to get a shot of some kind. Something to dull pain while he used those instruments of torture on me? Not that I wouldn't want it if that's what he planned, but what would be the point?

Oblivious to my squirming, Max continued speaking. The two men stepped back, waiting for something, both of them looking a bit bored, as though whatever was going on was a common occurrence.

Or maybe, like me, they were getting as tired as I was of his Bond villain-style monologue.

"Norman created a series of books that explored what a world might be like if the strong ruled and the weaker were enslaved. I did not find many of his methods for dealing with intractable slaves to be very practical, but he did have some fascinating ideas."

Max glanced at me over his shoulder, his eyes reflecting the firelight like glass as he lifted a long piece of metal that had been resting in the flames. The tip glowed the color of gray ashes, and my muscles seized at the realization that he intended to use that thing on me.

"There are less painful methods but I find the old ones work best to break a slave's will."

Blind panic was a term I thought I was familiar with. It evolved a whole new meaning for me in that moment.

There wasn't anything I could do to turn my head away, flinch back, cover myself—nothing. Wide-eyed, my focus went from a dull blur to razor sharp as he moved closer, praying desperately to whoever might be listening in to make this all some kind of nightmare that I could wake up from anytime now.

Once he was close enough, he held the iron rod so I could see the pattern on the end. An intricate symbol of a pigeon or something flying inside a wreath of olive leaves. If it wasn't on the business end of a branding iron, I might have called it pretty.

"Don't worry, my dove. This is a memory you will never be rid of."

As badly as I wanted to escape in that moment, I couldn't move an inch. Closing my eyes so I wouldn't have to watch what he was about to do, I whimpered around the gag, raging panic clawing at my insides.

Never in my life had I experienced pain like that before. The brand probably wasn't pressed against me more than a few seconds, but it felt like an eternity of agony as the metal bit into my flesh, hissing, searing, digging deep into the skin.

Marking me forever a vampire's property.

All the while I couldn't move, though I tried, almost biting through the leather that had been shoved so unceremoniously in my mouth. Nothing existed but that white-hot pain, the sizzle of it against my flesh. The sickening smell of my own skin and hair burning. Nothing mattered but escaping it.

And even after the brand was pulled away, the scent of charred meat heavy on the air, I was still screaming and fighting against the bonds to get away from it. In that moment, and for some time after, nothing existed in my world but the searing heat and agony radiating from my left hip.

Once my screams tapered off into hitching sobs, Max's cold fingers brushed against my cheek, tracing the trail of my tears.

"Be proud, pet. You bear the symbol of the coinage my people used when I was still alive. The city that I ruled. No one will doubt who you belong to when they see it."

I moaned against the gag and did my best not to throw up.

He ran his fingers through my hair, gentle, soothing, and it destroyed something in me to realize I was leaning into his touch in some wretched bid for comfort.

"As soon as you've recovered," he said, like it was nothing more than a momentary setback, as though he hadn't just branded me like cattle, "you'll be pleased to show it off. It means you have my protection. That you're my favored stock." He leaned in to press his lips to my temple in a cold kiss. "That Rhathos has no claim to you. Not anymore. Never again."

He removed the leather strap from between my teeth while his assistants took off the other restraints. I was too shocked to do more than shake uncontrollably in his arms as he picked me up, a tiny sound of hurt and fear squeezed out of me as I tried to focus beyond the blinding pain.

He carried me back upstairs, though he didn't immediately bring me back to the prison I was growing to know so well. Instead, he took me to yet another room I had never seen and laid me out on the bed. It was some kind of guest room, spacious and airy. A high ceiling featured snow-blanketed skylights rather than regular windows. All I could do was shiver there in misery, limp with pain and a soul-deep form of violation, surrounded by what felt like utterly incongruous luxury.

Once I was settled, he retrieved a tray of medical

supplies left on a nearby dresser. Painkillers, bandages, and some kind of aloe gel for burns. Knowing he had planned for this in advance didn't make any kind of difference other than leaving me feeling even sicker. He must have done this before to know exactly what supplies he'd need to have on hand and how to apply them once it was over. All I could do was try not to choke on the pills or pass out as he applied the gel. He made soothing noises as he did it, which didn't help in the least, though I wondered why he was doing it himself instead of leaving the task to an underling.

Strangely solicitous, he sat down beside me, angling himself so he could stroke my hair and wipe away my tears, like some twisted parent comforting a wounded child. I didn't want his touch to feel good, but the chill of his skin felt so soothing against my burning cheeks that I couldn't bring myself to pull away.

He didn't say anything, which I was glad for. If he did, I really would puke all over his nice silk sheets.

I hadn't forgotten he was a monster. Far from it. It was just too difficult to fight when all I wanted to do was pass out from the pain. It didn't take a genius to figure out he was shooting for some sicko version of Stockholm syndrome in hopes that I would become bonded to him, or that I would take this as some kind of lesson in obedience and servitude. And while feelings of disgust roiled in the back of my mind—not only for him, but for myself and everything that led up to this moment—

he was right. I wouldn't forget what he had done anytime soon.

Nor would I forgive.

Though I was certainly afraid of what else he could do to me, tonight I would dream of nothing but revenge.

Chapter Eleven

At some point, I drifted off. It must have been the pills.

Once I regained enough of my senses to realize I was still alive and that Max might be in the room, I sat bolt upright—and nearly passed out again.

It took some time for the agony to fade enough for me to focus. Max was gone. Sunlight filtered in through the skylights but the layer of snow made it dim and weak. There was a glass of water and a couple more white pills left on the end table within easy reach.

Anticipating my needs. Fancy that.

The pills took the worst of the edge off. The hazy, blurred vision and weakness like a weight pressing on my chest, making it difficult to breathe, were a small price to pay for disconnection from the constant itch and burn radiating from the mark on my hip.

For hours, I couldn't move my left leg or shift my butt without excruciating pain. The only thought

I could console myself with was that eventually I wouldn't even feel it anymore, and once that happened, I would do everything in my power to shove that hot piece of iron straight up Max's ass.

Even my thoughts rang with false bravado. Truth was, I was hurting and terrified and the pain was the only thing stopping me from trying to hide myself under the bed or in a closet, somewhere it might take him longer to find me again.

Branded. Scarred for life. The concept of enslavement had almost been abstract to me until this moment. Of course I realized I was Max's captive, but at this point there was no denying I had been bumped down in status from hostage and was now relegated to property.

Property didn't have feelings. Property could be broken or discarded on a whim.

Sick with the realization of what the brand symbolized, I scanned the room again, hoping there might be something sharp I could use to cut short his games with me.

Free will. At least I still had that much left to me. He couldn't control all my choices. I could choose my own way out. He couldn't control that part of me.

Desperation for escape—by any means necessary—was impetus enough for me to fight the pain long enough to sit up and focus through the tears.

The small container of ointments on top of the dresser wouldn't do much for me. I doubted there was enough there to overdose on. There were no sharp objects in the room. I wasn't confident that I could bring myself to asphyxiation, rather than just passing out, by using the sheets as a rope.

That gave me pause. I glanced up at the snow-dusted skylight. Then to the dresser.

It would be dangerous, but I could stack one of the end tables on top of the dresser and reach the window. The risk of breaking my neck didn't sound so bad a death compared to what might happen if I stayed quiet and still, meekly waiting for Max to come back.

Getting out was only part of the problem. I needed to run. Through the snow. All I had was the silk robe—no shoes, no jacket, nothing to protect me against the elements.

It didn't matter. It was worth risking a fall that might snap my neck or drifting off to a final sleep in a bed of snow. What did matter was getting the hell out of there before someone came back to move me out of this room to one with no escape routes at all.

I inched my way to the side of the bed, wheezing with every shock of heat and hurt that jolted up my side, my whole body gone slick with the sweat of desperate terror. Before going any farther, I grabbed a pillow and pulled off the casing, balling it up and shoving it between my teeth to keep from breaking them with the clenching and to muffle the involuntary cries of pain.

It was a good thing I'd thought to do that before actually standing up. Once I shook off the momentary blackout, I was terrified that someone might have heard me anyway. Slowly sitting up from my slumped position against the bed, I wavered on my feet, woozy with shock. Though I knew I should take my time, the thought of Max or one of his cronies checking in on me spurred me to movement.

Of course I ended up face-planting on the floor. The moment I tried to put weight on my left leg, the combination of the movement and the flare of agony that burned its way from my outer thigh all the way up to my rib cage was paralyzing. Before I could catch myself, I was down, stars in my vision and my knees and palms stinging from catching my weight. Hardly noticeable after the fire on my hip, but it still wasn't pleasant.

If anything, getting up off the floor was even more painful than getting off the bed. Everything hurt. Even my jaw, from clenching so hard against the cloth I'd shoved in my mouth. At least it kept the breathless whimpers muffled. Even to my own ears it sounded strange, inhuman, more like an injured animal than a person. Hard to believe those sounds were coming from me.

Limping across the carpet, I approached a closed door next to the bathroom—I assumed it was a closet—to see if there might be anything useful inside. Clinging to the handle for balance, I blinked in surprise at the contents.

Corsets. Dresses. High heels. Light dusters and jackets meant for show, not snow. Looked like someone had done their shopping in bulk at Hot Topic. This room had belonged to a woman, someone with a closet full of pretty, but not very functional, things. A guest? Or a vampire, maybe, impervious to the cold weather? No, a vampire wouldn't want a room with a skylight.

Not that the previous occupant, or why they left their wardrobe behind, mattered. Anything had to be better than what I was wearing now.

The white leather pants and matching corset with a long-sleeved shirt underneath seemed best. Harder to see against the snow. Leather would be a smidge more useful than the lacy or satiny numbers. There would still be far too much skin showing.

Whoever these belonged to before was bustier in the chest and longer in the leg than me, but I didn't care. Even with all the strategically fashionable slashes and holes, they covered most of my vital parts, and that made them infinitely better than the robe. I grabbed a pair of boots a couple of sizes too big, with heels much higher than anything I was used to wearing.

Limping across the floor, I searched the drawers of the nearest dresser, almost crying with relief when I saw there were warm socks in one, not just more fanciful crap that wouldn't do me any good outside. I could layer up and maybe stuff some inside the boots to make do until I could find something more practical and better-fitting.

I put on the clothes, then emptied and moved the dresser. *Before* putting on the heels. I might have been in a frantic state of mind, but I wasn't going to be *that* stupid about my escape attempt.

Through the tears, the burning, the pain, I managed to use the adrenaline and terror to find the energy to get the furniture into place. It took a couple of tries and another blackout before I managed to pick up and balance the end table. I did need a breather once I got that far, but I didn't wait too long.

Too much noise, too much time going by. I didn't dare stop to rest too long because every moment ticking by brought sunset, and Max's inevitable return, that much closer.

Slinging the boots over my shoulder, tied together by the wide lace shoestrings, and stuffing the bandages and medicines in my pockets, I tugged the sheets off the bed, wrapping them around my neck and shoulders.

Pulling myself on top of the dresser was even harder than putting on the pants. Not only did I have the leather rubbing against the brand, but the pull and strain of sore, hurting muscles and stretching the skin around the burn made everything *hurt*.

Once I got on top of the end table, I had to stop. Wait. Crouched, clinging to the edges, mentally grasping for equilibrium that wasn't there. Another blackout was coming, just there, graying the edges of my vision. Not now, not yet. I had to get out first.

Closing my eyes, I prayed for it to pass. A few breaths. A few heartbeats.

There was a sound outside my door. A scrape, like shoes scuffing on the marble floor.

My vision was still blurry but I forced myself to open my eyes and get to my feet. There was a bit of wobbling, but I managed to keep from falling over. Wiping moisture off my cheeks with the back of my hand, I blinked up at the skylight. A latch. One flimsy little latch was all that now stood between me and freedom.

I turned the knob, got up on tiptoe to push the window open. Despite the weight of snow, it lifted without much effort on my part. Cold seeped in, almost instantly chilling my fingers, followed by the scent of wood smoke and frozen earth.

A breath of freedom. It was sweet, but I needed to move fast. There was a wire alarm on the side of the window I hadn't seen. Someone, somewhere, would know something was wrong. No matter how much it hurt, I had to get going.

The pain of pulling myself up on the slick, icy ledge was different. Biting, but clean, the natural burn of straining muscles in my arms. Nothing like the scaring hurt on my hip.

The ice bit right through the corset, but it took a bit longer for the cold to seep through the leather pants. I was careful to lead with my right leg once I swung my body up. A quick roll, a flash of pain as I put weight on my branded hip, a muted thump from the window closing—and I was out. On the roof, alone and free.

I might have sat there panting and shivering for a minute or twenty while the knots of terror gripping my heart and lungs eased. The air was cold, but I savored the feel of unobstructed sunlight warming my cheek, sensing the glow through my closed eyelids. The taste of freedom and air not tainted by the musk of vampire and quiet desperation was sweet, but I needed to get the hell out of there before someone discovered I was gone.

Rising to my bare feet, I stood and surveyed my surroundings. Dark, heavy clouds spoke of an incoming storm, which would both hide my tracks and make my escape harder once it hit. From my vantage point on the roof, I thought this part of the house faced what might be the backyard. On three sides it stretched for acres. I didn't see an entrance or a back gate, but I was pretty sure I could reach and climb the rough stone wall surrounding the property. If I could get on the ground and kept on the east side of the property, I would be out in the open for a good stretch, but my chances of getting out unseen would be better.

The snow was thick, so I took it slow, easing myself toward the edge. The cold bit into my toes like tiny needles worming under the skin, but there was no way I was going to risk slipping in heels on a patch of ice and breaking my ass or neck. Aside from the discomfort to my feet, I didn't have much trouble shuffling down the slope of the roof, though I did have a brief bout of vertigo when I looked over the edge.

Three stories. I couldn't jump that. Not without breaking something.

Good thing I had brought the sheet with me.

Chapter Twelve

A few minutes later, the balls of my feet and ankles stinging—not to mention the incredible pain in my hip from the crouched landing after the short fall from the end of the knotted sheet—I was on the ground.

I didn't dare take any more time. The longer I waited, the greater the chance Max's cronies on security detail would figure out I was gone and catch up to me.

Stumbling through the snow, I made a beeline for the wall surrounding the property. I needed speed, and the high heels would cut into that enormously, more than the limp caused by my aching hip already did. I could put on the boots once I was over the wall and safe on the other side.

"Hey! Get back here!"

No. No, no, no. I wasn't stopping, not for one of Max's people, not for anything.

Everything hurt, but I still ran, limping every step of the way. Snow crunching behind me made it clear I had one pursuer who was catching up quickly. I wasn't going to stop, but I did slow down, breathing deeply, counting down the seconds as those heavy footsteps grew closer.

Just before fingers brushed my shoulder, I threw up my elbow, crying out at the shock traveling up my arm from contact. The guy crashed into my back, his momentum sending us both tumbling to the ground in a swirl of white.

He didn't make a grab for me once we were down. Both of us lay on our backs, but he was choking around a damaged, if not crushed, windpipe. Lucky shot on my part. He wouldn't be able to follow anytime soon.

It didn't take me long to gasp some breath back into my lungs, but I did need a couple of minutes to regain my ability to see around the blinding pain radiating from my hip. The guy didn't resist as I crawled over and rolled him out of his coat and took his gloves, his eyes bugging as he watched me shrug into the too-large garment.

After a moment's reflection, I patted down his pockets and took his wallet and keys while I was at it.

It was a bit of a struggle getting back to my feet, but once I managed, I met his wide-eyed gaze. There was fear there. Fear of me, maybe. The taste of it on my tongue, sweet like syrup, sparked a sudden, fierce hunger. When I raised a hand to tug on a glove and saw the claws and spidery black veins, I could imagine why he was afraid—but I was still human enough to remember not to give him any more reason than that.

"You tell Max he's going to pay. You tell him to let the others go or I'll be back, and next time I'll burn this place to the ground."

Even as I said it, the words lisping around growing fangs, I knew it was true. He had Sara. Iana. Vivian. Na'man. All those other people. As soon as I found a safe place, a pay phone, a cell phone to borrow—anything—I would get in touch with Royce and get his help to end Max's operation once and for all.

It still hurt to move, but I felt stronger, invigorated somehow. Like the violence was spurring some kind of survival instinct to heal and move at a greater pace. Whatever Other-ness was in my blood, it had some benefits aside from making me Hulk out with minimal provocation. I would have to be careful not to give in to the hunger cramping my stomach. Blood or flesh, either would do, but feeding that inner beast with something more tangible would send me down a path I didn't want to explore.

Once I reached the wall, I looked back over my shoulder. The guy who had attacked me was still on the ground and more dark figures were coming toward me from the house. I didn't hesitate, reaching for the lip of the wall well above my head. The jump was smoother than I expected, almost leading me to miss grabbing for the iron spikes set into the top. It was getting easier to ignore the cold and pain as I pulled myself up to the edge, toes curling against the ice.

Distant shouts followed me as I lowered myself over the other side and dropped into the drift of snow below.

And cursed as I landed on a rock or something. Ow, ow, ow.

At least I didn't break anything. And I wasn't bleeding. Yay, go me.

Hopping over to a nearby rock jutting above the snow, I brushed off the worst of it and sat down. Then I brushed as much snow off my feet as I could with one of the extra socks I'd stuffed in my pocket. That out of the way, with a groan, I pulled on the boots, wriggling my toes to settle them in the material I'd stuffed inside. My feet felt like blocks of solid ice, but hopefully the boots and socks would provide enough insulation for them to warm up before any damage was done.

Levering to my feet, I wobbled unsteadily on the heels. It was uncomfortable, and the ankle of the foot that had landed on the rock ached, but it was better than losing my toes to frostbite.

Glancing around, I looked for any sign of civilization. No roads were visible through the evergreens and skeletal bones of trees that had shed their leaves for winter. No man-made structures, either. There might have been something out there, but I didn't want to risk stumbling around lost in the woods at this time of year. Max wouldn't call for an official search party and anyone he sent to find me wouldn't make the trip back pleasant. Assuming there would be a trip back.

Stepping carefully, I made my way a few yards from the wall, always keeping it in sight and on my right. If I followed the wall, eventually I would find a driveway, which would lead to a road, which would (presumably) lead to civilization. I'd have to take care not to trip on anything unseen under the blanket of white, and to keep moving, no matter how much everything hurt. My feet, my ankles, my hip—the pain reminded me I was alive. I was free, and I had a chance.

That was all that kept me going. I wanted to lie down. I wanted to curl up and cry in the snow. I wanted to go back, to make sure Sara was okay. I just wanted to rest, for someone else to take over, to fix everything I'd broken and make it all go away.

And if I gave in to that temptation, Max would win. All those people still trapped with him would continue to suffer—maybe more, if he was as angry with my escape as I imagined he was going to be when he heard the news. I'd hate to be the messenger on his security team for that little tidbit.

I had to reach Royce as soon as possible, and pray it was before Max got it into his head to hurt Sara.

The collar was tugged up to keep the wind from biting too deep against my face, and I hugged the jacket tight to myself as I got moving. I kept checking back the way I had come and listening for any sounds of pursuit as I hobbled along. It was only a matter of time before the other guards came looking for my trail.

Every sound made me jump. Crunching ice. The muted thump of piles of snow falling from tree limbs. Snapping branches. Even telling myself that I had more strength than Max's human minions and that I knew enough self-defense to hurt them if they should find me didn't help. The thought made me feel even colder than I already was. Psyching myself up was a fine art I had never perfected.

Even though I was watching and listening, hypersensitive to anything out of place, I almost walked right into one of the guards looking for me. His clothing blended in with the snow, all whites and grays, and he was leaning against a birch tree with pale, peeling bark. I froze, the guy only inches away, hood pulled low over his eyes and head ducked with a glove in his teeth as he tapped on a cell phone. That distracting piece of modern technology was the only reason he didn't notice me.

Hands clapped over my mouth, I backed up, quick, silent, pain momentarily forgotten as I faded into the brush. Ducking behind a tree, I stayed there, pressed against the bark, trying not to hyperventilate or make a sound.

The strains of the James Bond theme started playing. I almost screamed, but managed to swallow back the urge once it sank in that it was just the guy's cell phone.

"Yeah? . . . What? No, haven't seen any sign." He quieted, but I couldn't make out whatever the other person was saying. ". . . Yeah, give me a minute. I'll be right there."

He stomped off in the direction I'd come from,

muttering under his breath. I made out "jackass," but that was about it.

I needed to be much more careful. That was too close a call. I stayed where I was for another minute, listening, making sure he was gone and that no one else was coming. They'd pick up on my trail anytime now.

On the bright side, they appeared human. I didn't think they had heightened senses, if cell phone guy was anything to go by. I didn't hear any dogs, so most likely they didn't have anything that could follow me by scent. Not until dark, when the vampires came out to play. If I could disguise my trail, maybe it would keep them from finding me.

I looked around, studying the trees. There was some kind of cedar not far from where I was standing. The short, stiff needles would make a decent broom to hide some of my tracks. I moved around the far side of it, opposite the wall, and broke off a small branch. The scent of the sap was sharp on the crisp air. Put me in mind of hamster shavings.

Brushing up my tracks turned out to be easier than expected with the way that guy had been moving through the snow. Sure, the depressions were still there, but my passage was far less noticeable when I swept away the signs. At one point when I backtracked I even found a place where cell phone bro had—I am pretty sure unknowingly—crossed over mine. A great and wily hunter, he was not. I made a few new tracks to make it look as if I had gone deeper into the woods before following his tracks the way he had originally come. Oh, and I held on to that cedar branch, just in case.

I did have to be careful. He had been moving closer to the wall than I intended to be, and despite my best efforts, I ended up dragging my bad leg a few times. Still, it made it easier not to trip on anything when I knew exactly where to step, and having a clear path to follow gave me the opportunity to move with more speed and certainty.

It took a lot longer than I expected to reach the recessed door in the wall where the guy had come out. On the bright side, there was a brick walkway leading up to that locked, wrought iron gate back into hell. A *swept* brick walkway that led straight to a winding, paved road only a few yards away. Hallelujah and praise be to whoever above was finally looking out for me.

Just before the urge to make a run for the road hit me, common sense reasserted itself. I stayed where I was for a moment, studying the path. If it looked too good to be true, it probably was.

I crouched down—bit off the screamed curse that thoughtless move almost spurred out of me—then peered at the upper slope of the archway above the gate after wiping away the tears of pain. As I suspected, there was a security camera angled to see the walkway and even the road. Probably to watch for anyone who might think to drop in unexpectedly. Knowing who was coming gave Max and his people a chance to hide the evildoing, hide the bodies, hide the human trafficking, et cetera, ad infinitum, ad nauseum. It wasn't like he didn't have a few dozen hidden closets or creepy basements to shove those skeletons into if the police should stop by, as I had already witnessed.

Even the thought of the last of his basements I'd visited was enough to bring up a sudden urge to vomit and a flare of unexpected heat on my hip. Shoving it to the back of my mind, I rose—much more carefully than I'd crouched—and faded back a few steps, sweeping up my tracks with the branch as I went. I knew where the road was now. Even if my everything hurt, I had a direction and a plan. Better than what I'd had an hour ago.

Then it hit me. The urge to walk to that gate. The naked desire to return to Max's side. To beg forgiveness.

I locked my muscles and closed my eyes, biting my lip until it bled. He knew. He knew I was gone and he wanted me back. Was *demanding* I come back, using that ephemeral connection between us.

It wasn't like hearing words or seeing images, exactly. The *feel* of him in my head was familiar from those few days when I had first been bound to him by blood. He'd been able to pull my strings then, puppet-like, making me walk and talk however he wanted. Since the connection was never fully set between us by another taste of his blood, now it was just a bone-deep knowledge that something greater than me was trying to take the wheel and make me do what it desired. Something that was pushing at the walls I erected to keep it out, spider-claws tickling over my brain in search of any weakness to worm their way inside.

Freedom tasted better. Even if it did taste like my own black, corrupted blood. Bit by bit, I shored up my defenses with memories of what he had done to hurt me, hurt Sara, hurt Mouse, and what he might do to me if I gave in to that urge to return to his side. The more I thought about the pain he'd inflicted, the easier it was to keep him out.

I wasn't sure how long I stood there, out in the open, easy pickings for anyone in his employ to find me. It was too overcast to be sure, but the angle of the sun seemed different once the worst of the urge to go running back to Max's side faded. Still there. Still urgent. Still painful.

But I'd just learned a whole new definition of pain at Max's hands a few hours ago, and his mental nudges couldn't hold a candle to that.

Fists clenched, eyes narrowed to the point I could barely see, I took a step toward the trees and the unseen road ahead. Then another. Another.

I remembered at the last minute that I needed to continue sweeping up my tracks behind me, but by then, it wasn't so hard to move independently.

I walked away from hell with my head high, knowing that I would be back. And that next time it would be to see it burned to the ground.

Chapter Thirteen

Keeping to the trees, I made my way toward the road. This area seemed a little too rural for much traffic, but maybe I could flag someone down to help me.

I didn't see them at first, but the murmur of voices told me there were people up ahead. Male. Low. Urgent. I slowed down, moving as silently as I could, peering through the underbrush to try to spot who was talking. I didn't want to accidentally walk into a gaggle of suited idiots, all under Max's thumb and ready to make me pay for running.

My heart leapt in my chest when I spotted the black-and-white parked at the side of the road. Then it stuttered and fell like a stone when I recognized Stokes, the man with the scarred face and eye patch, leaning against the other side and talking through the open window to the two uniformed officers in the car. His gravelly voice carried on the crisp, cold air, stopping me in my tracks and removing any last hope of rescue I might have been clinging to.

"Call me if someone spots her. Hopefully this crap weather will clear out so we can get the tracker working again."

"Creepy shit, man. I thought they only did that to dogs and cats."

The laughter of the guy with the eye patch chilled me worse than the snow and biting wind. "What do you think they are? They're pets, man. We've gotta protect our investments. They run away, we need to be able to find them again. Just remember, this one bites. Someone calls it in, you let us deal with her."

"We'll keep an eye out."

I hadn't thought it would be possible for me to feel any sicker about Max's slave trade activities, but that took it to a whole new level of what-the-fuck. Did that mean there was a tracking chip implanted somewhere on my body? Did the local cops get a piece of the slave trading pie in return for their silence and sometimes cooperation in returning escapees? I would have been violently ill at the thought if I had the luxury. The need for stealth outweighed my need to hork up the churning bile in my stomach.

I had made it this far and I wasn't about to give up and turn myself in without a fight. Maybe luck would stay with me and I could find a way out of town before their GPS kicked in. If they found me, I'd do everything in my power to make them work for every inch they dragged me back.

As I made my way through the woods, I lost track of time. It got dark. Cold. Well, cold*er*. The pain in my hip turned into a dull throb and felt like the only warm place on my body as I tucked my hands under my armpits and hunched over against the chill wind.

There was no way to know if any cars on the road belonged to Max or one of his cronies. No way to be sure which of the cops were in his pocket. I kept the street in sight but stayed in the trees, following the road much as I had the wall. Oddly enough—or maybe not oddly at all—I could see just fine in the dark. The blacktop shimmered under the moonlight, slick with ice in places, gleaming in monochrome shades to my no-longer-human eyes. Easily visible between the trees.

A few cars passed by now and again, including a cop car or two, but I didn't dare flag any of them down. There were also occasional driveways and dirt paths swept free of snow. I didn't know where those paths led, or who lived in the houses out here in the middle of nowhere. Even though I was tired and hungry and the blisters on my feet from ill-fitting shoes were making this trek even more miserable than it was already, I didn't trust a damned thing about this neighborhood. If they were Max's neighbors, even if they didn't know him directly, they would be too likely to call the cops or other unwanted attention down on me.

It might have been paranoid of me, but knowing what I did about how Royce ran his city, I would not be surprised if Max had his fingers in all the local community service pies. Police. Fire department. Hospitals. Who knew? By now, the word was likely out that he wanted me. I had no phone, no local contacts, ill-fitting clothes and shoes—but I did have one thing.

I had free will.

Funny, free will doesn't make your hurts any less painful, or your teeth stop chattering from cold, but it sure makes it easier to carry the burden and appreciate the smell of fresh air. And to mentally tell that creeping intruder, who was still insisting now and then that I return, to take a hike straight to the corners of Fuck and Off. I would be following my own path, not the one he wanted for me.

He probably figured out before too long that I had built up some resistance to his mind tricks, or that more pain wasn't going to be the goad that drove me back to him. The pressure of his mental intrusion didn't stay with me; it only came up intermittently. The savagery of it told me he was growing impatient, and might also mean their tracker probably wasn't working. I took it as a good, if uncomfortable, sign.

When I reached a crossroads, I stopped, uncertain. My sense of direction wasn't that great without the sun or any stars visible to guide me, but there were lights in the distance. Not just streetlights or house lights. A gas station or small store, I thought, though I couldn't be sure at this distance.

On the one hand, it was a well-lit, relatively public space, and they probably had a phone. On the other, Max might have sent someone ahead to keep an eye out for me, or told someone there to contact him if I showed my face. The tracker might even tell him where to send people to pick me up if I went to a local landmark.

It was a dilemma, but I preferred taking the risk of needing to run over dying slowly of exposure.

After making a note of the street names, limping a little faster, I focused on that light like it was the last glass of water in the desert. All that mattered was reaching my salvation—and Sara's. Even if they caught me and dragged me back, if I could get on the phone just long enough to tell Royce where we were, he'd send someone to save us.

It felt like an age crawled by before I made it to the edge of the parking lot of what turned out to be a twenty-four-hour gas station and mini-mart. Pulling out the wallet of . . . hmm . . . John Smith, if his license was to be believed (not in this lifetime), I checked for cash. Luckily, in addition to a few receipts, there were some bills in there. A couple hundreds, which just made everything easier, as well as a few twenties. I could make my call to Royce, get a cab, and maybe a night in a decent hotel.

It probably wasn't going to help much, considering what I was wearing, but I took a little time to finger-brush my hair and pluck the worst of the burrs and dead leaves off of myself. I'm sure I still looked like a slice of hell warmed over. I know I felt like it, anyway.

Pulling out a twenty, then stuffing the wallet in an inside pocket, I hobbled my way across the pavement and just inside the doorway, squinting against the bright lights as I got my bearings. The teenaged clerk behind the counter stared at me, his gum falling out of his mouth to land with a wet "plop" on the magazine he'd been reading.

"Um, hi," I said, then cleared my throat to sound less like an asthmatic smoker. "Got a pay phone?"

He shook his head, eyes never leaving my face, still giving me a mute stare. I scrubbed a hand over my cheek self-consciously, breaking eye contact to see if there was anything in the store I could use. Ooh, potato chips. That sounded awesome right about now.

Limping across the linoleum, I got myself a bottle of some red sports drink, a bottle of water, some chips, and a handful of protein bars. The coffee was tempting, but I didn't think it would be a good idea with how wind-burned my chapped lips felt. I dropped the stuff on the counter, plucked a container of lip balm out of a display bin next to the register, and put the twenty down.

"Look," I said, as the guy rotely began ringing up my items, finally remembering his manners as he focused on the pile I set before him. "I'm lost and I don't have a car or a cell phone. Do you have a phone I can borrow to make a couple calls? Please? I'll pay you."

He gave a nervous laugh. "Sure. Jeez, lady. Are you okay? Do you want me to call an ambulance or something? You don't look so good."

I shook my head, probably harder than necessary. "No. Thank you, but no. Just a phone. Maybe a number to call a cab?"

He pulled an ancient phone book out from under the counter and a very modern cell phone from his pocket. I took them and the sports drink with me and moved a few feet away to get a semblance of privacy. The kid watched me like I was his favorite reality TV show. Probably looked more interesting than whatever was in that magazine he was reading.

I dialed Royce first, sipping at the drink. I almost choked on it when he picked up. He was better at answering his phone to unknown numbers than I was, that was for sure.

"If this is a new number, Euphron, I'm having it blocked. You put the agreement in writing and send it via Athena, or no deal."

"I'm . . . uh . . . it's not Max."

Royce didn't respond right away. When he did, his voice was hushed, strained, like he didn't quite believe it was me. "Shiarra?"

"Surprise," I said, sounding lame even to my own ears.

"I—gods above and below, I thought—"

I wanted to tell him how much I missed him. How much I needed him, and how scared I was— but I didn't have time for it. If the words passed my lips, I was going to start crying and never stop. I didn't want to end up falling into hysterics and scaring the poor kid who was watching me so avidly. There would be time for that later, once I was alone.

"I'm on a borrowed phone," I said, voice thick around the lump in my throat. "I just—Royce, I need—I just got away from Max. Sara's still there. Still with him. She needs help. Please."

"Gods be damned. Why didn't Francisco say— your pain—the fear and the . . . I thought I'd lost you. What in the name of the gods happ—no. No, there will be time for that later," he said, sounding more rushed and flustered than I'd ever heard him before. I was a little too shell-shocked to be startled that he knew I was hurt, but a part of me was glad that our connection was strong enough that he understood just how bad off I was without me having to explain. He took a shuddering breath, audible even over the cell phone connection. "Where are you? Give me the address."

I turned to the clerk, who scribbled it down on a piece of paper for me when I asked. We were in a suburb of Illinois I'd never heard of. Of course. Max's home stomping grounds were in Chicago, so why was I even surprised? After cursing my luck, I then repeated the information back to Royce. The vampire didn't ask twice, which was good, because I wasn't sure I had enough strength or nerve left to focus on that chicken-scratch writing to repeat it again.

"Stay right there, love. I'll have someone pick you up, take you somewhere safe. Don't call anyone else, and don't go with anyone unless they tell you I sent them. I know you're hurt, but stay away from the local public services, police and hospitals. Do you understand?"

"Yes," I said, wanting to say so much more, but not finding the words.

Love. He'd called me *love*. I almost didn't hear anything else he said after that. For one brief, blessed moment, I forgot my pain and fear. He really did care about me. I wasn't just property. Not to him. Not to anyone, ever again.

"Call again if you need me. *Stay there.* I'll send someone right now. Ask for Analie's name to confirm they're one of mine. We'll speak again once you're safe and sound."

I nodded. Realized he couldn't see my reaction to the command, and rolled my eyes heavenward at my own airheadedness. "Okay."

He clicked off without another word. I wasn't sure I had anything else to say either.

Chapter Fourteen

The coffee was scalding my tongue, but I barely felt it. The taste didn't really register either. Cradling the cup in my hands, trying not to slosh it all over myself from the head-to-toe shivers wracking me, I watched the parking lot and tried not to think too hard about what might happen to me now.

The kid, Dustin, had a raging case of white knight syndrome. When I steadfastly refused to let him call the cops or an ambulance, he insisted on loaning me his coat and gloves. Sat me down in a plastic chair that he dug out of the supply room in the back and set next to the register where I could keep an eye on the parking lot. Paid for a microwave soup and the coffee, too, and made me drink it instead of the sports drink. Said it was more important that I warm up, and deal with the dehydration after my core temp was raised. He was very insistent that I needed to submerge as much of my body as possible in a hot bath as soon as I got wherever I was going.

There was no small measure of fear in me that

Max would send men out looking for me beyond the bounds of his own property line. That they would find me here, kill this sweet kid who smelled too strongly of Noxzema and breath mints, just for presuming to help me. Putting his life in danger was no way to repay his kindness, but I had to wait and hope that Royce's contact would get here first.

The soup was long finished and the coffee tepid by the time a black pickup truck with flames emblazoned on the side pulled into the lot. The oversize tires made me think of the monster truck rallies my dad used to watch on TV, and it was blaring some kind of pop music so loud I could hear it inside the store.

A tall, slender Asian woman stepped out, hopping from the step on the driver's side down to the blacktop. She was practically engulfed by a glaringly pink down jacket lined with faux fur at the cuffs and collar. She was working it with skinny jeans and matching pink Uggs with fur trim. It looked like the kind of outfit you'd see a model wear as she strutted down the runway, not somewhere in the back woods of Middle of Nowhere, Illinois. It was the kind of outfit Ken, Royce's fashion director for his nightclubs, might have instructed some of the eye candy at The Underground to wear.

I was a little too busy gaping to remember to hide myself before she came in. Dustin was pretty amazed, too, his eyes bugging as he took in the girl's striking figure. If she was one of Max's people, I was screwed—but I found it a little hard to believe he'd have someone who voluntarily dressed like that on his payroll.

Her mouth twisted into an *O* of surprise when she spotted me, cotton candy pink lacquered nails soon lifting to cover her expression. Cripes, even her eyeliner was sparkly pink. "Oh, Shiarra, I'm so sorry. I got here as fast as I could. Alec didn't say you were . . ."

Her voice trailed off, and I wondered what she thought had happened to me. I probably still had twigs in my hair and blood under what stubs remained of my fingernails.

Though I wanted to get out of this place more than anything, first I had to make sure she wasn't sent by Max to lure me out. "What's the name of the little girl staying with Royce right now?"

She didn't hesitate, and didn't seem offended by my paranoia. "Analie. We both know she's not just a little girl. I promise, Alec sent me, not who you're thinking."

And I could have wept, knowing I was safe.

"Come on, we need to get moving."

I put the coffee down. Braced myself to get out of the chair. A riotous shock of pain flared from my hip, jolting down to my knee and up to the base of my skull, so harsh and sudden I nearly blacked out. Sitting down for so long had made something—either some kind of pus seeping from the brand or maybe the salve Max had used—adhere to the pants. Sitting up felt like I was tearing whatever nerves were left down there out by the roots with rusty pliers as the material peeled away from my skin.

Dustin was by my side before the woman, practically flying around the counter to get to me first so he could put a hand on my shoulder to keep me in the chair. Though I flinched from his touch, he didn't seem to notice. Instead of sympathy, he scolded me, which did a better job of taking my mind off the pain than her nervous fluttering.

"Why didn't you say you were hurt? I should have called that ambulance. Stop moving, I'll call them right now—"

"No," I croaked, grabbing his arm to keep him from pulling his phone from his pocket. "Don't. Please. Just trust me on this, Dustin. Don't tell anyone I was here. Not a soul."

"You're afraid you'll be arrested?"

I started at that. He didn't fight my grip, but he did give me a hard look that might have made me shrink back if I had felt guilty about something, and if it wasn't coming from a kid who was probably half my age.

"I remember who you are now. I remember seeing stuff about you in the news."

The girl moved in, her expression darkening as she tapped his chest with a pink lacquered nail. "Look, kid, you don't want to get involved—"

He gave her a withering look as he cut her off. "It's a little late for that." His expression, when he turned back to me, was pained. "Look, I'm sorry you're afraid to get help from anyone, but you're hurt and a lot of people are looking for you."

"You're telling me," I said. "Dustin, thanks for everything. I'll find a way to repay you, I promise. But I need you to stay quiet about this, pretend you never saw me. Just for right now."

His eyes narrowed, and he took a step back out of my reach so he could pull out his phone. "I can't do that. I'm sorry. You'll thank me for it later."

The lady, who still hadn't told me her name, held out a hand to me. "Come on, he's not going to listen. Let's get out of here."

She was a lot stronger than she looked. Though I had a hard time moving my left leg, with her support, I got out of the chair and on my own two feet again. She scooped up my bag of goodies and acted as a crutch, letting me lean on her as I limped to the door. Dustin, though obviously frustrated, didn't try to stop us. His voice followed us out as he spoke into his cell, describing me and my injuries to the person on the other end. Probably a 9-1-1 dispatcher.

The moment she held the door open for me, a gust of cold wind carrying a few stray flakes of snow blasted me in the face, reminding me of my brush with hypothermia. Shivering, I hobbled outside first, clinging to the door for balance. My frantic, adrenaline-fueled strength had long since deserted me, but there was no time for delays. If an ambulance or cops were on their way to investigate, we had little time to get out of here, and less chance of going unnoticed in that beast of a car.

A sense of foreboding crawled over my skin, colder than the hint of fresh snow on the wind.

Once I was outside with enough room for her to

squeeze past, the lady grabbed my arm, hauling me to her car at a faster clip than I was ready for. Dustin followed us out, still on his phone. Though the pain and dizziness made it hard to focus on anything other than putting one foot in front of the other, I scanned the tree line at the edge of the parking lot, then stiffened. If she hadn't been dragging me along, I might very well have given up then and there.

Max was watching us, hands pocketed, head lowered, only the embers of red glowing in the depths of his eyes giving him away. That, and the brutal wrenching in my psyche the moment our eyes met as he fought to tear my control away from me and force me to come to him.

Away from the lights. Witnesses. The security cameras.

Panting, I tore my gaze off him, sudden warmth oozing down my lips and chin. Blood gushing from my nose. "Hurry," I begged, though I was the slow one here.

Her fingers tightened on my arm, but other than that she gave no sign she heard me. Once we reached her pickup truck, she practically threw me inside, somehow shoving me up to reach the cab in next to no time.

Hands shaking, I settled myself in the huge leather seat. She raced around the other side, hopping in. When I looked up, Max was standing on the edge of the pools of light cast by the headlights, his eyes reflecting a phosphorescent sheen like a cat's. There was some kind of dark, sleek sedan parked under the trees on the side of the road, not visible from the front door of the store. No wonder I hadn't known he was there. Probably laying in wait to ambush or follow me somewhere without any security cameras.

"Fucker moves fast," my new friend said, her tone conversational as she started up the diesel engine with a roar and shoved the monster into gear. Blessed heat blasted from the vents, briefly fogging the windows. "Buckle up. There are napkins in the dash and, I think, a bottle of water under the seat if you want to clean up."

I gasped as I was thrown back, the tires squealing on the pavement as she hurled us straight at the vampire. One hand on the dash to brace myself, I squeezed my eyes shut, waiting for the inevitable collision—but it never came. Squinting one eye open, I looked ahead, but there was nothing but empty road before us. Twisting around to look behind us, I saw the convenience store fading fast in the distance, though one . . . two . . . four pairs of headlights flicked on and began to follow us.

Max was still visible, a darker shadow against the tree line. I pressed a hand to the glass, mouth going slack with horror as he held his arm out to the kid, who was moving away from the lights and cameras and safety of the store to the vampire's side. Dustin was making straight for the deeper shadows, where a sure, ugly death waited for him, all because he had done me a small kindness.

"Stop! Stop, we have to go back!"

She shot me a look. "We've got a tail, and you just

narrowly escaped a nasty fate. I am no match for that thing and, in your state, neither are you."

"You don't understand! Dustin! He's going to kill Dustin!"

"And you, too, if we go back there. Save your strength. You're going to need it."

I stayed plastered to the window, staring back. I couldn't see anything else. The wood and shadows swallowed up man and beast, and soon even the store was lost to the night.

My vision blurred, tears stinging my eyes as I stared back, willing for some sign that Max was after me and not that poor kid. Though the vampire had severed the mental contact between us, cutting me off from feeling what he wanted, I was sure he had done it on purpose. He must have wanted me to sit and stew and feel guilty for leading him right to someone whose only crime had been to offer me temporary shelter.

It was working.

"Kumiho."

I wasn't sure I heard her right, but I was too busy staring back the way we had come and feeling like a Grade A, gold-plated turd to ask her to repeat herself.

"I could be wrong, but I thought the polite thing to say when someone introduces herself is, 'Nice to meet you, and by the way, thanks for saving my ass.'"

A faint sound somewhere between a laugh and a sob rattled in my throat. I turned away from the window, pressing my fingers to my eyes to keep the tears in. If I let them spill now, they'd never stop. "I'm sorry. Kuh . . . Kim . . ."

"Kumiho. Or Soo-Jin, if you prefer." She patted my shoulder. "Don't worry about it. I shouldn't be giving you a hard time, but old habits die hard. Listen, I'm sure all you want to do is sleep for a week, but as soon as I put some distance between us and that tail we're going to have to stop somewhere so I can dig the tracking chip out of you. Do you think you can handle it without any meds? I don't have anything to give you for the pain and Alec said the only flight he could get for the magi won't arrive until tomorrow night."

Numb, I dropped my hand and looked at her, blinking owlishly like that might help her words sink in better.

Her gaze flicked over to me, then back to the road. Her lips thinned. "Sorry, Shiarra. I really am. But I can't take you to a safe house until the chip is out, and I don't have the skills of a healer." She flashed me a smile full of sharp little teeth, prompting a shudder out of me. "I've always been much better at removing things than fixing them."

From the hands of one monster and into another. What the hell was she, and why was Royce trusting her with my life?

After my time spent with Clyde Seabreeze in California, I couldn't help but question Royce's judgment and taste in allies.

"Do whatever you have to," I said.

"I'll do what I can. We'll put a few miles behind us, then I'll take care of it."

"Dig it out of me, you mean?"

She nodded, gaze focused on the road stretched out before us. I swallowed back rising bile and looked ahead, too. I wondered how she knew about the chip. If she knew where it was on my body. Had she worked for Max at some point? Or was she an escapee, like me?

Chapter Fifteen

Kumiho, or Soo-Jin, or whatever her name was, did a great job of shaking Max's cronies following in our wake, and giving me a raging case of carsickness. Once we were about a mile from the convenience store, she yanked the steering wheel to one side.

I almost peed myself, certain we were going into a roll.

Instead, she sent us in a turning slide that put us in the ditch at the side of the road. The tires of the huge truck bit into the snow and mulch, sending us rocketing into the trees. The cars following us, on the other hand, slid a good distance as they attempted to stop, two of them crashing into each other. The other two managed to make the turn, but one skidded into a tree when the driver drifted off of our tracks, making an accordion out of the driver's side. The last managed to stay on the path we made, following us into the woods.

Branches slapped against the doors and my hip

flared with agonizing regularity as we bumped and jolted over unseen obstacles in the dark, hidden beneath the blanket of snow. The regular thumps and screeching of branches were punctuated by the occasional *whump* of snow piles being dumped on us from above.

Kumiho wasn't deterred and showed no visible signs of alarm as she navigated around the bigger trees. I clung to the oh-shit handle with both hands and stared at her in a mix of shock and a weird sense of unreality as she sang along to the song blasting out of the radio, looking for all the world like she was having a great time. I didn't recognize the song, and it took a few minutes for it to sink in that the lyrics were in another language.

Flashes of light from the headlights of the sedan behind us as it bounced over the uneven terrain occasionally lit up the interior. I had the surreal sensation that I was in some kind of strange nightclub, complete with strobe and exotic electronica music.

During a drum solo, Kumiho shouted conversationally at me over the music. "That fucker better not hit my car. Bad enough I'll probably need a new paint job after this."

I just gaped at her.

We burst out of the trees and into a small clearing. There must have been a frozen pond or something under the snow, because Kumiho had to wrestle with the steering wheel and my heart crept up into my throat as we started drifting into a sideways slide. Just as I thought we were going to slam into a looming oak, the tires got traction and hurtled us through a gap in the trees, back into the forest.

Behind us, the car fishtailed, sailed into a spin, and careened into a huge snowdrift. Even over the music, I heard a sickening crunch and the shriek of twisting metal.

Kumiho smiled, her eyes narrowing to thin slivers, but she didn't let up on the gas. We rocketed through the woods at alarming speed, putting more distance between us and our pursuers.

In the span of two more songs, we were beyond the wooded barely-there path and back on a paved road. I don't know how she found it, or how we managed to get through that mess without hitting any trees, but I was grateful for it nonetheless.

My fingers hurt with strain from clinging to the handle as I flexed them open and let go. Under the gloves, I was sure my knuckles must have gone white.

Once through the shortcut, she took a lot of back roads and winding streets until we reached a dirt road that ran through an empty field blanketed in snow. Visibility behind us was good, so we could see if anyone else had followed us, with plenty of time to get back in the car and take off.

She was a lot more solicitous now that we didn't have Max or any of his men within spitting distance. Of course it hurt like hell to move around. On the bright side, she said the chip was on the back of my right hand, so I didn't have to get out of the car while she removed it.

After handing me a wad of tissues from the dash

and giving me a purse strap to bite down on—the best she could do under the circumstances—she came around to my side of the car. Standing on the step on my side, she felt around the back of my hand and then between the webbing of my thumb while I huddled in the cab, shivering. She found what she was looking for and used a razor-sharp nail to make an incision. It didn't hurt nearly as badly as I was braced for, probably because everything else hurt much worse already.

As she squeezed around the cut, a small object about the size of a grain of rice popped out. Like a splinter I didn't know I had. I caught it in my other hand before it could slip away and disappear in the snow. Rubbing the blood off, it looked like a tiny red-and-black computer chip encased in glass. Not very ominous on its own, but the implications of having it inside me chilled me to the core. I wondered if Max had put the chip in me back when I first met him in New York, or if he had waited until I was in his clutches here in Illinois.

As a P.I., I had done quite a lot of investigation into the technology of tracking missing persons. A GPS chip that could broadcast a signal through human skin wasn't supposed to be possible. Yet, here I was, looking at what amounted to a human LoJack system. I supposed money really could buy anything when you were as rich as Max Carlyle. That, or, when you had as much time on your hands as a vampire, you could spend decades or centuries studying a technology to twist and perfect it for your own uses.

Kumiho extended her hand for it. Once I gave it to her, she snapped the tiny device between her fingers and then tossed it to the ground. "Good riddance. You ready to rock and roll?"

At my nod, she got back behind the wheel and started driving again. Though I had no clue where she was taking us, she must have been familiar with the area since she turned off the plowed trails to angle into what seemed to me like a minor depression in the woods. These always turned out to be side roads, some of which led onto other private properties, others into villages or towns.

Unable to do much else, I stared out the window, trying not to think too hard about what Max must have done to Dustin and what he would do to the people left behind who still needed to be saved. A cold, empty place in my heart filled with dread at the thought of how he might take out his frustrations on Sara since I had escaped his clutches.

As we ate up the miles, the towns and other traffic on the road became more frequent. The one- and two-story buildings we were encountering were soon scattered with a few taller ones. There were modern office buildings and fast-food chains I recognized. There was a muted glow on the horizon that Kumiho told me was Chicago proper, though she was headed somewhere else.

It was very late by the time she pulled into a gated community somewhere out in the wilderness beyond the greater city limits. After she punched a code into the monitor beside a darkened security guard station, the gates swung open on silent hinges to grant us entrance into the walled estate.

We passed a huge clubhouse overlooking a pond that had not frozen over except at the edges, water spraying from a fountain in its center, and a couple of tennis courts. I studied the houses. Most were single-story, sprawling over decently sized lawns. They weren't built right on top of each other like most communities of this type that I had seen. A few of the homes had swing sets in their front yards. I guessed the majority of the homes were two and three bedrooms, and it looked like this was a community for upper-middle-class families with children.

Kumiho navigated the well-lit streets with familiarity, pulling into the driveway of one of the bigger houses. I caught a glimpse of a lake in the backyard, and the Tudor-style home was tucked into the end of a dead-end street, giving the place a vibe of security and privacy.

The place was designed like a miniature castle, complete with a rounded turret on one side. A weathervane topped the cone-like slate roof, which tapered to a point higher than the rest of the house.

It looked warm and inviting and mostly I was grateful that we were stopped so I could finally lie down and sleep. Now that the worst of the danger was behind me and no one had followed us to the gates, I didn't feel too awful tucking away my worries about Sara so I could get some rest. Despite my concern for her, we wouldn't accomplish anything else today, and I would be pretty useless to make plans or describe anything about Max's hideout until I was better rested.

I hadn't been given any opportunity to sleep off my shock or my hurts. As badly as I wanted to help Sara, Iana, Dustin, and everyone else I had left behind, I could barely string two thoughts together, let alone figure out how I was going to get them to safety.

Kumiho killed the engine, then turned to look at me. Though I could feel her gaze on me, sensed her scrutiny like a physical touch, I just stared ahead. Reacting was a bit too beyond me just then.

"Are you going to be able to walk? Or do you need help?"

It took me longer than it probably should have to process her question. Even then, my answer was hoarse and wavering. "Help, I think."

Getting from the car to the house was a bit of a blur. Mostly I remember cold, seeping right through my shoes and pants and gloves, more than it should have over such a short distance. Pain ate at my vision, darkening the edges a little more with every step. Her strength was all that kept me on my feet. Not normal. Not human. I still had enough cognizance to be able to tell.

It felt like forever until she set me down, leaving me to sink into a pile of soft cushions. Spent from the combined exhaustion and pain, I barely managed to note that there were indeed four walls around the couch that was now the center of my universe.

I closed my eyes and was gone.

Chapter Sixteen

The distant jangle of a phone jarred me out of sleep. I woke up to watery sunshine on my face, the rest of me cocooned like a blanket burrito. I was filled with warmth and a thousand tiny aches all over my body. Oh, and one hot, dull throb from my hip.

"Good morning. Or afternoon, technically."

Kumiho was far too cheerful. But I smelled coffee, and that lured me out of my burrito-shaped hideout.

"Where are we?" My voice sounded like I had swallowed about a pound of wet sand followed by a gravel chaser.

I had to squint against the sunlight streaming in from some rather large picture windows overlooking an ice-rimmed lake and snow-dusted trees. The room was a strange conglomeration of Eastern-influenced furniture and artwork depicting some fox-like creature with many tails, mixed with a couple of custom neon signs and what I thought might be framed K-pop band posters on the pale yellow walls. Kumiho was visible beyond the breakfast bar, puttering around in a large kitchen full of new-but-made-to-look-old appliances, apparently content to ignore the phone ringing in another room. It cut off before long, probably going to voicemail.

"Welcome to my humble abode. You're lucky Mr. Royce sent me to be your hostess, tour guide, and guardian for your stay in my little slice of paradise." She grinned, saluting me with a mug. "Here's to rich benefactors, eh? Come on, up and at 'em. Get some food in you and then I'll show you to the shower. We need to get you cleaned up and into some new clothes because, girl, I hate to tell you, but white is *so* not your color."

That startled a laugh out of me, followed by a brief coughing fit. Once I got my breath back, I rearranged the fuzzy—need I say it?—hot pink blanket, swinging my legs around. Though the pull and burn was sharp, and my muscles protested every step of the way, I managed to get to my feet under my own power and pad across the heated tile floor to the breakfast bar. Getting up on one of the stools was a little much for me to manage, so I stood there, blistered feet aching, leaning heavily against the counter.

"I'm not really the Betty Homemaker type, so I hope you don't mind a simple dish. I was making *hoeddeok*. It's a little like pancakes."

I nodded, taking the cup of coffee she offered me as she turned back to prepare me a plate.

"That sounds great. Thanks for the coffee and everything." I sipped, closing my eyes in bliss as the rich, sweet taste rolled over my tongue. "And thank you for coming to my rescue," I belatedly remembered to add.

"Hey, anytime. This is a drop in the bucket compared to what I owe your master."

That gave me a start. "Whoa, now. He's not—"

"Oh, sorry. Slip of the tongue," she said, though I got the impression from the light in her eyes and the sly twist of her lips that she had meant exactly what she said. "I forget what the PC term is for it these days. What is that ridiculous word . . . Your host?"

My cheeks warmed, but I met and held her challenging stare as she pulled the plastic wrap off of a bowl and reached inside to roll a handful of some kind of dough in her hands. "I'm not a blood donor, if that's what you're implying." Not really. I hoped. Maybe just that once—but that didn't make the title stick. Did it?

"Funny, that's not what the newshounds say. And he is awfully fond of you, if the number of phone calls I've received from him since last night are any indication."

That filled me with an altogether different kind of warmth. Was it possible the vampire had deeper feelings for me than my bruised and battered ego dared hope? When he sent me to stay with Clyde in Los Angeles, I had done my best to make myself believe that he was doing it for my own safety. Royce must have had a good reason for sending me away, and that reason couldn't have had anything to do with being dissatisfied with my performance in the sack after I finally grew a pair and admitted I wanted him to do every dirty thing to me I had ever read about in those romance novels I hid from my mom as a teen.

Don't judge me.

The guy had done everything I had hoped and more, fulfilling fantasies I hadn't even known I'd had. Things that made me flush just to recall. To be sent away on the heels of experiencing the kind of afterglow that Chaz, my alpha werewolf cheating scumbag of an ex-boyfriend, had never been able to give me, may have made me a bit paranoid that Royce was not as enamored of me as I now was of him. My many worries about Royce's motives and what he really wanted from me took a backseat after the night we had shared.

Kumiho's sly, knowing smile made it hard for me to come up with a way of explaining my relationship with Royce that didn't make me feel like I was giving up a state secret. After my awkward silence extended a bit too long, she laughed and placed the ball of dough on the flour-dusted counter.

"It's all over your face, sweetie. I know what it's like to fall under his spell. I'm just surprised you managed to snare him, that's all."

Somehow I managed to keep my tone neutral. "Oh? Why is that?"

She didn't miss a beat, rolling out more circles of dough while her gaze and widening smile were focused intently on me. "He's always been a regular

Don Juan. Using his looks and his money and everything else to get what he wants, only to leave his lovers once he's had what he was after. Don't look so shocked. It's the nature of the beast when dealing with vampires. I just find it fascinating that you're the one who melted one of the coldest, most jaded hearts I've ever encountered."

I fiddled with my coffee mug, staring down at the contents so I wouldn't have to look her in the eye anymore. Though I hardly expected him to be a saint, I didn't want to think about Royce's "conquests" before I came along, either. Considering how he oozed sex appeal like the world's most effective cologne, I shouldn't have been surprised.

"Hey," she said, tapping the back of my hand with a flour-coated finger. "Sometimes I let my mouth run. Don't worry about any of that. He's a damned fine catch, and word on the grapevine says he's a wonder in the sack. A walking, talking wet dream, as one of my friends put it. Ride it while the riding's good!"

My mouth dropped open, and I'm pretty sure my cheeks matched the color of my fire engine red curls.

Humming some jaunty tune under her breath, Kumiho focused on whatever she was making, driving her thumbs into the center of each ball, using a spoon to dump a mixture of what looked like brown sugar and some kind of crushed nut in the center before rolling them back shut.

In minutes, she had the balls frying in a pan, flattening them with a spatula in one hand as she shook an admonishing finger from the other at me when she caught me staring. "Don't look at me like that. You Americans and your hang-ups on relationships and sex are so beyond me, you know that? Don't question a good thing. Enjoy what you have with him while it lasts. I may not live in New York anymore, but I remember enough of what he was like to know that he must feel more than just a bit of tingling in his dangly bits for you to go to as much trouble as he has. Here, eat this while it's hot."

She set a plate before me with a large, thick pancake in the center. I took advantage of this ready-made excuse not to put my foot in my mouth by filling it with something else. Picking up the pancake with my fingers since she didn't give me any utensils with the plate, I took a big bite. Though it scalded my tongue, the outside was crunchy and the inside tasted like sweet, gooey, cinnamon-sugar heaven.

Clearly she was pleased with my sounds of approval. Before I knew it, my plate was heaped with three more of the treats. She made a plate for herself and settled down next to me, and the two of us ate together in companionable silence. Except for the phone ringing in the other room again, which she continued to ignore.

After we ate, she gave me a tour of the rest of her home, abbreviated when she noticed how I grimaced with every other step. She sent me into a large, luxurious bathroom with a walk-in shower, Jacuzzi bathtub, and hand-painted tile with scenes of bamboo groves and more of that fox thing that was on all of the art in her living room. She gave me a pile of pink, fluffy towels and a clean pair of sweats she thought might fit me. I would have to roll the cuffs of the pants up to my ears, but aside from that, it was more than I could have asked for. She waved off my attempts at gratitude and left me to clean up after myself.

No doubt, Kumiho had given me a lot to think about where Royce was concerned, but I agreed with her that I didn't need to analyze his motives that deeply. She was right. He must have felt more for me than just a spate of lust, or even some sense of obligation because I had saved his life. Whatever it was he felt for me, it had to be more complicated than simple desire, and I would make it a point to ask him about it as soon as we were face-to-face again.

The hot water helped soothe a lot of the immediate aches, though the mark on my hip stung like crazy when I unthinkingly turned my left side into the shower spray. Even the cut on my hand didn't hurt that badly when I put soap on it. Gritting my teeth, I hurried the rest of my business, washing my hair and scrubbing the remaining blood, dirt, and dried sweat off everywhere else.

Though I felt much better, I was exhausted by the time I was done toweling dry and dressing myself. Wrapping my hair in a towel, I shuffled out of the bathroom, giving her the dirty clothes in my arms.

She wrinkled her nose in distaste. "I'm going to throw these out. Girlfriend, the minute you feel up to it, I'm taking you shopping to fix that wardrobe issue."

I gave her a weak grin and went back to collapse on the couch again, throwing my arm over my eyes to block out the sun. The sounds of her puttering around went distant as she moved deeper into the house, then stopped altogether when her ringtone shattered the quiet for the umpteenth time.

This time she must have picked up. The rise and fall of her voice nearly soothed me to sleep, at least until she came back into the living room and leaned over the back of the couch to give my shoulder a light poke.

"Testicles McGee is on the phone for you." Kumiho covered the mouthpiece with her hand before handing me the phone, whispering her next words and adding a wide grin and a suggestive brow waggle. "You'll have to tell me your secret. He's totally smitten. Since you've been up, he's been calling every fifteen minutes to check on you, I swear. I held him off as long as I could."

I was so exhausted, I couldn't find the energy to laugh. The thought of Royce being so worried about me also did plenty to raise my flagging spirits and filled me with a deep, fuzzy kind of warmth. I tucked the phone between my ear and shoulder, closing my eyes. "I'm here."

"Did she just call me what I think she did?"

"Yes. What, you don't think you make a good hero from a romance novel?"

Royce made a gruff sound, neither disputing nor denying the idea. It was the first time—probably the only time—I ever thought of anything about him as adorable.

"Speaking of which, when are you going to come here to sweep me off my feet? And help me get Sara back?"

He hesitated. "Shiarra, I'm sorry. I'm not able to leave New York right now."

That stunned me silent.

"You won't be alone," he continued, regret coloring his tone. "I wish I could be by your side right now, but there are too many issues here for me to come to you. I'll be sending help to rescue her, but I want you on the road back to New York as soon as possible. I can send a plane or helicopter to pick you up once you cross the state line into Kentucky."

"Please tell me you're joking." I barely managed to get the words out from behind the forming lump in my throat. "You can't seriously be asking me to leave her behind."

"I'm not asking you to leave her behind. I'm asking you to come to safety and let my people and your mage friend take over to get her out of there. I don't want you putting yourself back in danger, and I can't afford to have traces of my bloodline found in connection with what Max has brought down upon himself."

"No. I'm not leaving without Sara."

"Shiarra, going back would be suicide. I might never get you out of his hands—"

"No. Don't even say it. Don't even think it. I won't go in alone, but I can't leave her there. Not after . . . I can't."

Royce growled, the sound garbled and staticky over the phone. "Stay where you are. Don't go charging in."

"I don't think I can walk without help, let alone charge off to rescue Sara. Besides, I'm not stupid or suicidal." I paused. "You're really not coming?" My voice was thin, strained, even to my own ears.

"I cannot. If I leave now, Max or one of my other enemies will seize the opportunity to move in on my territory. Aside from which, I can't have our sire believing me directly responsible for any harm that may come to him."

That didn't sound very good. While both Max and Royce had made passing mentions of the vampire who turned them in the past, I had never given her much thought. Considering he ruled three states, I had thought Royce was beyond answering to anyone but himself anymore. I wondered what Athena must have thought about Max's attack on New York and his attempt to kill Royce, before shaking my head and concentrating on the issue at hand.

"I don't want to go back there, but I've got to do something to help Sara. To stop Max. I feel so useless, and I don't know what to do—"

"Don't worry," he cut in before I could get too worked up. "The arrangements have been made. You'll stay with Soo-Jin while the others collect Ms. Halloway. You'll both return to New York, safe and whole."

Whole. Something I would never be again. I didn't say it, nor did I voice how betrayed I felt that he wouldn't ride in with the setting sun to save me.

It was irrational, and I knew it, but it still stung that he chose to let someone else do the dirty work.

"I feel your pain, my little hunter. Don't fret. You're safe now, and Ms. Halloway will be soon, as well."

That didn't do much to make me feel better, but I wasn't going to argue. The important thing was getting Sara free, not me doing something foolish to endanger myself or my new friends. Even if Royce wasn't there, with Arnold's help I had no doubt we'd get Sara out. It was saving everyone else who was trapped there, and putting a permanent halt to Max's slave trading business, that worried me.

It took a bit of courage to get my next words out, knowing I was asking a lot more of Royce than he owed me or Sara. If he chose not to help me get everyone else out, I hoped Arnold might feel differently.

"I need you to tell Arnold to bring whatever he needs to remove a collar like the ones on Christoph and Ashi."

Royce paused. The smooth, deliberate tone to his next words told me he was pulling on his I-know-better-than-you pants and felt I was treading on dangerous ground. "You may think Christoph or even Ashi might help you, but let me assure you, the moment those collars come off—"

"I didn't say I wanted them to come along for the party," I said, interrupting. "There's someone else. She's trapped in there, too. Probably more than just one Other, considering what I saw, plus a bunch of normal people who don't deserve what's happened to them."

"The other humans you mention are one thing. I was intending to have any other captives my people came across brought back here. However," Royce continued, still choosing his words with care, "I may not always agree with Max, but if he has an Other wearing a collar that suppresses magic or shape-shifting, it's probably for very good reason. Removing it may not be wise."

"That's true, but she helped me when she didn't have to. She's probably not going to be a danger to anyone but Max. Besides, I promised I would help her."

He made a soft, frustrated sound. "Very well. I'll pass on the request. What is she? Do you know?"

"No," I replied, trying to hide my embarrassment. I could practically feel his disapproval radiating through the phone. "Her name is Iana, if that helps. She mentioned being with him since a police riot or something."

"The police strike in Boston?" The disapproval turned to alarm. "I thought she was dead. She cannot be released. Keep your distance from her if she ever finds her freedom."

"She might be dangerous, but she's my friend, and she's more broken than anyone I've ever met. I made a promise to her and I'm keeping it."

Royce didn't respond immediately. I held my breath, praying he would understand how important it was to me to keep my word to Iana. Out of all of the people in Max's menagerie of slaves, she was the only one who had done anything to help me or show me any compassion while I was there. Something about the thought of her being left that way, trapped forever as something she wasn't, rankled too deeply for me to shrug off my promise to help her.

"As you wish," he said.

If only it hadn't sounded like a condemnation.

Chapter Seventeen

Royce didn't keep me on the phone long after that. He asked to speak to Kumiho, who took the phone with an exaggerated eye roll and flapped her other hand in the universal gesture for talking too much. Her antics did dredge a smile out of me, even if I wasn't feeling too great just then. Her expression soon shifted to one that looked too serious for her candy-coated exterior and she moved away from me, disappearing into the hallway, an unseen door soon shutting with a quiet *click* behind her.

Whether Royce was asking more favors of her or giving her some instruction to sit on me to keep me from pulling a Lone Ranger, it didn't matter. I had talked about this with Sara while we were in Los Angeles. I was going to do what I could to be smarter about how I dealt with my problems. Rushing in, as Royce had said, would be suicide. Even if he was plotting with Kumiho to keep me out of the action, for once I would consider those plans without disregarding them on their face.

I could admit to myself that I wasn't strong enough to face Max alone and maybe not even with an army at my back. The thought of being in the same room with him again filled me with a terror so deep that the constant, minor trembles in my hands became full-body spastic shudders. Though I wanted to be brave and strong, to think that I was capable of better, I knew the limits of my courage.

Taking a deep breath to quell the growing fear and frustration, I finally did what I had been avoiding since it happened.

I peeled the loose shirt and pants off my left side to see how badly I had been burned. The brand didn't hurt the way it had yesterday. It had subsided to a dull heat that grew into a sharp burn when I moved in a way that rubbed or pulled the damaged skin, but it was still an ugly, irritated red around the edges. The mark itself was a mottled indentation of black and red, with a touch of yellow.

The scar it would leave would be a permanent reminder that my time with Max was not some impossible, horrible nightmare. That bird and that circle of olive leaves, once the symbol of the currency of Max's homeland, was now a symbol of how *I* was some form of currency to him. Property. The sight of it fixed me with a confusing mix of fear and fury and a hollow emptiness, but there wasn't anything I could do to erase it.

He hadn't been lying. No matter how long I lived, I could never, ever forget.

A box of tissues landed in my lap. I jumped, stifling a scream and scrambling to adjust the clothes to cover up the mark.

"You looked like you could use them."

Kumiho padded on silent feet to the kitchen, leaving me to wipe my shame away in relative privacy. I wanted to promise myself that these would be the last tears I would shed over what Max had done to me, but I knew that promise would be a lie. There was so much about it that hurt, more than I had words for, more than what was etched into my skin.

It took a bit of time for me to shove that hurt back into a locked box and bury it in the region of my heart. The discontent stayed there, lodged deep in my chest, ready to burst open again at any moment—but I would keep it hidden away for as long as I could.

Dashing the last of my tears away with a wad of tissues, I took a deep breath, held it until my lungs felt they would burst, then let it out. Thus composed, I got back to my feet and limped to the kitchen, leaning my good hip against the counter.

Kumiho turned, looking me up and down as though she'd never seen me before. Maybe she was seeing me with new eyes after whatever Royce had discussed with her.

"Well. Apparently I am to be your bodyguard for a bit longer than expected," she said. "The war has reached my doorstep, whether I wish it or not."

"War? What war?"

Her scrutiny turned sharp, her brows knitting. "Were you not aware that there have been uprisings—

vampires wresting control of long-held cities from each other, werewolf packs destroying or consuming one another, shifters and the undying clashing in terrible battles in contested cities? New York was one of them, and I thought there were some rumors of your involvement with the werewolves there."

I started to shake my head, but then paused and considered. The night I broke into Royce's apartment building, urged by the spirit of a dead man inhabiting the hunter's belt I'd been wearing at the time to take some twisted form of revenge against the vampires inside, there was supposed to have been some big fight between two local packs of werewolves. The Sunstrikers, led by my ex-boyfriend Chaz, had some kind of beef with the Ravenwoods. The human hunters—White Hats—who had been helping me at the time had chosen to side with the Sunstrikers, but I refused to join their fight.

"Maybe," I said, choosing my words carefully. "I know there were some problems in New York, but I was trying not to get involved."

"That's probably for the best. Unfortunate business. You're lucky you missed Alec's show of temper after his properties were burned down. I heard the carnage was a marvel to behold."

Her eyes glinted with a vicious light, her teeth bared in a feral grin that said better than words that she enjoyed the thought of bloodshed. That slick pink lipstick, like her lips had been coated with melted taffy, somehow made her appear more fierce and predatory. Then what she said sank in, and I had to collect my jaw off the floor before I could sputter out a few words of my own.

"Wait . . . excuse me? Did you say burned down?"

"Yes. I take it he didn't tell you?" She rubbed her chin, musing. "There was some fracas with a Were pack. They destroyed one of his clubs, and then that apartment building near Central Park. Burned them down. Alec has kept his battles in the courts and shadows since . . . oh, the 1700s, I'd expect, but since the arson he's been raging a rather bloody war with the wolves. If he kept it from you, I imagine he didn't want to alarm you."

I bit my lip, not sure how to respond or what to think. It seemed like something so important would have been one of the first things for us to discuss, but I couldn't argue with her logic. I already had plenty of problems on my plate. Worrying about what happened to Royce's properties and if everyone who lived in that apartment building was okay wasn't going to do me any good. Of course, that had never stopped me before. I hoped Mouse, Ken, Wesley, Christoph, Analie, and all the others who had lived there were alive and unhurt. They may not have been dear friends, but they had all looked out for me in their own way.

Also, I didn't *think* Chaz would have been so stupid as to try to burn down Royce's properties, but if he had, a tiny—*very* tiny—part of me was worried about him.

I still thought Chaz was a sleazy douchenozzle of a shitstain, but—damn him to hell—I couldn't turn off all my feelings for him. I hoped the scumbag was okay.

Kumiho folded her arms, resting her butt against the counter as she regarded me. "You aren't in any danger while you're here, if you're worried. No one—*no one*—would dare intrude on my territory. Not even in a time of war." Her fierce grin widened until I could swear I could see her molars. It was easy to believe her, even if I had no idea what she was. "And your beau is quite a fierce creature when roused. I wish I could be there to see it when you fully grasp what a beast he is under the veneer. I imagine that will be something to behold."

I cleared my throat, unable to meet her gaze. "I've seen enough. I know what he is and what he can do."

"Oh, I doubt that very sincerely."

Before I had time to question what she meant by that, she uncrossed her arms and pushed herself away from the counter, striding past me and out of the kitchen. Her movements were swift, liquid, the smooth stride of a predator on the hunt. Very reminiscent of how Chaz moved close to the full moon, when the beast roiled just below the surface of his skin, apt to slip its leash at any moment.

She returned a few minutes later, a purse in hand and swaddled in a thick, fur-trimmed ski jacket.

"Give me your measurements. I need to run a few errands. I'll pick up some new clothes and shoes for you while I'm out," she said, shoving a pen and small pad of paper in my direction.

Though I didn't want to look a gift horse in the

mouth, the abrupt change of topic and thought of being left alone here sent a pang of dread through me. Seeing my stricken look, she placed a hand on my shoulder, heat and a tingling sense of possession radiating from her touch.

"Remember, you're safe in my home. Not even Euphron of Sicyon would dare violate the sanctity of these grounds."

I nodded, pulling away with a shiver. She did not try to touch me again.

It felt a little like I had left one cage only to be trapped in another.

Pushing that thought to the back of my mind, I wrote down my shoe and clothing sizes. Then, as an afterthought, I added Sara's sizes before I handed it to her. She glanced over the paper, arched a brow, then stuffed the note and the pen in her purse.

"While you're out—will you check if Dustin is okay?" I asked.

Her features darkened with a flash of pity. I got the idea it was more for my hopeless naïveté than worry about Dustin's welfare. It was soon hidden behind a mask of brisk industry as she adjusted her clothes and made a point of rearranging some things in her purse.

"I'll check," she said. "Remember, stay inside. I'll be back in a few hours with some new clothes and the cavalry. There's some paper in that desk over there. If you can, make a map of what you know of the grounds and where your friends might be hidden away. It will help us make plans once the others arrive."

Right. Royce's vampires and Arnold were on the way. Knowing that I could contribute something useful that would keep my hands busy eased some of the guilt and tension that had built up between my shoulders. It took a few breaths to steady my voice enough to speak.

"Thank you, Kumiho. For everything."

Her expression softened, and she bowed her head, her hair sliding forward like a dark satin curtain to obscure her features. "Don't thank me, girl. I'm not good or kind or moral. You'll never know how lucky you are to have me on your side. Vampires are not the only ones with dark appetites, and repaying the debts I owe your master will see mine well fed."

For the first time, I felt a thrill of fear of this woman.

Her eyes were a strange, orange color, glinting in the shadows cast by her hair. Her gaze bored into mine for what felt like an eternity before she turned away. Silent, even in those stiletto heels, she stalked to the front door.

"Wait."

She stopped, hand on the knob, but didn't turn around.

"You may not think so, but you're not a bad person. You're kinder than you think."

"You're speaking from a place of ignorance," she said. Though the words were sharp, I still heard the edge of pain and longing in them. "You don't know what I am or what I've done. You don't know anything about me."

"I know you dropped everything in the middle of the night to pick up a perfect stranger whose life was in danger."

"Because I was bound to repay a debt. Someday you'll understand what it means to owe a debt to an immortal. When that day comes, the world will be darker for it."

"I think I do. I saved his life, remember? I know how much he thinks he owes me, even after I told him he doesn't."

That got me an over-the-shoulder glance. Her lips quirked in a thin smile. "No wonder he loves you."

Without another word, she slipped out into the cold, a swirl of snow trailing in her wake.

Chapter Eighteen

Angus looked like the kind of guy who could strangle you with his beard and grind your bones with his teeth. Every part of him not covered in scars was matted with curly red hair. Built like a brick shithouse, he would have been formidable even without the strength of a vampire coursing through his veins. This was not someone I wanted to mess around with.

"Blast and be damned with ye, woman," he snarled down at Kumiho, who was glaring up at him with her hands on her hips. She showed not a bit of fear for his great size or bared fangs, nor did she show the slightest hesitation as she went toe to toe with him until their chests nearly touched. "I'll be the one what decides who goes on the raid, and that's final!"

"My home, my territory, my rules," she snapped back at him. "I was promised a feed in return for my services. Are you giving me one of yours?" Those strange, orange eyes flicked to one side, focusing on a young mage who blanched under her hungry scrutiny. "I'll be happy to take one of them in payment instead—"

A fist the size of a dinner plate struck the counter with a resounding thump, blocking her path to the mage. "Haud yer wheesht, ye bloody besom! Ye'll do nae such thing."

Man, I was glad he was on my side.

Arnold stood by my side, practically vibrating with tension. There were half a dozen magi with him, all of them nervously watching the vampires and doing their best to keep their distance from Kumiho. I didn't recognize any of them, but I wasn't terribly familiar with his coworkers from The Circle. He never brought them along on any of our social outings. I had the feeling he didn't get along with many of them outside of the professional relationship he was forced to maintain to do his job as head of security of the coven.

As for the vampires, I knew Angus but had never met any of the others. There were over a dozen of them, and they and the group of magi had arrived in a trailing convoy of matching black SUVs less than an hour ago. Kumiho had dropped off some supplies and new clothes for me before picking them up at the airport, leading them back here just in time to avoid the first rays of the rising sun.

It hadn't taken long for the arguments to start.

Angus had been given the instruction to keep me away from the coming battle at all costs. Kumiho, on the other hand, had been promised violence, and babysitting me or not, she wouldn't be denied. She wouldn't leave me here, but Angus didn't want me to come with them, even if I stayed in the car or at the fringes of the fight. They had been arguing almost nonstop since they arrived, neither one backing down, both unwilling to find some kind of compromise.

Not that I had much clue what might work as a compromise in this case, but anything had to be better than those two coming to blows. The house and everyone in it probably wouldn't survive the battle.

I had started to open my mouth, but the two of them had both turned to *look* at me, and that had been sufficient to get me to shut my jaw with a snap.

As Angus and Kumiho argued in the too-crowded kitchen, Arnold touched my arm and gestured me aside. The other magi followed after us as we made our way to the living room, the vampires lounging against the walls all watching us go with hungry eyes.

Once we had a little distance from the arguing Others, I gave Arnold the hug I hadn't had a chance to when he had first arrived. Though a bit startled by me throwing my arms around him, he was soon returning the gesture, blowing a shuddering sigh into my hair.

"Oh, Shia," he whispered, his voice breaking, "I never should have let you and Sara leave New York. Or I should have gone with you. I've got to get her back."

I tightened my grip on him a little, trying to will into him a sense of comfort I didn't feel. Then I leaned back to meet his green eyes, misting up behind the thick Coke-bottle lenses of his glasses. "I'm sorry, Arnold. It's my fault she was taken. That necromancer is probably the only reason she's still alive."

He grimaced, pulling back and turning away. "I'm sorry I didn't get back to you in time. When you called, I mean. Not that I could have done anything about it from across the country. At least that thing isn't here."

Clearing my throat, I shuffled aside a few steps to sit on the arm of the couch, rubbing the back of my neck. "Um . . . about that . . ."

"Shit. Don't tell me we're fighting a necromancer, too," one of the other magi said, his voice high and squeaky with fear.

Arnold lifted a hand to rub the bridge of his nose, dislodging his glasses and his grimace deepening. "Fuck," he said, summing up my feelings in a nutshell.

"Sorry," I replied lamely, knowing it was inadequate. There were no words to make any of this mess easier to deal with. "He's on our side. Sort of. He's got an agenda, but I have no idea what it is. Before I got out, he made it sound like he wanted to help us. And Sara told me he was doing what he could to protect her."

Arnold and the others all had varying expressions of disbelief. I hoped I was right. Gideon wasn't on any side but his own, but whatever his goals were concerning Max, I thought they might align with ours to one degree or another.

Granted, he would probably turn on us the moment we ceased to be useful to him, but having a necromancer on our side, even if only temporarily, might make the difference between Max walking away from this coup—or being left behind in pieces.

Since the magi were already nervous from being outnumbered and trapped in a house all day with a flock of hungry vampires, I thought I might try distracting them from their added worries about the necromancer with some social niceties.

"Let's not worry about that right now. Will you introduce me to your friends? I don't think we've met."

With a start, Arnold gave me a wan smile. "Sorry, I must still be jetlagged. Everybody, this is Shiarra Waynest." The six magi inclined their heads, one of the two women giving me a shy finger-wave. "Shia, meet Xander, Kim—"

"Kimberly," she said, giving me a lopsided smile.

Considering she shared a name with the woman Chaz had been sleeping with behind my back, I did my best not to instantly hate her. She was just a kid: young, fresh-faced, and innocent. I had to wonder what she was bringing to the table in this fight and hoped to God Arnold knew what he was doing when he invited her along for the party.

"Yes, right. Kimberly, Jacob, Connor, Lucas, and Bonnie."

I shook hands all around, though when Bonnie's fingers slid over my own, she gasped and tightened her grip. "You didn't say you were hurt. Sit down, let me see what I can do."

Arnold's expression shifted to one of concern. The other magi gathered around the couch as Bonnie ignored my halfhearted protests and made me settle in the cushions. She placed a hand a few inches above my heart. Her eyelids fell to half-mast as a fae light deep inside her irises stirred to life.

A pins-and-needles tingle bit into my skin below her hand, spreading into a bone-deep warmth that was like a soothing balm to my sore, aching muscles. Bonnie's look of concentration became a wince when the warmth hit the brand. I blew out a little hiss of pain, surprised by the pangs of hunger hitting me, but it wasn't so bad that I couldn't handle it. The magi exchanged looks among themselves, some of them shifting their weight awkwardly. Though she didn't stop whatever she was doing, the burn on my hip grew into a brief, intense itch before fading. Then it continued down, easing the aches in my legs, ankles, and feet.

The hunger, though. That was becoming a problem.

With a gasp, she withdrew, a bit pale and drawn. The tingles cut off so abruptly that I winced. Her eyes had turned a bright green, lit with a fae glow, alive with the magic in her blood. The smell of it was like a taint—strong, too near, sweet and corrupt at once. Some part of me wanted to bathe in it, destroy the source. The rest of me wanted to drink it down until nothing was left, and I felt fangs and claws extend despite my best efforts to hold them back.

My stomach had never felt so empty. A low growl rumbled in my throat as I fought the urge to launch myself off the couch toward the nearest source of warmth and drumming life, beating a faster and faster rhythm as the prey realized it was far too close to a hungry predator.

"Shia?"

Arnold's voice. Questioning. Frightened.

Familiar. I latched onto it. A reminder that I didn't need to be a monster.

"Food," I said, clutching my stomach, feeling the bite of my own claws. I gasped and lisped around fangs. "I . . . meat, blood, anything . . . now!"

"Oh, no you don't." Kumiho's voice. Something hot was pressed into my hands. The scent of herbs wafted from the bowl of broth. I drank it down, not caring it was burning my tongue. "Bloody idiot magi! You trying to get yourselves killed?"

"I didn't know she wasn't human," Bonnie said, stung and defensive. "They told me she was human! That wasn't supposed to happen."

"Yes, well, you use up a hybrid's reserves, you can expect them to seek sustenance wherever they can get it. Give her some space."

The broth helped. It wasn't meat or blood, but it was hot and substantial enough to dull the edge of the hunger. When I lifted my gaze, peering over the edge of the bowl, the magi had moved away and were staring down at me with varying expressions of fear and fascination.

Arnold was the hardest to face. There was pity there. Pity for me. Whatever I was now.

I looked away first.

"Rhathos said nothing about a half-breed," one of

the vampires said, his eyes gleaming red as he spat
out that pronouncement around growing fangs. He
had an accent I couldn't place, speaking almost in
singsong and rolling his "R"s. Combined with his
sharp, pixie-like features and wispy reddish-blond
hair, it made it really hard to take him seriously. "We
should kill her."

Well . . . maybe not.

Angus scowled, turning a newly appraising gaze
in my direction. "That's not for us to decide, lad."

Too bad he didn't sound like he believed it.

The other vampire was still coming my way.

I didn't have the energy or the inclination to get
in a pissing match with an Other I didn't know, but
he was moving in my direction with obvious intent.
Arnold and a couple of the other magi made a few
sounds of protest, but none of them looked willing
to get in the guy's way. With a snarl of warning, I
braced myself to get up, but Kumiho put a hand on
my shoulder to keep me from rising.

"Knock it off, both of you! Fane, you know
better."

The vampire bowed his head and took a step
back, though his jewel-bright eyes remained focused
on me with a depth of hatred that seemed far too
intense, considering we'd just met and hadn't even
officially exchanged names yet. That had to be a
record even for me.

Kumiho then looked down to me, her eyes gleaming that odd, burnished orange that startled me
badly enough to flinch and look away. She didn't
have to say a thing.

"We'll fix this," Arnold said, with such conviction I almost believed it. "When we get back to New York, I've got some things we can try. I found a few texts. There's got to be a way."

"With so much fresh blood so close? Good luck," Kumiho muttered, sarcasm threading her voice.

Keeping a wary eye on Fane, I levered to my feet. "Fighting each other isn't going to solve anything. Can we all get some rest and save the testosterone for tonight? Please? I want my friends to get out of that place alive, and you're all I've got."

Though Fane was still looking at me like I was the Antichrist, he gave me a tight nod. The others soon followed suit, their postures relaxing, eyes no longer gleaming red. Kimberly mouthed "thank you" at me, her grateful expression telling me all I needed to know. Magi might be capable of wielding arcane power, but they were nowhere near as fast as vampires and their parts were easily squished. If they weren't careful, they could end up on the menu if one of the vampires got peckish.

Having been in her shoes, I knew exactly how she felt.

Chapter Nineteen

After settling the vampires and magi, Kumiho dragged me along with her into her candy shop-cum-bedroom as she made phone calls, changed clothes, and sent a particularly savage all-caps text message to Royce telling him to kindly go fuck himself if he thought he could renege on their bargain. If he replied, I didn't see it.

While she was busy texting or e-mailing or doing whatever on her phone, I peered at the brand again. It didn't hurt anymore. The skin was shiny and smooth, pinkish at the edges instead of a raw red. Like it had happened months ago, not less than twenty-four hours. All my other little hurts had faded away, even the world-class blisters on my feet.

"Fane is a problem. Until my agreement is fulfilled, there will be no walls or doors between us."

I started, then adjusted my shirt and pants to cover the mark. That out of the way, I folded my arms, frowning at her. "That seems a little unnecessary. I can take care of myself."

"Yes, but seeing as there is still enough humanity in you to be controlled by another Other, I won't take the risk of him calling you where I can't see so he can finish what he started."

That sent an icy pang of dread through me. Even if Max didn't always succeed at forcing me to do things against my will, I had enough experience with vampires messing with my thoughts to know just how dangerous Fane was to me. All it would take would be a moment of distraction, just long enough for him to slip close and slit my throat.

Shoulders slumping, I dropped the posturing and gestured in the general direction of the living room. "This is crazy. I have to go back there, but I can't even trust my own allies not to stab me in the back on the way out."

"That's vampires for you, kid," she replied. "Avoid the temptation to drink, and you might live a few nights longer. Oh, and speaking of crazy, I'm going to tell you now so you don't run off when we're in the thick of things. No matter what you see, remember that my first priority is to protect you."

"What, you mean if you cast some hocus-pocus or take off your skin-suit or something?" I grinned, but it faded pretty quickly when she nodded too vehemently for me to believe she understood I was joking.

"That, and I want you to remember that I am very aware of what I am doing when I am not as you see me now. I have greater mental faculties than Weres do when shifted. I will never do you harm, and for as long as we are allies you will never have a reason to run from me, no matter what you might see me do to others. And I will take my due."

Recollection of her talk about "feeding" made my stomach turn. I could have guessed what she was talking about before, thinking she might be some kind of vampire demanding blood as payment, but she had gone out in daylight to run errands. Her touch was hot, not cold. She ate human food with me, and she admitted to having some other form, though she wasn't Were.

Whatever it was she planned on eating, it wasn't going to be pretty. Was her price for helping me save Sara the life of a human? A vampire? Maybe it didn't matter, but a sick, twisted part of me was curious. Even still, I didn't dare ask.

I may not have been able to say the words out loud, but I knew that by going back there I was condoning the death—most likely an ugly, brutal, painful death—of one or more of Max's men. Not because they were fighting to protect Max's home and assets, but because I chose to go back, eyes open, knowing it was the bare minimum price to be paid.

It wouldn't be the first life I was responsible for ending, directly or indirectly, but somehow this felt like I was letting go of some important aspect of my humanity. Taking a life to buy the freedom of another. Several others, really.

It might have made me cold, it might have made me ugly, and it might have made me a monster, but in the long run I would be saving lives. If I could cling to that thought, maybe I would be able to live with myself when this was over.

"Get some rest while you can," Kumiho said.

She pulled a cord, loosening some thick curtains that turned the room from a cheerful sunlit space into a twilit haven full of shadows. In the dark, her eyes glinted orange and her shadow seemed . . . different. Dangerous. Like it didn't match the shape of her petite frame, like it hinted at more limbs than she had.

Her shadow reminded me of jack-o' lanterns and their silent, grisly smiles flickering with dim light on Halloween nights. Maybe that was a glimpse at what she would look like when she wasn't human. Maybe that was the thing hiding under her skin, masquerading as a person. A bit of niggling doubt told me that the instincts screaming at me to put as much distance between us as possible might be on to something.

She plopped down on her bed, sinking into the thick comforter, then patted the spot beside her. Swallowing hard, I rolled my shoulders and flexed my hands in an effort to get rid of some of the building tension in my muscles, but the knots only grew tighter.

She wasn't Max. She wasn't going to hurt me. I knew it, but I couldn't fight the unreasoning fear of her that sprang up at the sight of those strange shadows.

"Remember, I am no danger to you."

I nodded, willing myself to believe it. I forced myself to take the few steps necessary to join her, settling into the other side of the bed and curling up so I wouldn't have to face her.

Every movement, every shift of her weight and breathy sigh made my hackles raise. Fane had already gotten my blood pressure up, bringing out the beast lurking inside me and all of the hidden instincts and desires that entailed. Beyond the room, I sensed warmth and life, the pounding of several hearts, and the unnatural cold of creatures that had something almost as sweet under their skin.

My fingers twitched with the desire to let the claws come out so I could properly hunt. The soup sat heavy in my stomach, alleviating the worst of my hunger but not dulling the desire to have something more like hot copper filling my mouth and throat.

Arnold would probably let me close enough to hurt him. Just a little cut. It didn't have to be so bad, and then maybe the cravings would go away for a little while.

I wanted to be sick with myself, that I could be so single-minded and even consider hurting one of my friends. Wanted to be. I just couldn't shake the thought that there was flesh and blood in this house that could feed these new needs of mine.

Keeping my eyes shut tight, I repeated a silent mantra to myself, biting the knuckle of my right thumb to keep myself focused.

I would not hurt my friends. I would save Sara. Arnold would find a way to make this stop.

I. Would. Not. Hurt. My. Friends.

It took a very long time for sleep to take me.

Chapter Twenty

I huddled in my new jacket, my gloved hands shoved into my armpits for warmth and my head bowed. Kumiho was on my left, Arnold my right. The magi were spread out in a semicircle behind us and the vampires had their backs.

The night was clear and cold, a fresh coat of snow dusting the road like a glaze of powdered sugar. Well, powdered sugar with a bunch of fresh tire tracks. Before selecting a gathering spot, we had done a couple of passes around the property checking for cops doing surveillance or a security detail. Both were conspicuously absent. There were no cars parked on the side of the road, and the only tire tracks were our own.

After Kumiho and Angus decided it was worth risking and that no one was around to see, we parked on the street near where I had escaped, the wall surrounding Max's property not yet visible through the trees. The theory being that, while Max might feel my approach and figure I had backup, if we avoided the security cameras, he wouldn't realize how many people I had with me. It was the only element of surprise we could hope for.

That, and the magis' plan to burn down the outer buildings like the guesthouse and the guard shack at the main entrance.

There had been some bitter arguments between Angus and Arnold before we left. Angus wanted to preserve the property for some reason he refused to divulge, but Arnold wanted to cut off escape routes. Kumiho sided with Arnold, which put an end to the initial argument but brought up another one about how they planned on covering the exits.

My eyes had glazed over while they all strategized and bitched and snarked at each other. A couple of times I was asked to point out locations I knew, like the entrance to the underground cells where I had first woken up and the room on the upper floor where Max had kept me. Producing the maps I had sketched out while Kumiho had been running her errands, and then stuffed in a pocket, forgotten, kept them busy for a few minutes. Since we had no idea if Sara would still be in that room, Arnold didn't want to risk burning down any part of the main building.

Angus and Kumiho disagreed with him on that, arguing that something should be done to hem the rival vampires inside and leave them only one way out. Fire was a great deterrent to all creatures, alive and undead, so setting the outside ablaze so no one could escape through windows or any other exits seemed like a great idea to them.

Arnold didn't want to risk losing Sara or anyone else in the fire and was arguing for a less dangerous spell.

Seeing as I had no idea what the magi could do, aside from firebomb the place, I didn't have much to add to the conversation. They eventually decided that five of the magi, along with several vampire bodyguards, would remain outside to cast some kind of protective shield to trap everyone—Max and his people, the rest of Royce's vampires, Arnold, Kimberly, Kumiho and me—inside.

It might have been cold outside, but knowing I was walking right back into Max's clutches was the real reason my knees were knocking together.

Along with Kumiho, Arnold planned to stick by my side, and Angus vowed to add himself to my bodyguard detail. It should have made me feel safe, but I had seen what Max could do. The gun tucked into the holster at my waist would have given me a confidence boost if I wasn't going up against a vampire fast enough to dodge the bullets.

Angus hadn't mentioned what we were waiting for, but when another car pulled to a stop behind our line of vehicles, I figured it was for the last of our backup. More fool I.

The driver, a man in a chauffeur's suit, who had dark dreadlocks threaded with white beads that clicked with every stride, moved to open the back passenger door. Lo and behold, out stepped Francisco, the sloe-eyed Cajun. This time his suit was some kind of shiny satin material, the color somewhere between brown and gray. It screamed of too much money and not enough taste, kind of like that sly, cunning smile. Just as it had been when I first met him in Max's home.

My hand whipped straight to the gun holstered at my hip, but Kumiho grabbed my wrist before I could draw the weapon and shook her head in warning. Angus stepped forward, the Highlander going so far as to bow in deference to Francisco. The other vampire didn't return the gesture.

The driver stepped aside and cleared his throat, his voice a smooth drawl with a hint of a heavier accent. "May I present Monsieur Francisco Dane Zafis LaFontaine, premier *prince du sang* of the Americas, and Master of Louisiana, Mississippi, and Arkansas."

"Master of New Orleans, it is an honor," Angus said, though he didn't sound like he meant it. Judging by the way Francisco's eyes narrowed, I had the feeling that Angus's choice of words was considered some kind of an insult, too.

I opened my mouth to protest this farce, but Kumiho's grip tightened to the point where the bones in my wrist ground together. I ended up biting off a yelp of pain instead.

Angus shot me a warning look, then completed his spiel to Francisco with a bit more sincerity. "The Master of New York sends his greetings."

"I'm sure he does," Francisco replied, glancing at me over the rims of glasses tinted to match the color of his suit. "I prefer he send me his statement of release."

"Once the goods are exchanged and my Master

receives confirmation ye haven't interfered, it's yours."

I watched this exchange, tense, wondering what the hell was going on. Francisco had been a guest in Max's home, had taken advantage of his hospitality, and had quite possibly purchased people from the slave auctions. I couldn't remember if he had been one of the vampires to walk away with a shiny, new, better-at-everything-than-me human, but, based on what I had seen of him, I had to assume he was too chummy with Max to be trusted.

"Why is he here?" I hissed the question at Kumiho, never taking my eyes off him.

He answered me before Kumiho could. "Because I owe your Master a favor, *cher*. And I always pay my debts."

"How can we trust you? I saw you in there. With him."

He just smiled.

Fucking vampires and their smug attitudes.

"He's nae threat just now, lass. He knows what it will cost him if he tells anyone what we're about."

"Later is another matter," Francisco added.

"Aye. Let's be quick about this. We've got a war to win."

Francisco inclined his head, then reached into his jacket to pull a small packet out of an inner pocket. He held out the packet, which Angus took and tucked away in his own inner jacket pocket. The two exchanged tense nods, then stepped away from each other. As Francisco's driver held his door open, he tilted his head to peer at me over his glasses one more time.

"Tread carefully, *mon cher*. You are an interesting piece. I would hate to see you taken from the board before the game is through."

I . . . wasn't sure how to respond to that. He winked at me, then ducked into the car, out of my view. We all watched the chauffeur in what was probably uncomfortable silence for him as he picked his way through the slush and around to the driver's side. The car was soon pulling into a U-turn, the taillights disappearing back into the night as the vehicle whisked around a curve in the road.

Whatever the others may have thought, I was certain Francisco couldn't be trusted, and that he must have done something to screw this up for us. Not in an obvious way. There would be some trap waiting for us once we were too deep inside to get out again, I just knew it.

Angus's voice rumbled in the darkness, as close to a whisper as the Highlander could get. "Are we ready?"

No. Nope, nope, nope, never, ever, not in a million years.

Despite my misgivings, a soft string of whispered "aye"s and "yes"es spurred us on. I beat my survival instinct into submission and led the way through the trees, ignoring the voice screaming in the back of my head to turn around and run while I still could.

It didn't take long for us to reach the wall. When I was running away, it had felt like there was a much bigger stretch of forest between me and the road, but that was probably because at the time I had been trekking through the underbrush in ill-fitting heels and in the most pain I had ever experienced in my life. The hiking boots Kumiho had given me for tonight's venture fit far better, as did the sweater, jeans, and jacket she had bought me. Arnold had a small pack slung over his shoulder with the clothes and shoes she'd bought for Sara. I hoped I had remembered her sizes correctly.

I also hoped she was still alive and would need them before the night was out.

Once we reached the wall, two of the vampires climbed to the top, fingers finding purchase or biting into the frozen stone with sharp cracks. At the top, the pair peered over to check for any patrols or other signs we would have a welcome party waiting for us on the other side. Before long, they were signaling it was clear, holding out their hands to help the magi over while the other vampires climbed or leapt to the top.

I accepted an offered hand, though I bit back a yelp of surprise when I was yanked up, only to find myself face-to-face with Fane. My free hand shot out, clutching his arm for balance. He grinned at me with a hint of fang, a glimmer of red flashing deep in his eyes as he helped me steady myself on the ledge on top of the wall.

"Watch your step."

The rolling lilt of his voice didn't sound like a challenge, even though his stare and smirk told me it was. Tempting though it was to the animal side of me, I didn't rise to his bait, yanking my hand free. His footing slipped and he had to make a quick grab and shift his weight, barely keeping his balance. Without bothering to lend him a hand, I leapt down to land in a fluid crouch. He didn't say anything else, but I felt his eyes on me, burning holes in my back.

I took a deep breath, focusing on the sprawling mansion perhaps an acre away. Max hadn't made any attempt to get into my head yet, so I hoped he hadn't noticed I had returned. He'd know soon enough.

Once everyone was safely over the wall, five vampires paired off with the five magi who would trap us inside, four of the pairs striking off to set up their impromptu circle around the property. Nothing would go in or out of it until they let the shield fall. Two hours, they said. That was the maximum amount of time they could hold a circle of that size, even working together.

I had the feeling we had far less time than that to decide how this battle would turn.

It took longer than I expected for them to find their places. The property was *big*, and they had to do everything they could to avoid detection. The vampires didn't appear bothered by the wait, but Kumiho was growing restless, flexing her hands repeatedly and staring a bit too intently in the direction of that mansion. There wasn't any trouble, but Xander, the mage who had stayed behind, commented how it was also taking them so long because they had to shift the local ley lines into alignment.

"Too wild and untapped" was how he put it, moving his hands like a conductor of an orchestra to shift something I couldn't detect.

He and Arnold both stiffened and looked to the north at the same time. Something was moving against the snow. A human shape. Not one of our people. Running back to the main building.

Kumiho grinned in a way I didn't like. "Start your distractions, little wizardlings. I'll return in a moment."

She took off at a sprint, far faster than the other figure was going. She would catch up to whoever that was soon.

Arnold shouted something I didn't catch, some guttural-sounding word, gesturing in the direction of what I thought might be a guesthouse. It looked like a firework shot from his hand, lighting up the snow in a glittering yellow-red arc as it raced to the building.

The impact was like a missile from a rocket launcher, punching through the outer wall and exploding with a shock wave that sent most of us staggering back and throwing up our arms to protect our eyes from the flash. The ground shuddered under my feet, and a straight, narrow depression formed in the snow like a miniature valley. It led directly from the guesthouse to the mansion. Angus had been right. There was—had been—an escape tunnel there.

On the other side of the house, more fireworks went off, the flash briefly blinding me. I hoped whatever they were casting didn't cause the prison rooms beneath the house to collapse like the escape tunnel had.

Though my ears were ringing, I still heard Arnold just fine. "Holy shit. That was fucking awesome!"

Xander laughed. The rest of us sidled a few steps away. Yes, even me.

"Careful there, lad," Angus muttered, giving me a nudge to get me moving along Kumiho's tracks. Kimberly and the remaining vampires, save for the one assigned to be Xander's bodyguard, were soon following us. "Don't let the power go to yer head. We need ye focused on the task at hand."

"Don't worry. I know what I'm doing," Arnold said.

No kidding. Shaking my head to dispel the lingering ringing sound, I focused on Kumiho's tracks in the snow, scanning ahead to spot her as I sped up. Angus quickly passed me, taking the fore, and Arnold picked up his pace to run beside me.

I came to a screeching halt when I saw what Kumiho was doing, Arnold plowing into me from behind to send me into a spectacular face-plant in the snow.

Chapter Twenty-One

Arnold landed in a sprawl on my back, and I was momentarily blinded by snow. It didn't take him long to roll off me. Rough, huge hands dug into my jacket between my shoulder blades and yanked me back to my feet. I flailed and batted at them with one arm, the other scrubbing furiously at my face to get the snow out of my eyes.

"Are ye ruddy daft, woman?"

Blinking the last of the melting snow out of my eyes, I squinted at Angus, then the hulking form of the creature looming over the blood-spattered corpse of the person who had been fleeing from Kumiho.

I knew it was her. Shreds of her jeans and unmistakable hot pink jacket dotted the snow around her. Even with the thick smell of blood on the air, I recognized her scent. It made sense now, why she smelled musky and strange, Were-but-not.

The creature lifted its head, and bright orange eyes peered at me. It had a body that reminded me of a shifted werewolf. A kind of animalistic half-man, something equally at home on two legs or four, with claw-tipped black hands that could easily be mistaken for paws. Silky orange fur covered the top of its muzzle and most of the body, with black, tufted ears, white on the underside of its jaw, belly, and on the tips of all nine of its poofy tails flicking and swaying like serpents.

Nine. Tails. I shit you not.

It let out a yip-like sound that might have been a laugh before dipping its muzzle back to its gruesome business.

I turned away, putting a hand to my stomach and breathing through my mouth to keep the meaty scent and ripping, tearing sounds from making me toss my cookies. Arnold was sitting in the snow next to me, staring, gone a sickly shade of green.

"Kumiho. *Kitsune.* I should have known," he said, voice hollow.

"Kitsune?" I asked. The term was vaguely familiar, like something I might have known before but forgot.

"What, you thought Soo-Jin's name was Kumiho?" Fane's derisive voice startled me. "That's *what* she is, not her name. She got her pound of flesh. Let's get ours, aye?"

"Aye," Angus affirmed.

He reached out to pull Arnold to his feet, helping him on his way toward the mansion. I avoided looking at Soo-Jin, or Kumiho, or whoever she was, and her impromptu meal as I trudged past, focusing as best I could on our target. Every rip, tear, and crunch made me flinch, but I managed to keep the bile down, and not to run screaming from the demon-fox Soo-Jin had turned into.

Once Kimberly caught up with us, gasping for breath, she barely managed out a "Hey, what's happ—" before she spotted what the rest of us had already seen and barfed.

Fane surprised me again by staying behind with her, waiting to one side for her to collect herself while the rest of us moved on. I didn't want to be the one to tell the young mage, but chances were high she would see much worse before the night was through. Her reaction did not bode well for how she would handle the fight to come.

I wasn't sure what it said about me that I was getting used to seeing carnage like that, and knew to expect worse.

Arnold pointed up. I tilted my head, scanning the sky—and soon realized those little sparkles weren't stars. They were from a crystalline shield far overhead, colors swirling like you might see on a soap bubble in the sun, arching over the property and surrounding the building. Our two-hour mark had begun.

It didn't take long for some of Max's men to rush from the building to meet our charge. Arnold's splayed hand threw one of them back with some kind of unseen force, a guttural war cry from our would-be assailant warbling into a scream of pain, soon cut off as the figure . . . dissolved? Christ, whatever Arnold had cast, it turned that vampire, or whatever he was, into ash right before our eyes.

There was no time to stop and consider what the mage had done. I focused on the three people still coming in our direction, not realizing until I was already four or five strides closer that I had let fangs and claws extend before thinking to reach for my gun.

I shouldn't have bothered. Long before I was close enough to be in any danger, Angus and four other vampires shot forward with a burst of inhuman speed. One moment they were all around me, and the next they were halfway across the field, tearing into the remaining vampire and two humans who had come out to face us. The fight was over before I, Arnold, Kimberly, Fane, or Soo-Jin ever reached it.

Soo-Jin had joined us and was close at my back. There was something oddly comforting about that—though Arnold didn't seem to think so, giving us a wide berth once he noticed how close she'd come to him.

We slowed down and took a more cautious approach once we got close to the side door we were planning to enter. This was close enough to where I had escaped that I thought I could figure out how to get around once we were inside.

Angus put his shoulder to the door, the other vampires crowding around us and shoving me and the magi behind them. A vampire whose name I didn't know gave me a nervous, fang-filled smile. For the first time since my escape, I thought to look—*really* look—at my allies.

Arnold's brow had a sheen of nervous sweat, and

Kimberly was not only green around the gills, but her gloved hands were visibly shaking. The glint to Soo-Jin's fox-eyes and cant of her head gave me the idea that the *kumiho*, or *kitsune*, or whatever she was, wasn't bothered in the least by the thought of the battle to come. Most of the vampires, though they didn't fidget the way the magi did, showed other signs of nervousness. Their quick, unneeded breaths and slight flicks of their fingers, like they were flexing claws they didn't have, worried me more than the thought of Kimberly's squeamishness.

If the vampires were afraid, then they weren't as certain of the outcome as Angus and Soo-Jin appeared to be.

After the doorjamb splintered and cracked, the door popping open under Angus's weight, we all shuffled inside. It opened into a game room. A series of billiard tables and a wet bar on the far wall took up the bulk of the space. Angus was grinning ear to ear, beard bristling and eyes glinting like rubies, clearly enjoying this. He wielded a sword with a long, broad blade like a baseball bat as he scanned the place for any foes lying in wait.

Aside from the first rush, there was no sign of any defense prepared against us. Still, I was nervous. I knew how many people Max employed for security and we hadn't seen a fraction of them. There was also Gideon to contend with, not to mention Max himself. Then again, this place was so big, the rest of Max's security might have been focusing on something on the other side of the building and we'd never know.

"What's the heading? Which way?"

I started to take the lead, but Angus's hand on my shoulder stopped me.

"Just tell us the way, lass. Ye nae take point."

"Sorry," I mumbled, reddening. I should have known better. I gestured to a set of doors at the far end of the room. "That way, I think. We should go upstairs first. If Arnold can free Iana, she can help us."

Angus went first, cracking the door open and glancing either way before moving into whatever was beyond it. I recognized the next room. I could figure out where to go from here, thank goodness.

"Hey, I know where we are. The way to Max's room is that way. The way downstairs is over there."

Arnold gave Kimberly his familiar, Bob, the tiny black mouse, so that he had a way of keeping tabs on the other half of our little war party. She had no familiar to trade him, but didn't seem to mind letting the mouse settle himself between her neck and collar, its twitching nose and whiskers barely visible between strands of her long, blond hair. Kimberly and three of the vampires, including Fane, broke away to find and free any captives in the underground rooms after I gave them directions and explained how to find the hidden door. The rest of us hurried to find the stairs.

Arnold and a couple of the vampires boggled at the opulence and glitter, but I knew all the beautiful furniture and art had been bought with blood money, funds raised on the suffering of humans and Others alike. Besides, the stink of rot and formaldehyde was too strong for me to enjoy anything about the view, considering how badly my eyes were watering. No question, Gideon and his zombies were still here, and close.

The others must have been noticing the stench, too. Soo-Jin was the only one who didn't seem bothered by it. Aside from Angus, all of the vampires had that just-bit-into-a-lemon face that said they had gotten a whiff of something rotten. Arnold had his arm up, his nose pressed into his jacket. His hunched shoulders, little furrows between his brows and narrowed eyes told me he was more determined than ever.

It was a good thing, too, because when Angus threw open the wide double doors leading into Max's bedroom, there were half a dozen zombies waiting for us. The sting in my eyes wasn't just for the smell when I saw Tiny was among them.

Angus waded into their midst with a roar, his blade cutting three of the shuffling dead men down before anyone else even made it into the room. His eyes matched the color of his hair, red as blood. He moved with inhuman speed and agility, destroying the walking dead before they could so much as brush a finger bone against him.

The other vampires swept in, though a bit more cautiously. No one could miss their distaste in their curled lips and grimaces. Arnold stayed beside me, gaping at the zombies. Soo-Jin stayed behind, too, but I think it was more because she didn't want to get zombie bits stuck in her fur and teeth than because she was afraid. Rather than join us, she turned to guard our backs, squaring herself in the center of the hallway.

Arnold sounded a bit strained. "I . . . man, I mean, I heard about them but I never thought . . ."

I patted his shoulder, watching from a safe distance as the vampires gingerly attacked the zombies. It was almost funny to see how squeamish they all were, save for Angus, about getting zombie goo on their hands and clothing.

The dead men snapped their teeth and clawed at the . . . uh . . . well, the *un*dead men who were tearing them apart. Some of them had small blades, but those didn't do much other than punch holes in decaying skin and set loose an even worse wave of stench on us. The zombies didn't appear to notice or care about their wounds, stumbling around and clawing at the much faster vampires dodging their groping hands and snapping teeth.

It didn't take long to dispatch them. Once the vampires figured out that it took breaking limbs and dismemberment to disable the zombies, not piercing them, it sped up their work tremendously.

I had to turn my gaze away as one of the vampires slid an arm around Tiny's neck, and I couldn't suppress a flinch at the cracking, tearing sound that followed.

It was necessary, but it still hurt.

No one else would do it for him, so I mouthed a prayer that whatever might have remained of Tiny and the other zombies were at peace now. Arnold and one of the vampires surprised me by joining in, our voices rising and falling in sorrowful whispers.

"Eternal rest grant unto them, O Lord, and let perpetual light shine upon them. May the souls of the faithful departed, through the mercy of God, rest in peace. Amen."

When we were done, I turned a questioning look on the vampire who said the prayer with us. He brushed a piece of zombie gunk off his jacket before tugging the collar aside and showing me the gold cross that hung at his throat, giving me a tight smile.

Huh. A Catholic vampire. How about that.

There wasn't enough time for us to linger. I picked my way across the carpet, careful not to step in any puddles of dead people parts and chemical-laden blood. Arnold followed in my footsteps, choking back little gagging sounds. Angus busied himself with wiping zombie gunk off his blade onto Max's bed.

I tugged the painting away from the panel that hid the lock leading to Iana's prison. Arnold took my place in front of it, studying the buttons and the section that required Max's handprint to unlock it.

"I know the code, but I don't know how to handle the other part."

Arnold shook his head. "Not necessary. Just give me a sec."

He set his hand against the scanner, tiny arcs of blue-white electricity flickering around his fingertips. Whatever power he was using, it looked like it was seeking a way into the panel, touching all the edges and moving into the cracks and crevices where the buttons and cover plate fit together.

The panel went dark, and the door slid back.

Gideon was waiting on the other side with the most predatory smile I'd ever seen outside of a vampire's. He raised his hand, his tattooed palm pointed at Arnold. "Lube up and bend over, sweet stuff. You're about to have a very bad day."

Chapter Twenty-Two

Arnold flinched as a wave of some unseen power shot in his direction. There were no flashing lights or sparkles or glitter like I had come to expect from magic, but I felt the unseen wind of its passage, making all the small hairs on my arms and the back of my neck prickle. I could smell it, too, the scent of ozone briefly overpowering the stink of dead things.

Nothing else happened.

Gideon's look of puzzlement quickly turned to alarm as Angus tackled him to the ground, a blade pressed to his throat and drawing a slick line of red across it.

"No!"

At my outburst, everyone looked at me like I was deranged. Hell, I would have looked at me like I was deranged, too.

It took a second for me to find the words, but once I did, I got them all out in a rush.

"I bet he knows where Sara is. He can tell us. He tried to help us before. Please, don't hurt him."

Angus growled, the blade biting just a smidge deeper. Any more than that, and he would nick something vital. "Have ye lost yer wits? He's no ally to us."

"I can be," Gideon managed, his fingers digging into the carpet.

"Tell us where Sara is," Arnold demanded.

Gideon's green eyes narrowed, flickering with suppressed power. "Let me up and I'll show you the way. I'll even help you take down Max."

"Lies," one of the vampires spat. "He tried to attack us. You saw it."

"I was trying to save myself! Wouldn't you have done the same? I wanted a shield since you took the ones I had away, and fuck you all so very much for that."

Arnold gritted his teeth, glaring down at the prone necromancer. "It's true. I felt it. He was trying to snare a vampire."

"Well, you're so pale. Honest mistake."

Arnold huffed. "Too many MMOs. What do you expect? This isn't getting us any closer to Sara *or* Max. Tell us or I'll . . . I'll . . . I'll bind you. We've got enough magi here, and don't think we won't."

Gideon struggled just a bit under Angus. The vampire growled and gave him a little shake until the necromancer stopped. Whatever "binding" meant, it was enough to put the fear of God into Gideon.

Panting with fear, fingers twitching like he was itching to cast a spell, Gideon nodded, staring up at the ceiling. "Fine. Fine! I can take you to the girl.

I'm not sure where Max is, but I can find him if you let me up."

This was far too easy. I wasn't sure if we should trust him, but I didn't know how else to track down Sara in this maze. Apparently Arnold didn't trust him either.

"Keep an eye on him and don't let him cast anything. Stuff his mouth and tie his wrists together."

"Sara didn't tell me you liked to play those kinds of games."

A thundercloud of rage passed over the mage's face, and he lifted a fist. "You show us the way or I will personally burn every last iota of dark fae out of you, consequences be damned."

Gideon's eyes flared with power, like green gemstones lit from behind, but he didn't make any more smart comments. Angus smiled like he was taking great pleasure in shoving the balled up pillowcase someone handed him into the necromancer's mouth, only stopping once the poor guy was gagging on it. Someone else found a few ties and handed them over. Those were used to hold the gag in place and for tight, efficient knots around his wrists. If he hadn't been such a deceitful bastard, I might have felt sorry for him.

Once he was trussed up to Angus's liking, the elder vampire hauled Gideon to his feet. "Lead the way, little *uilebheist*."

Gideon shot him a dirty look, but didn't bother to make a run for it. Not like it would have done him any good considering he was surrounded by vampires fast enough to snap his neck or kneecaps before he took more than two steps.

He paused once in the doorway, his eyes widening at the carnage. It was rather impressive, but Angus had no patience for it, giving him a little shove from behind.

After stumbling, he threw a glare over his shoulder and then resumed his trek forward, leading us to wherever Sara was hidden. He didn't seem surprised to see a towering fox-demon with nine tails in the hall, merely giving her a wide berth as he led the way. He must have seen her before at some point.

I don't care how blasé you are about supernatural creatures. Something like Soo-Jin would be cause for comment in my neighborhood, and I'm from New York, fer Chrissakes.

'*You owe me.*'

The voice was a whisper in the back of my mind, but I did my best to ignore it. Gideon gave no outwardly visible sign that he was mentally badgering me with demands, much like the spirit in the hunter's belt used to whenever I wore the enchanted artifact. I didn't want Angus or Arnold to hurt Gideon, so I tried not to show any signs of how creeped the hell out I was, either.

I promised to get you two out. I intend to keep my word. After all, if they hurt me, she'll feel it, too.'

That made me falter. Arnold's hand on my shoulder steadied me, but I couldn't bring myself to move again right away.

'*She's mine now. If I go down, she goes with me. Keep that in mind.*'

Great. Just fucking peachy. Like I had any way of explaining that to Arnold or the vampires that wouldn't make them *more* inclined to forcibly separate his head from his shoulders.

On the bright side, by keeping Gideon tied up, Max might not jump to the conclusion he'd turned traitor and kill him first.

Shivering with a combination of nerves and dread, I trailed behind the others. Arnold kept his hand on my shoulder, and I set my hand over his. We'd been through bad times like this before. Maybe not quite this bad, but we'd figure out a way to fix this, just like we always did. Somehow.

The necromancer led the way downstairs, down a corridor I wasn't familiar with, and then to a recessed oak door with a padlock on the outside. It was deep in the house in a shadowed alcove, easily overlooked. Gideon jerked his jaw at it, then rubbed his cheek against his shoulder, trying to dislodge the gag.

Angus elbowed him aside and reached for the lock. Gideon kicked the back of his knee until the vampire swung around and planted a fist through the wall next to the necromancer's head. Slowly, deliberately, he then set the knuckles of the hand with the sword on the other side.

Gideon's back thumped against the wall, and he stared up at the vampire. A new scent wafting from him filled the air, one that made me consider him with new eyes. A predator's eyes. Hunger cramped my stomach so badly I had to bite my inner cheek hard enough to fill my mouth with my own blood to quiet the building need.

Plaster chips pattered on the floor as Angus yanked his hand free of the wall. His thick fingers hooked under the cherry red tie, pulling it down, then tugging the balled up pillowcase out. Gideon gasped and coughed, then choked out a few words.

"Some . . . Ow! There are some vampires in there, too, you ungracious Neanderthal."

Angus growled, but backed off. I eyed the hole he left in the wall, suitably impressed. Vampires didn't often make such an obvious show of their strength around me. Knowing they could do it and seeing it were two very different animals.

The necromancer stayed where he was, not protesting as one of the vampires took his arm. Angus wrapped a hand around the lock and wrenched it off, tossing it over his shoulder. So much for going in quietly. He hefted a booted foot and kicked the door in.

I was getting the idea he really enjoyed doing that.

We moved in, the vampires leading again.

There were an awful lot of Max's vampires inside, and they were well prepared to fend off our assault. Many of them moved like Angus, with the same fluid grace and speed, which meant they were all elders. They had guns, too, which had Angus and Soo-Jin quick to backtrack and yank me out of there. But not before I spotted Sara, Iana, and several of the other girls by the far wall, trapped behind a set of bars bolted into the wall like some jail in the Old West and backed up as far from the fight as they could get.

They left me in the hall outside with Gideon and the vampire holding him in place, even Soo-Jin slinking back through that door to rejoin the fray.

"Well, this is lovely. I feel so useful like this," Gideon said.

"Shut up," the vampire holding him snapped.

The shriek of wrenching metal made me cringe and cover my ears. My hands didn't drown out the sounds of the battle as they became more of a fever pitch, the snarls and growls and yelps outnumbering the gunshots. There was a flash of light, and a roil of flame rolled out of the room and into the hall, scorching the door frame and the wall opposite. We all scrambled out of the way. A particularly chilling cry rang out, quieting everything else for a moment.

Smoke drifted out of the doorway and filled the hall.

"Jesus, Mary and Joseph."

Gideon quirked a brow at me. "I don't think they had anything to do with that, Copper-top. Looks like your little mage friend got pissed."

"Didn't I tell you to shut up?"

Gideon turned a flat stare on the vampire. "Why, yes." He then returned his gaze to me. "So. How about you undo these ropes so I can be of some use, hmm?"

An urge to do just that rose in me. With a growl, I stalked closer—and slapped him, hard. "Don't you *ever* fuck with my head again or I will rip yours off. You hear me?"

The vampire stiffened. "What did he do?" Then shook Gideon. "Hey. What did you do?"

Gideon smirked and tilted his head up, slowly licking the blood from his split lip. The scent of it drew me closer, and that was when I realized there was some on my knuckles. Before I knew it, my hand was inches from my mouth, my throat burning for the taste of it. The only thing that stopped me from licking it off was how very interested Gideon appeared to be in my actions.

"Go on," he purred, "drink up. It's what you've wanted to do all night, isn't it? Drink until there's nothing left."

The vampire shook him again. "If you don't shut up, I'm going to stuff an old sock in your mouth next. Can it and leave her the fuck alone."

I met the necromancer's too-interested gaze as I swiped the back of my hand down my jacket, wiping the blood off. He frowned, then shrugged, as if he hadn't had some kind of investment in the outcome a moment ago.

Soo-Jin had warned against giving in to the urge for blood. I was starting to get the idea that it might make the monster inside of me come out to play if I gave in to the need.

That would, in turn, make me easier for Gideon to control. What a dick.

After successfully tamping down the urge to smack him upside the head again, I sidled closer to the door to peer inside. The smoke made it hard to see well enough to tell who was winning, but there were still plenty of bodies clashing, moving with inhuman speed.

Three figures were headed this way, shadowed by smoke and clinging to each other, edging around the fighting. I thought about going inside to work off a little steam, too, but better sense prevailed. I backed up a couple of paces until I was beside the vampire, drawing and leveling my gun at the door-way in case whoever was coming wasn't on our side.

Chapter Twenty-Three

I snapped the safety back on and put it away as soon as I saw it was Iana, using her great strength to half carry, half drag Arnold and Sara on either side of her. The two of them were coughing and limp in her arms. I got on the other side of Sara, putting her other arm over my shoulder and helping her along until we were a good distance from the doorway.

Gideon and the vampire both watched us with avid interest as Iana and I helped Arnold and Sara settle on a nearby settee. Iana was breathing hard, but the blood on her hands and smearing her white robe weren't hers. As soon as he stopped coughing so much, Arnold wrapped his arms around Sara, who clung to him, tears streaking down her pale cheeks.

"Oh," Gideon said, his tone giving away his delight. "Oh, ho, ho! They've got it worse than I thought."

"Shut. The. Fuck. Up."

Gideon rolled his eyes, but obeyed the vampire. For the moment. The way he watched Arnold now was different and sent a pang of worry through me. Nothing that monster was planning could be any good. Not for the mage or Sara or anyone else.

Iana placed a hand between my shoulder blades, making me jump with the unexpected contact. Even with my heavy jacket between us, her blood ran hot enough to burn through the material. She sidled up beside me, her eyes alight with a deep golden glow as she stared down at Arnold. "Is this the one you promised me?"

The husky words might have sounded like desire coming from someone else. It was a type of desire, but there was nothing sexual in it. Just a deep and abiding longing for her freedom.

"Yes, that's him. I think he needs a minute."

"He does," Arnold managed between coughs. Sara added a vehement nod, tightening her grip on him.

I backed off a bit, focusing on the doorway to give them a semblance of privacy. Not that they'd get it with Iana, Gideon, and the vampire all staring at them like bugs under a microscope.

Arnold sat up a bit straighter, his eyes going wide. Though still hoarse, his words were clear enough to send a chill through me.

"Shit. We need to move. Max found Kimberly and the others. We've got a serious problem."

The sounds of fighting from the other room were still going strong. If I'd had one, I would have been tempted to pull out a stopwatch just to see how long they would keep it up. Considering the fight in Royce's basement with Max had lasted half a night, it wouldn't surprise me for this one to drag out for an hour or two as well. There was no way Angus, Soo-Jin, or any of the others would wrap that mess up in time to find Kimberly and the vampires who had gone with her.

Gideon cleared his throat. "I can help."

The vampire smacked him on the back of the head. He cried out and shot forward, cheek and chest smacking against the opposite wall. He couldn't catch himself, sinking to his knees with a groan.

Iana stalked over to him, grabbing his jaw and forcing him to look up at her. "How can you help, dark one? I know what you are."

"The mage is tapped. I can fix that. Once I fix that, he can fix you."

I stood a bit straighter, tension building in my arms and shoulders. "That doesn't sound right. Don't trust him. Not with that."

Gideon growled and fought the bindings on his wrist. "For fuck's sake, I want Max dead as badly as you do. Fabian will never be mine as long as Max is alive to control him and take all his wealth in tributes. We want our freedom, just like you! Let me go and I'll do whatever you want."

Iana studied his face briefly, then smiled without humor. "It sounds like truth, but smells like deceit. Nice try, heartless thing. I know you for what you are. I see you."

The necromancer inclined his head, his own

smile sly but humorless, as much as admitting defeat. There was something comforting about knowing Iana was Other enough to smell his lies. At least one of us had that power. "Fine. Not all lies. Half truths, maybe."

"Come on. We don't have time for this. Kimberly needs help," Arnold said.

Iana frowned and shoved the necromancer down, leaving him to get up on his own off the floor. She stalked over to the mage, baring her teeth in a semblance of a smile. "Fine. Remove the collar and I will save this woman, assuming there is anything left to save."

Arnold, holding Sara against him and stroking her hair, studied Iana. He reached up to nudge his glasses farther up on his nose, then gestured for her to come closer.

"I'm not too tapped for that. Turn around and kneel for me, please. And hold your hair out of the way."

She did as instructed, practically vibrating with suppressed excitement. Arnold winced when he saw how red and raw the skin was around the collar. A few feet away, despite looking a bit put out, Gideon pretended not to watch and had taken to sulking in a crouch by the wall.

"We'll heal this. When it's off. When we get out of here, there's someone—"

"If you remove it, that will not be necessary," she said.

Arnold didn't waste any more time with small talk. With one arm around Sara's waist, he reached out to circle his fingers around the collar. He closed his eyes tight, an expression of intense concentration crossing his features. Iana didn't move, but her eyes closed as well, her teeth bared in anticipation.

A sharp crack sounded. The metal grew dull, losing a sheen I hadn't quite realized it had until it was gone, and it fell away to clatter on the floor.

Iana surged to her feet, her eyes and skin blazing with a warm, golden glow as she spread her arms. That warmth began gathering in her palms like she was holding growing balls of condensed sunlight. A low growl rumbled in her throat and rattled my bones like the thunder of a diesel engine as she turned her focus on the necromancer, who was making an effort to inch away from the pissed off Other leaning meaningfully in his direction.

"Don't," I warned. "We need him to find Max."

She looked less than pleased and didn't give any sign that she heard me. Instead, she took a step closer, her fingers curled into talons around the globes of light in her palms. Even the vampire was looking nervous by this point.

"Iana."

She paused, fingers twitching, never once turning her fierce gaze off of Gideon's cringing frame to focus on me.

"Listen to me. We need him. Now is not the time for this."

Gideon, pale and shivering, bobbed his head up and down. "Right, I'm useful, remember? You need me."

Her growl deepened in pitch, then cut off. The

sense of a storm gathering around her, all crackle and electricity, faded. "So be it." The light gathering in her hands disappeared like it had never been. She moved on the balls of her feet, still too predatory for my liking, and yanked the necromancer around to slice through the bonds on his wrists with her nails.

The vampire dashed forward, grabbing their arms so neither could slip away. His features twisted in a what-in-the-hell-is-wrong-with-you glare I was more used to seeing being leveled in my direction.

He didn't keep it up for long. Gideon's free arm slid around until his palm—the one with the tattoo—rested over the vampire's heart.

That was all it took. In the space of a breath, the vampire's expression went blank, a chill wind with no origin I could detect sliding through the hall. Every hair on my body stood on end, an electric tingle skittering over my skin until I broke out in goose bumps.

The vampire loosened his grip on Gideon, and the necromancer took a step back, favoring Iana with a dazzling smile as he straightened the lapels of his suit jacket. All traces of his earlier fright were gone.

"Much better. Oh, don't look so put out. I'll let him go once I'm done with him. The girl, on the other hand . . ."

Sara made an inarticulate sound of protest and I gasped, somehow managing to be surprised at the necromancer's duplicity. Arnold struggled to his feet, putting himself in front of Sara and raising his hands. Blue-white sparks crackled around his finger-tips. Gideon laughed.

"Come on, now," Gideon said, his grin widening. "You really want to see who has the bigger magical—or otherwise—*cojones* here? I promise you it's me."

The sparks whirling around Arnold's hands were gaining speed and size. The need to find Max spurred me to move before he might do something we would all regret later.

I dashed forward and grabbed Arnold's arm before he could cast whatever it was he was on the verge of hurling at Gideon. Arnold might have had the power of the cosmos at his fingertips, but his physical strength paled against mine, even before I was infected. He struggled a bit, then harder when Gideon started humming the strains of a song I recognized from all those times Arnold made me and Sara sit through it on game nights at his place. It was "Do You Wanna Date My Avatar."

Sara spoke up, her voice hoarse and cracking with strain. "Don't, Gideon. Please."

The necromancer kept his gaze on Arnold for a long, strained moment. His focus flicked to Sara, following the line of her shoulder and arm, noting the way her fingers caught in Arnold's jacket. Gideon rolled his shoulders and tilted his head back, his soft laughter making my skin crawl.

"I know, I know," he said, throwing his arm across his eyes in an overly dramatic gesture I had seen him make before. "I'm why we can't have nice things. What a world."

"You promised you'd get us out of here," I hissed.

Gideon looked at me, frowned, then started patting down his pockets with a faraway, thoughtful expression. After a moment of this, he shoved a hand in a back pocket of his jeans, groped a bit, then pulled it out. His face lit up as he triumphantly held up the invisible whatever it was pinched between his thumb and forefinger.

"Look at that! I found exactly one fuck to give. It is my gift to you."

Arnold tugged against my grip again. This time I didn't stop him. He went chest to chest with the much taller necromancer, glaring up at him. "Let her go!"

"I'll think about it. Don't worry. I have no intention of hurting anyone who doesn't deserve it. Not tonight."

Iana hissed. "Enough. I taste your lies. Cease your foolishness and use that magic of yours. Find him."

Gideon gave her a raspberry, then turned away from the two, snapping his fingers. The vampire turned to follow him, glazed eyes focused on his back. Iana stalked after them, her anger a palpable thing.

Arnold and Sara were slower to follow. He waved me off when I tried to help, and I flinched under the accusatory look he leveled at me. I wanted to protest that none of this mess was my fault, but a teeny, tiny, hateful voice in the back of my head was giving a gleeful singsong rundown of all the reasons it *was* because of me.

It didn't help that Iana and Gideon were moving

at a much faster clip, not bothering to see if we were behind them. They'd outpace us and leave us alone, lost in this den of monsters to fend for ourselves if we didn't hurry.

Then it occurred to me that if Gideon faced Max without me, Iana certainly wouldn't do anything to keep the duplicitous little shit from becoming a smear on the wall. If he was hurt or killed, I didn't even want to *think* about what that would mean for Sara's health.

Fighting the creeping terror that thought inspired, I started to run to catch up with Gideon.

"Hey, wait up!"

Chapter Twenty-Four

Gideon led the way, Iana and his enchanted vampire minion following up the rear from either side. Though I was sure Iana would rather tear Gideon's head off and play kickball with it, the effect made it look like he was in charge. I wondered how Max would view this situation, and how the hell I would keep him from killing Gideon out of hand.

At some point, Arnold and Sara fell too far behind for me to see them. The mage had said he could find us wherever we went, but I wasn't sure if he just wanted to get me out of his sight or if he really meant it.

I was tempted to give in to panic and despair, but that wouldn't help anybody, least of all Sara.

Iana stopped in her tracks so abruptly that I ran into her, sending us both stumbling forward a couple of steps. Her fingers closed around my upper arm so tight that it hurt. Gideon paused, glancing over his shoulder.

"Weapons," she said.

"All I've got is the one gun. They wouldn't let me have anything else," I said, apologetic.

"No." She shook her head. "We need to arm ourselves. I don't have the strength to shift yet, and you need more than a pistol. Come, he has an armory on display."

Couldn't argue with that. Gideon opened his mouth like he wanted to say something, but closed it with a snap once Iana got moving at a much faster clip. She led us through a room full of paintings and sculptures, an echoing, empty ballroom with at least a dozen crystal chandeliers reflecting the moonlight into a thousand tiny stars on the polished floor, and an indoor arboretum full of exotic flowers and ferns arranged in a labyrinthine maze. There were small lights here and there, but most of the place was dark, and I was afraid the shadows might be hiding more than just a couple of ornamental rosebushes.

We didn't run into anybody along the way. I spotted security cameras here and there, tiny red lights or the sheen of a lens giving them away. Either everyone in Max's employ was otherwise occupied, or Max didn't care that we were running around unchecked. Neither option boded well for us.

We must have run half the length of the building before Iana led us into a room that looked like something out of an exhibit I had once seen at the Metropolitan Museum of Art. The arms and armory display there had been full of swords, daggers, shields, helmets, and other kinds of armor. Max's collection was similar, but rather than sticking with a particular theme or time period or even culture, he had a little bit of everything. Spears with bronze, iron, and stone tips, armor made of leather and metal and other materials I couldn't immediately identify, knives with handles of stone, bone, and wood.

The difference between what I saw here and what I had seen in the museum was that each piece on display here still looked just as serviceable and dangerous as it must have been the day it was made. None of it was hidden behind display cases, either. All of the armor looked to be about the same size. Made for a man of Max's proportions.

As I took a breath, aside from the scent of dust and metal and leather and oil, I could taste the old blood in the air. Long dried, long dead, and so much remembered violence radiated from these pieces that I could have choked on it if I breathed too deep. These weapons weren't the purchases of a collector. They were trophies, retired reminders of a life of violence and a river of bloodshed. Lifetimes of it.

Iana viewed the place with distaste, her lip curled in a sneer as though she'd gotten a whiff of something rotten. I had the feeling she was sensing the same thing I was. Maybe more than I, considering she was a far stronger Other than whatever I was turning out to be. Her senses were likely more attuned to these things in a way I would never experience.

Something told me that there was a history behind each and every piece in this room, and that if I held it long enough and breathed it in, the blood soaked into the material would tell me the story. My connection to the one who had worn and wielded these instruments of torture and murder would be enough to let it unfold like a grisly picture book in my head.

Never had I felt so ill at having a piece of Max inside me.

Iana studied the collection on the wall before selecting a short, double-bladed sword with some kind of raised line running down the flat of the blade. It was old. Ancient. Cast bronze, now myriad shades of green, but not so pitted or oxidized that the metal couldn't hold an edge. The pommel was far newer than the rest of it, but even still, the leather around the grip was cracked and so faded that I couldn't tell what the original color must have been.

She held it out to me expectantly. As soon as my hand closed around it, a jolt of something dark and hungry radiated off the blade. Countless images of angry, frightened faces, splashes of blood, and other things assailed me.

Hair like sunshine. Eyes like the sea. Taken away in a flash of red, replaced by the shadow of Rhathos—*Royce*—and then Iana was shaking me, and the images were gone.

"These things will haunt you if you let them."

"No shit," I replied.

The sword Max had used to fight against Royce for the life of his ladylove, Helen of Volos, was in my hands. A fight he had lost, and with it, any hope of reconciling with the only true friend he'd ever had. Thousands of years old, and the weapon was still so well preserved and cared for despite its age that it could cut through flesh and bone like butter.

I was tempted to throw it away, to find some other way of dealing with Max, but I knew it wouldn't matter which weapon I picked up. They would all carry memories of death, and it was up to me to keep it under control. "I'm fine. Let's get the hell out of here."

Gideon ran a fingertip down the edge of a much newer blade, smiling at the red smear he left behind. "We'll have to come back here before we leave. I could use a few vamp-blooded blades for some rituals I've been meaning to try."

"I don't think so," came another voice. That hated, familiar voice.

Max stood in the doorway, his eyes gleaming crimson and his hands and clothes spotted with flecks of red and black. He must have run his hands through his short, dark brown hair at some point, because half the curls were plastered to the top of his head by I-really-didn't-want-to-think-about-what.

Iana grabbed a sword and rushed forward, her eyes full of murder. Before she was halfway across the room, Max was behind her, one hand on her wrist and the other wrapped around her throat, holding her tight against him. Christ, I hadn't even seen him move.

Her skin reddened under his touch, and she cried out in a mix of rage and pain, dropping her weapon with a clatter. I raised my sword with shaking hands and edged closer to Gideon. Iana twisted and writhed like a snake, but Max didn't pay either of us any mind. He bared his fangs and growled, glaring at Gideon over her shoulder as he tightened his grip around her neck.

"This is the thanks I get for taking you into my home? Allowing your union with my progeny?"

Gideon laughed, slumping against the wall next to the vampire minion staring blankly up at the ceiling like a mannequin. "I've done nothing to betray you. I kept your property safe, distracted, and out of the battle. You should be thanking *me,* you decrepit antique."

My gaze shot to the necromancer. "You . . . you *what?*"

He wiggled his fingers at me. "I did what I needed to. And so will you."

An all too familiar sense of something taking the wheel in my head set in. I shut my eyes and shook my head, but it didn't stop the fucker from propelling me like a goddamned puppet straight at Max, sword raised in a suicidal run while blood filled my mouth as fangs popped into place.

If it didn't mean Sara would hurt too, I would strangle that fucking necromancer the minute he loosened his mental grip on me.

Max threw Iana out of the way, sending her crashing into a display of armor that wouldn't have been out of place at King Arthur's Round Table. The vampire caught my sword arm on the downswing, but he didn't move fast enough to block the gun as I shot him in the gut with my off-hand until the gun gave nothing but a series of dry clicks.

It made him jerk, but he didn't otherwise react to

the bullets. He gave no sign of pain or anything beyond a furious glare. A glare that became a great deal more pointed when he noted the sword in my hand.

"You don't deserve the honor of touching that sword," he hissed, digging his thumb into my wrist until the pressure became so painful that even with Gideon's goading I couldn't keep my grip on it.

"Neither do you," I spat out, simultaneously fighting his hold on me and Gideon's mental talons.

He shoved me down to my knees, and I winced at the force of it, knowing there would be bruises later. "You suicidal little bitch. As soon as I clear out the rest of the rabble, I will flay the skin from your body and break every bone until you beg me for death. The minute you do, I'll sire you just so you heal and I can start over again. Then I'll send you, a piece at a time, to your precious Rhathos."

Glaring up at him, I thumped a fist against the bullet holes in his abdomen, already closing. If I was going to die anyway, I was going to stand up to him the only way I could before I did—by running my mouth.

"Revenge is not the spackle that will fix the Helen-shaped hole in your heart. Making someone else feel sad because they made you feel that way is childish, and I'm a person, not a toy for you to steal and break so you can piss in Royce's sandbox. Grow the fuck up."

"You know *nothing* about me or my motivations, you vacuous, insignificant shant of a blood whore."

"All you live for is someone else's pain! You're

nothing but an empty shell, making everyone else hurt just because you can't stand that someone did it to you. You're nothing. Helen knew it, and so did Royce. I'll bet Athena did, too."

Max growled softly, grabbing my other wrist before I could hit him again and his grip tightening to the point of pain. I still met his glowing red eyes unflinching. He'd already taken everything else from me, so forcing his way back into my head would only further prove my point.

"You're a ghost," I said, voice soft, knowing how much my words were cutting him and wishing I had a way to make more than his heart bleed. "A ghost who should have faded away with whatever shreds of humanity you had left when Helen died."

"Get her out of here before I forget I still need her alive," he hissed in Gideon's direction, though he still stared down at me with the promise of pain to come written all over his features. The pressing cloud of barely leashed power swirling around him gradually tamped down as he got his rage under control, but I knew that wouldn't save me from the world of pain he was planning to deliver on me later.

I glanced over at Gideon and—the vampire that . . . wasn't there anymore?

Then I screamed in pain as Max's grip tightened even more when the other vampire latched onto his wrist and blood-crusted hair from behind, fangs digging into his neck. Max voiced a furious howl and shoved me away as he twisted and clawed at the other vampire.

"You filthy little betrayer!"

Gideon waggled his eyebrows, moving his hands like he was orchestrating a symphony as he gave Max a fierce grin, showing his teeth all the way to the molars. "Abra-cadaver, you fucking bastard."

With a move too swift for my eyes to track, Max was across the room, his fangs embedded in Gideon's throat even as the other vampire remained latched onto him like a freaking monkey riding his back. It would have been hilarious if I wasn't terrified Gideon would be killed, and, with him, Sara.

The necromancer didn't even have time to cry out, his look of shock fading into a slack-jawed combination of pain and ecstasy. His eyelids drifted shut as Max pinned him against the wall.

Gideon's hold on me was fading. Not a good sign. I had to find a way to stop this, fast.

The vampire drinking from Max jerked his head back. Alarm quickly turned to panic and disgust, and he let go, stumbling back to spit out a red glob before he swiped his arm over his mouth.

Before he could get far, Max released Gideon's limp frame and whirled, bloody fangs bared. The other vampire backpedaled, but he barely got two steps before Max was a blur again.

Sharp cracks were followed by a wet ripping sound, and a fine spray of cold, red mist hit my face and hands. Panting with terror, I dropped my empty gun and scrabbled for the sword with my off hand.

Before I could reach it, cold fingers slid around the back of my neck and yanked me up to my feet.

Chapter Twenty-Five

I screamed so loud and shrill I managed to startle myself.

Max whirled me around and then slapped me so hard, stars filled my vision and blood filled my mouth from the blow and from my own fangs cutting into my lower lip. Before I could fall, his fingers curled around my throat, cutting off my breath and lifting me until my feet dangled off the floor.

The ringing in my ears didn't last long, but between him cutting off my air and the blood in my throat, I was starting to black out. He ran his thumb over the blood dribbling down my cheek, making it a point to flick one of my fangs, then sucked the smear of liquid off with a grim, red smile.

"I'm going to enjoy sucking the life out of you. Giving it back just to take it away again."

Then he stumbled and dropped me as Iana plowed into him from behind, a curved scimitar jutting out between his ribs. My knees were like jelly, collapsing under me as I fell. A choked off cry was all I could manage as pain jolted up my wrist when I tried to catch myself. Max must have sprained or broken it when he shook the sword out of my hand before.

Iana snarled and clawed at Max from behind, her legs latched around his waist and her body pressed tight against him to keep him from dislodging the weapon. Her hands were glowing again and everywhere she touched him, terrible burns appeared on his skin. He kept trying to grab her arms but every time he got a grip, her free hand would swipe along any exposed part of him she could reach and tear at the skin and muscle until he let go.

With a roar, he twisted around and body-slammed her into the ground, which had the added effect of shoving the scimitar even deeper into his chest. The lights on her hands winked out and she let go with an inhuman, ululating screech of pain. They both rolled away from each other to rise into wary crouches, each looking for an opening.

Max kept his eyes on her as he gripped the flat of the blade and started to push it out. Aside from a slight tightening around his eyes, I saw no sign that he felt any pain. The slow, taunting smile that spread over his lips only seemed to infuriate her further.

"Just like old times," he whispered.

Whatever that meant to her, it struck home. She moved with the clear, vicious intent of a monster, and I could almost see phantom talons and the shadow of something far bigger than her petite frame sweeping down on Max. It wasn't enough. He swatted her aside, sending her into an ungainly sprawl she quickly recovered from. Seething, she regained her footing and reached for another weapon as he moved toward her.

"I will rain fire and blood on this house. I will end your life and bloodline, and all you hold dear. I will—"

"You will shut up and go back to your cage, or I will find that last hidden temple you thought I knew nothing about and destroy it."

Iana lifted her chin, her golden skin turning crimson high on her cheeks. "I would rather see the last temple fall than for you to remain on this earth a minute longer. I'd sooner die than return to you."

"As you wish."

Once again, Max moved too quickly for me to follow. Between one blink and the next, he was across the room, a dagger buried in Iana's gut. The rotting peaches scent that was quick to permeate the room was mixed with the charnel reek of ruptured intestines. Her eyes flared gold as she gasped and bent double, clawing weakly at his chest.

He helped her sink to the ground, one arm over her shoulder to support her on the way as he cradled her jaw, the other keeping the dagger in place.

"Poor sweet," he said, stroking the back of his hand over her cheek. "If you think it hurts now, just wait until I have the time to properly salt the wounds."

And that was when I drove the ancient, bronze sword into the sweet spot between his neck and collarbone, deep into his body, angling for his heart.

Bet the sack of shit wasn't expecting that.

He arched his back, gasping and releasing his grip on Iana to claw at the air. I leaned in from behind, my lips brushing against his ear as I put my weight into the blade to shove it even deeper.

"I know you won't be around to appreciate this little life lesson much longer, but . . . no means *no,* you fucking unrelenting *asshole.*"

His mouth moved, a crimson froth bubbling on his lips. Then he was twisting, on top of me, black, molasses-thick blood dribbling from his mouth onto my face as he snarled down at me. I clenched my teeth and pressed my lips together so none of his blood would get in my mouth.

All it took was a good, adrenaline-fueled yank on the pommel of the sword to make him roll aside, twisting in agony. He tried to speak, his voice a breathy gurgle.

"Ath . . . Athena . . . will kill you . . . for this . . ."

I rolled too. Once I was on top of him, I wiped his blood off my face and then met his crimson eyes, leaning in to make sure he couldn't miss my utter contempt. "Wow. Look at all the fucks I don't give. Save me a ringside seat in hell, you son of a bitch."

Though I had to use my weaker wrist thanks to how he'd mangled my dominant hand, I still managed to put a twist on the blade and jerk it to the right. I had no idea where all the blood came from considering how much he'd already lost, but a gush of cold, black fluid jetted over the pommel and my fingers and pooled around us on the floor. His struggles became less and less, then stilled, the red glitter in his eyes growing dim and then dying out forever.

I leaned over to grab the blade Iana had dropped, using it to slice off the fucker's head. Had to be sure. There was no other way to know with certainty that he wasn't coming back. It took a bit of sawing, and my hands, arms, and knees were coated in a wash of blood, but the sharp blade made the gruesome task easy despite having to use my off-hand.

When it was done, I sat up, tilting my head back and closing my eyes, gulping air. Bands of steel around my heart tightened, a mix of relief and an unexpected sense of loss swirling through me in a wash. Though I wasn't sure why, tears stung my eyes and an empty, gaping chasm had settled in the region of my chest.

Distantly, the sounds of screaming, loss, agony, rattled through the walls and buzzed in my bones. Vampires. Blood-bound donors. The ones who felt that he was gone.

I knew how they felt. Some part of me was gone. Not like the loss of humanity and self when I had killed someone. Not like the piece of me left behind when I acknowledged I was turning Other.

No. This was something else. Like a hole had been chewed in my heart, a black hole of need that would suck me down into some dark abyss if I let it. The temptation to use the blade on myself didn't seem so weird on the surface. After all, I would put an end to all the pain and misery and suffering I was already going through.

I would be with Max again.

That was enough of a reminder to tell me that I was still a few beers short of a six-pack, and I needed to rethink my priorities.

Swiping the tears off my cheeks with my palms, I looked around, bleary-eyed. Gideon was still slumped over by the door. The other vampire was a few feet away. The rest of him was close to Gideon, except for that one chunk in the corner.

Iana groaned, and I shook my head in an effort to rid myself of the weird urge to do something to follow Max into oblivion. She needed help. Whatever was going on in my head and whatever afterlife Max had gone to could wait a damned minute while I checked on her and Gideon.

Ignoring the desire to slide into that black void, I crawled on hands and knees—awkward, with my hurt wrist—to Iana's side. I hadn't seen it before, but Max must have used a nail to slice her jugular. Even though that cut had mostly healed already, she had lost a tremendous amount of blood. It was pooled around her head and soaked into her hair like a pale, glittering halo. The wound in her stomach was too jagged and wide for me to do anything about. She'd already pulled the dagger out on her own, but I had no idea how to stop the bleeding.

One of her hands, coated in a thick, sticky layer of her own blood, settled over mine. Though she couldn't manage to speak much louder than a whisper, and must have been in a horrific amount of pain, she managed a beatific smile for me. "I'm going to give you a parting gift. You gave me freedom. I thank you for that."

"Oh, Iana, no." My eyes blurred with fresh tears as I twined my fingers with hers and leaned over her. I did my best to be gentle as I pressed my bad hand to the seeping wound at her throat, ignoring the pain rocketing up my arm to put some pressure on it. There was so much blood already, all around her, but I had to try to keep some inside.

"Hush, I have little time. There is no saving me. Better to die free than live as a slave," she whispered, her eyes closing as her fingers tightened around mine. "Your spirit is good, if not pure. My gift is twofold. I will cleanse you of the taint you carry. I ask only that you carry what remains of me to the Sleeper."

She stared up at me expectantly, obviously waiting for me to say something. I blurted out the first thing that came to mind. "I can't drag your body back to New York with me, Iana."

That prompted a short-lived laugh out of her that quickly cut off into a little cry of pain. She had to catch her breath before she could continue.

"No, Shiarra. I just need your agreement. My . . . essence, or soul, I suppose you might call it, will join with yours. Then you must find her. She'll know what to do."

"Wait, what? You can't have my soul!"

"Foolish child," she said, voice weak, thready. "Your soul *is* you. Not a part of you. My presence will do nothing to change that. Your body is but a shell, and it can house two for a time. Yes or no? I won't have the strength to do this much longer."

Even though I wasn't certain what I was agreeing to, I didn't think Iana would do anything to hurt me. If she thought this Sleeper could help, then I would track her down and play the part of metaphysical delivery person.

"Okay. Yes." I couldn't see through my tears anymore. I didn't want her to die, not this way, but I didn't know what else to do.

She breathed a relieved sigh. Her chest stopped moving, and her pulse no longer fluttered under my fingertips. For a second I thought that was it—that she was gone—but then a subtle heat began creeping up my arm. I started to pull away, but her hand tightened on mine so hard that I couldn't have withdrawn without hurting her or myself. The heat sank into my skin, working up to my shoulder, growing hotter as it went.

"Iana! What the hell?"

She didn't answer. The heat began to tingle and burn, settling into my chest, digging into my muscles, climbing up to my jaw and even my teeth.

I couldn't move. My muscles locked up, and when I closed my eyes, all I saw was a hazy, golden glow, growing brighter by the minute.

I'm not sure how long that inner fire blazed through my veins, but when it was over, it left me shivering with sudden cold, and night-blinded.

No. Not night-blinded. My night vision was *gone*. I hadn't realized how freaking dark it was in here without any lights on.

Not only that, but a thousand myriad sounds and scents that had assaulted me before had gone silent. Temporary deafness, blindness, and loss of my sense of smell? No, I could hear Gideon moaning in pain somewhere nearby, and the smell of blood and butcher shop leftovers assailed me. Not as acutely as before. It was like my ears and nose had been covered in gauze. My mouth tasted god-awful, too, like the lingering taste of copper pennies left on my tongue. Old blood. I felt around with my tongue, and detected no hint of fangs anymore.

Holy shit. Iana hadn't specified what she meant by "cleanse" me, and I hadn't thought to ask.

She'd made me human again. She'd burned away the infection. Healed me.

All because I gave her a few minutes of freedom.

I had never let go of her hand. Though I couldn't see her body anymore in the dark, I curled both of my hands around hers, already going cold, bowed my head, and cried.

This wasn't a victory. What had I really done that merited her giving up her life in the process of saving me or making me whole again? It wasn't rational, but I wished I hadn't taken her gift, thought that maybe she'd still be here if I hadn't said yes. Maybe she could have used that strength to stay alive a little longer. Maybe I could have gotten to Arnold or Bonnie in time to save her. Maybe one of the vampires could have turned her, even if she would have hated them—and me—for it.

It wasn't fair. And all the wishes and regrets in the world wouldn't bring her back.

As I rocked back and forth, holding her limp hand to my cheek even if she wouldn't feel it anymore, something changed. It felt like some of that warmth in my chest returned, a phantom touch, filling up some of that emptiness where Max used to be.

Though she hadn't told me, whatever part of herself she'd given over to me was expressing comfort the only way it could. Passing on a taste of her motivation. She had given up everything to put an end to Max's evil. She knew and accepted that she would not survive the encounter. Her reasoning wasn't solely to avenge her imprisonment. Like me, she had wanted to put a halt to his activities to save the others, and future generations, from his cruelty.

It wasn't like having the vampires or the belt in my head. Nothing about it was like a voice or a goad. Just a feeling. A knowingness that told me I wasn't alone.

I'm not sure how long I sat there, silently grieving over someone I barely knew. Her body was gone, but she wasn't. Not really. A part of her was with me, and I would carry it with me until I found the Sleeper. Even when she was gone, I would never forget what she had done for me, and that I would never be alone.

Chapter Twenty-Six

Though I no longer felt like I was going to jump off the nearest cliff at the earliest opportunity, the reminder that I was so close to Gideon sent a pang of fear through me.

Then I remembered that I was no longer harboring a semi-vampiric nature for him to manipulate. The charm that should have kept vampires and magi from messing with my head was long gone, but I didn't think there was anything he could do to me as long as I avoided meeting his gaze. I hoped.

I didn't dare wipe away my tears considering what must be on my hands and clothes. Though I couldn't see shit, I followed the sounds of his heavy breathing and groans, fumbling on hands and knees in the dark. Every time I touched a puddle I cringed and wrinkled my nose. My senses might have been dulled, but the stink of rot wafting off the necromancer was easier to follow than the sounds of complaint he was making, even over the powerful odor of blood and other gore in the room and coating my clothes.

We both yelped when I put my hand down square on his junk. There was no mistaking it, either. I really hoped he couldn't see as well in the dark as I had been able to, because I was pretty sure my cheeks must have been glowing like beacons.

"Sorry! I didn't mean—"

"Stuff your sorry!" he croaked.

"I'm sorry! Cripes. I can't see shit in the dark."

"Fuck," he whispered. "I'm dying. First my blood, now my balls. What the fuck is next?"

I huffed, sitting back on my heels and feeling around for a more neutral body part of his to grip. "Shush. If you can complain about it that much, you're not dying. I said I was sorry. Can you cast a light or something?"

He snorted. "Not that kind of mage, remember? I see fine. I guess I can direct you."

"Doesn't hurt to ask. Come on, let's get out of here."

Gideon grumbled a bit under his breath, but he gripped my hand when he felt me fumbling for his arm, and accepted my help getting him to his feet. Once he was up, he lurched against me so hard we both almost toppled back to the ground. Good God, for such a beanstalk, the guy weighed a *ton*.

Oh, ugh. He was still bleeding from the bite, too. It was getting all over my cheek from where half my face was mashed against his chest near his armpit due to the disparity in our heights. Worse, aside from a liberal splash of Eau de Zombie and formaldehyde giving him a formidable stench this close up, I was pretty sure the guy had never heard of deodorant.

"You stink," I grumbled, half dragging, half carrying the necromancer back the way we had come. Up ahead, I thought I could see the outline of the door leading to a hallway we had passed through earlier, but it was hard to tell in the dark.

Gideon didn't seem very grateful for my help. Or my observation. "Yeah, well, you don't smell so good yourself, Copper-top. Did you have to bathe in the blood? You reek of butcher leftovers and putrid produce."

"At least I don't smell like a rotting body in a boys' locker room. Freak."

"Blood bag."

"Turd burgler."

"Twat-waffle."

"Douchenozzle."

We both fell into a fit of entirely inappropriate giggles. Once the last of his snorts tapered off, he tightened his grip around my shoulder in what might have passed for a hug.

"We're still not friends, you know," I told him, putting a cap on my own laughter with a bit of difficulty.

"No, maybe not. But you better get used to having me around. Even if I could go back to San Francisco, I doubt your partner or her boyfriend would want to come with me."

I stopped so abruptly that he lost his grip on me and fell forward with a cry. Cursing under my breath, I felt around until I found his arm and shoulder again, helping him sit up. He pushed me off him, breathing heavily and fabric rustling in a way that made me think he was checking for new bruises or something.

This wasn't in the plans. He hadn't said a damned thing about coming back to New York with us, and only then did I realize why Iana had said he was lying. It wasn't about hurting us—not in the literal sense. It was about his actions having anything to do with his ties to Fabian. He must have been planning this from the start.

Even though I knew he was serious, the words still exploded out of me. "You've got to be kidding! You're supposed to let Sara go and leave us all the fuck alone."

"Yes, and everyone is supposed to live happy ever after with a pony, their very own Prince Charming, and a winning lotto ticket under every pillow. Sorry to break it to you, snookums, but we don't always get what we want."

I punched in the general direction of his shoulder. I may not have had Other blood to fuel it, but I still landed a satisfying hit somewhere in the vicinity of his shoulder.

"Ow! The hell was that for?"

"For being a lying asshole! For scaring the piss out of me! For betraying me, betraying Sara, for thinking you have *any right*—"

"Shut the fuck up, you stupid little angst factory!"

His vehemence, more than his words, did surprise me into silence. He continued in a tirade, so obviously frustrated and hurt and frightened that any lingering desire I had to continue to berate him faded into an unexpected and unwelcome sense of pity.

"You have no fucking idea what coming out in the open has cost me. You have no clue what it means to be a necromancer, what the Other community wants to do to me. I can't go back."

"Why not? That doesn't make any sense. I thought you loved Fabian?"

"Ha! Fabian desires the power I wield, not me. Now that his sire is dead, he'll know I had a hand in it and that he hasn't got a prayer of controlling me. He'll do his best to kill me if I ever return to the West Coast. I can't stay here—it'll be the first place he'll send assassins to find me."

I considered that, wrapping my arms around myself for warmth. Even with all the layers of my clothing, I was cold. Gideon had murdered people. Innocent people. A group of White Hats had committed the grievous crime of being in the wrong place at the wrong time, getting in Gideon and Fabian's way when the dastardly duo stole into Los Angeles to wrest control of the city away from Clyde Seabreeze. The hunters paid for it with their lives.

Gideon was not a nice guy. He'd proven that time and again. So why did I feel so bad for him?

"I don't get you. You've lied your ass off, participated in a hostile invasion, killed people, nearly killed Clyde, and now you're telling me you won't let Sara go. Not to mention helping Fabian kidnap

Devon. I'm having a really hard time figuring out why the hell you think I owe you anything except helping you get out of here in one piece so Sara doesn't get hurt in the crossfire."

A twin set of glowing green orbs flared in the darkness. Must have hit a sore spot. I scooted back, putting some distance between us.

"Devon lived and escaped because of me, and thanks for asking about my motivations before leaping to conclusions. As for Sara, if I let her go, do you know what her lover and his coven will do to me? They'll make me into a fucking magical eunuch, that's what. I'll never be able to cast so much as a simple fucking corpse location spell, let alone call up a guardian to protect me. I can't have that."

"Maybe you should," I countered. My relief to hear Devon was alive and free was short-lived after hearing how selfish Gideon was being, keeping Sara trapped to save himself. "Like it or not, you're dangerous. If the magi don't stop you, then you can bet your ass Royce and the other vampires will."

Probably in a much more permanent fashion, though I didn't say that part out loud.

"Your concern is touching," he replied, laying on the sarcasm, "but I'll take the risk. Do you know why I wanted Max dead? He was *hunting* me. He thought I didn't know that he had broken the accord between our kind and enslaved or killed every other necromancer in the country. I am the last one, Copper-top. If I hadn't helped Fabian, I never would have had the chance to make it look like I was trying to get into Max's good graces. The deaths and pain I caused were regrettable, but everything I've done has been in the name of survival, to get close enough to destroy him before he could make me into another collared curiosity for his collection."

I stared at the vague shape slumped a few feet away, somewhat visible now that my eyes were adjusting to the darkness. There wasn't much I could say to that. I may not have had Iana's ability to taste his lies, but I had the feeling he meant every word this time. There wasn't even a hint of slyness or duplicity to his voice that I could detect.

This changed everything. He was dangerous and awful and I hated myself for feeling sorry for him—but I didn't want him or anyone else to die. Enough people had already suffered. There had to be some way of getting Sara out of this mess without putting Gideon at risk. He wouldn't let her go without some kind of reassurance from The Circle and the vampires in New York guaranteeing his safety, and I didn't have a clue how to manage that.

If he was telling the truth, and he really was the last of his kind, it made sense that he would go to extraordinary lengths to save himself. Sara was his life insurance policy now, so he probably wouldn't hurt her. He'd do whatever it took to protect himself. The problem was that he had proved himself willing to kill in the process.

Considering I was a murderer, too, and had even considered killing Gideon on multiple occasions, I couldn't exactly throw stones.

His voice had gone low, but the frustration in it was still evident. "You think I'm a monster, too. I bet you think I'm no better than Max, lying and using those vampires and killing like I did."

"No," I replied, "but I am thinking you and I seem to excel at making the same kinds of terrible life choices."

He scoffed, the derision evident in his voice even if I couldn't see his expression. "Please. Don't patronize me."

"What, you think you're the only special snowflake who ever made a bad decision? Get over yourself."

Another disbelieving snort. He was starting to piss me off. Mostly because I saw far too much of myself in him, right down to the bad decisions, smart-ass responses, and martyrdom complex. He wanted to do the right thing but went about it all the wrong way—just like I always managed to do.

"You know what? Fuck you and your attitude right to hell." I glared in the general direction of his shadow. "I've killed people, too. Probably for much more selfish and much stupider reasons than you. You're not the only person in all of creation who ever did something terrible they regretted later. If you want to go play the part of the victim, you go right ahead—but you damned well better get over it quick and start looking at how you can atone for the wrongs you did. Start with figuring out how to let Sara go and make nice with Arnold. Maybe then you won't have to look at The Circle and the vampires in New York like they're all out to play the next round of let's-see-who-tries-to-kill-me-this-time."

His eyes flared again, glowing like a pair of tiny green lanterns in the dark. He didn't come back at me with a snarky reply, so I hoped he was thinking about it instead of brushing off the idea out of hand. There was a conscience in there, buried somewhere under the fierce drive to survive. Without Max in the picture, there was a possibility he could afford to be a better person now. Maybe I could find some way of convincing Arnold and Royce to help him start over.

Chances were I'd have to talk them out of tearing him to bits first, but—hey—one problem at a time, right?

The gleam of his eyes gradually died away, shifting fabric rustling as he scooted closer to me again. "I'll think about it. Let's find your friends and see if you can convince them to let me out of here in one piece first, hmm?"

Cringing at the prospect, I helped him back up, resigning myself to the battle ahead. I would have to use my wits instead of a sword this time, but that didn't make it any less intimidating to consider. Facing down Angus, Arnold, and Soo-Jin's protests wasn't going to be fun. And who knew what Royce would have to say about it once he found out.

Grunting with effort as he leaned his weight on me again, I wrapped my arm around his waist and shuffled forward. I managed to huff out a few words between pants after we made it to the door.

"Hey, if I can get you out of here in one piece, promise me something?"

"Depends. What?"

"First thing you do, take a shower."

He laughed, and I was starting to think maybe we'd be all right after all

Chapter Twenty-Seven

It took awhile for us to find Arnold and Sara. Gideon had some kind of connection to her that told him roughly where she was, but the problem was that, like me, he had been confined to a few specific rooms and wasn't familiar with the layout of the building. He couldn't tell what floor she was on, only when he was getting closer to her. It was a royal pain in the ass when we both realized that he'd taken us in a circle because she was either on the floor above or below us.

Plus he wasn't a very good navigator in the dark, getting frustrated when I didn't turn *right that second* when he told me to, usually when it was too late for me to cleanly maneuver us through doors or around corners. Ass. At least there weren't too many rooms with the lights off.

Considering Kimberly and the vampires with her had gone after the captives belowground, I was willing to bet that Arnold and Sara must have gone in search of them once they lost track of us. They must have thought that was where we went, too.

By the time the thought occurred to me, I was already on the verge of exhaustion and Gideon's grip on me had slipped a couple of times due to his growing weakness. He'd tied his handkerchief around his neck, and he'd stopped bleeding awhile ago, but being upright wasn't doing him any good. He needed rest, and so did I.

The only bright spot in my day was that the way to the underground cells wasn't hard to find once we did a bit of backtracking. The trail of blood helped.

Dark red footprints led to and from the hole that had been pounded in the security door. Judging by the way the metal behind the veneer of shredded silkscreen wallpaper was twisted and bent inward, one of the vampires had decided busting through was a more expedient method of getting inside than letting Kimberly try Arnold's tactic of shorting out the locking mechanism's circuitry.

I examined the entryway with a wary eye, then glanced up at Gideon. The muscles in his jaw were tight, but I wasn't sure if it was from pain or nervousness. "You got any magic tricks up your sleeve if we run into trouble?"

"Not really, but desperation is the mother of invention."

"I thought that was necessity."

"That fits, too."

The temptation to run my hand down my face in exasperation was strong, but thanks to the tacky coat of ick on my hands, I wasn't about to touch any part of myself without washing first. It was no wonder half the Others in the country wanted him dead. He was an annoying smart-ass, just like me. Blowing out an exasperated breath, I gestured as best I could with my off hand.

"Look, there's no way I can carry you down those stairs. Stay up here and be ready to do your thing if something follows me back. And for God's sake, don't wander off."

He made a face. "Like I could, even if I wanted to. You're my Get Out of Jail Free card, Copper-top, so don't go getting yourself killed. That would be really inconvenient for me."

I rolled my eyes, tone gone dry. "How sweet, I didn't know you cared."

After setting him down by the top of the stairs, where he would have a clear view of both the hallway and the blood-spattered stairwell, I made my way down. I took it slow, fighting a growing sense of terror and claustrophobia. The last time I was down here, Max had kept me locked up in a tiny room, telling me I was nothing but a piece of property to be used or discarded on a whim. The vampires who had participated in his slave auction had been down here, every bit as ancient and formidable as Max. Some of them might have hung around, and I had no doubt I would be dead long before Gideon or anyone else could help me if they were waiting in the dark.

Still, there were other people trapped in the rooms below. Even if I didn't have the advantage of claws and fangs and supernatural strength anymore, I had to do something to help them.

Telling myself that wasn't making it any easier to take each successive step. Neither was the blood on the walls.

When I rounded the bend and could see down the corridor, I grimaced. The beautiful gold inlay in the hardwood was lost under a sea of red. There were bodies in the hall, not all of them in one piece. People-sized holes had been made in walls and doors, the smell of death and piss and desperation an overwhelming, smothering blanket. Every door was open, most of the rooms dark.

I'm not sure how long I stood there, but voices at the end of the hall, from the room with the statues, drew me forward. Beating down the growing sense of panic, I picked a long, sharp sliver of wood, which might once have been part of a door, out of the red muck, and stalked toward the rectangle of light at the far end.

Once I reached the doorway, I sagged in relief and dropped my gore-covered, makeshift weapon with a clatter. Arnold looked up from where he was wrapping a bandage around someone's leg, and Sara rose from comforting a pale, shaking woman to wrap me in a fierce hug. Returning the gesture, I peered over her shoulder, taking stock of the survivors.

There were only two vampires standing, both looking distant and pale. I wasn't totally thrilled that Fane was one of them. Kimberly was crouched by one of the statues, her head bowed and arms wrapped around her knees. Over a dozen people in shredded, red-spattered white robes huddled together, including an elf with a black eye and some kind of Other with patches of tawny fur that kept sprouting and disappearing on various parts of his body as I watched.

"Is everyone okay?"

Sara briefly tightened her grip, then pulled back and shook her head. She was a bit shaky, and there were a few tight lines of pain around her eyes, but there was a hard edge to her voice that spoke of her determination and courage.

"Max killed half our people before he rushed off. We've been patching up the survivors. Where did you go? Where's Gideon and that woman?"

"Gideon's waiting upstairs." I moved inside, addressing everybody this time. "Max is dead. We need to get out of here. Come with us, we'll help you."

Most of them looked up at me, even Kimberly. A few huddled deeper into themselves, and one or two of the people in robes started sobbing in relief. I shifted in place, uncomfortable with the wave of thanks and grateful hugs and touches some of them gave me as they worked up the courage to approach.

One of them jabbered something in a language I didn't recognize. German, maybe? She sounded scared and a little angry, but I wasn't sure how to respond. Neither was anyone else, judging by the blank looks all around. She complied when the others gestured for her to follow us out, even though she was obviously wary and kept as much distance between herself and the vampires as possible.

I led the way back up, Fane making his way to the front of the crowd to walk beside me. His sharp features had gone stony and drawn, and he didn't say anything, though he radiated tension. Whether from the battle or fear or hunger or something else, I couldn't tell.

When we rounded the stairs, Gideon braced himself against the wall and struggled to his feet, relief etched across his face. The vampire stilled beside me, then was nothing but a blur.

Half a second later, he was holding the necromancer against the wall by the throat and the wrist of his tattooed hand.

"Fane, don't!"

The vampire's fangs were bared, eyes gleaming crimson as he hissed up at the squirming mage, whose face was going purple from lack of air. "You have no idea what this is. It can't be suffered to live."

I pounded up the stairs after him, tackling him around the waist before he could choke the life out of Gideon. The three of us fell with a heavy thump outside the hole in the wall. Something sharp sliced across my upper arm as we fell, and I was pretty sure the other two hadn't made it through unscathed, but it had the desired effect of startling Fane into letting the necromancer go.

Gideon clawed at the runner, trying to drag himself out from under us, but all he managed to do was pull the strip of carpet closer. The vampire snarled and struggled to grab at the necromancer again, but I straddled his back, putting all my weight into him, and whacked him as hard as I could on the back of the head.

"Leave him alone! He's not a danger to you!"

"Like hell," Gideon panted, then yelped as the vampire's hand came down on his shoulder. The yelp quickly turned into an agonized shriek as Fane's fingers bit into his skin, sinking deep into the muscle.

Somewhere on the stairwell, Sara gave an answering cry of pain.

I didn't have the strength to pull Fane back, and he was still hell-bent on the kill. I did the only thing I could think of.

"For fuck's sake, somebody help us! Get him off!"

The Other with the fur was the only one who bothered to help. He rushed forward, baring a mouthful of fangs at Fane as the vampire fought to keep his grip on the necromancer. Fingers tipped with wickedly curved black talons closed around Fane's wrist, dislodging his grip with a sickening sucking sound from Gideon's shoulder.

I traded places with the Were or whatever he was. The guy did a much better job than I had at keeping Fane pinned. The vampire stared at Gideon's limp frame with raw lust in his eyes, but stopped fighting to reach for him when he realized he was at a disadvantage.

Shuffling forward on hands and knees, I gingerly touched Gideon's back, relieved when he cursed and flailed. He couldn't be too badly hurt if he was still fighting. "Stop that, I'm checking the wound."

"Son of a motherfucking *whoremaster,* that hurts," Gideon replied, and with feeling.

Yeah. He would be just fine.

Arnold shouted my name. I gritted my teeth and gave Gideon a light smack on the small of his back, far from the seeping divots in his shoulder. He flinched anyway. "Don't move. I'll see what Arnold needs. Maybe he can do something about that."

He cursed at me again, and I managed a weak grin, relieved. Except when I turned around, the other vampire had Sara in his arms, Arnold holding her hand. She had gone paler than before, pain twisting her features into an unrecognizable mask. With a gasp, I dashed to her side, putting a hand to her cheek.

Her skin was cold, and there was a faint, reddish light glowing on her arms in the shape of the runes that Gideon had supposedly removed. Even as I watched, they faded away, leaving her arms unblemished. I whirled, only to see he was sitting up, rubbing his bad shoulder with an apologetic expression.

"Sorry. I tried not to," he said.

Arnold made an inarticulate sound in his throat, his free hand lifting like he was thinking about hurling some kind of magic—but held back only by the thought of what it might do to Sara. His fist clenched, tightening until his knuckles cracked. Gideon had the grace to redden.

"I'm sorry, I can't undo it. The siphon or the bond. The minute I do, I'm a dead man. Don't deny it. I see it in your eyes."

Arnold gave him a grim, humorless smile, all teeth. "You're already dead. The minute I figure out how to fix this, I'll hunt you down and end you."

I stepped between them, hands up, though I was suppressing the umpteenth urge to throttle Gideon myself. "Look, we need to keep him safe for now, and he needs to come with us back to New York. We'll figure out a way to undo it and keep *everyone* alive and well in the process, got it?"

Gideon gave me a tentative nod, but Arnold didn't answer. I turned my attention to the mage, giving him a significant look, one eyebrow arching. His glare shifted from Gideon to me, lights flickering in his green eyes like lightning flashes in a thundercloud.

It was the first time I ever felt anything close to genuine fear of Arnold.

His stare stayed on me for a long, uncomfortable moment. Then he turned away without answering to focus on Sara, whispering something to her too softly for me to hear.

It wasn't a promise not to hurt Gideon once the spell binding Sara to him was broken, but for now it would have to do.

Chapter Twenty-Eight

Collecting the remaining survivors and finding Soo-Jin, Angus, and the others didn't take long. The vampire who had been holding Sara handed her off to Arnold before rushing off at inhuman speed to track the rest of our party down and bring them to us. Fane, after promising not to attack first and ask questions later, was released. He made a point of sucking the blood off his fingertips, staring at the necromancer in a meaningful way as he did it. The perv.

Arnold and Sara weren't speaking to me, even though she had for the most part recovered. Gideon had shuffled off as far from everyone else as he could get while remaining in the same room.

It was uncomfortable as hell, made worse when Angus and Soo-Jin returned with the others and gave me the kind of soul-chilling, disapproving looks I thought no one but my mother could pull off. Maybe the case of the shivers they gave me was because the capital "L" Looks I was getting were coming from an angry, ancient vampire and a nine-tailed fox-demon. They didn't have to say a thing to make me feel like a heel. Considering I already did, all they accomplished with their unspoken condemnation was making my embarrassment deepen once I got over the urge to pee myself.

Rather than look either of the two in the eyes, I took stock of who was with them, searching for familiar faces. Max had moved his harem of unwilling donors to the same cages Sara and Iana had been in, which meant that the women I had shared a prison with should have been among the humans being ushered along by the surviving vampires. All of the mortals were terrified, eyes wide, limbs trembling, clinging to each other for comfort. One of them looked relieved when she spotted me, but the rest were far too scared of Soo-Jin and the vampires still sporting fangs and glowing eyes to relax.

There were a couple of familiar faces, but not enough. Not nearly enough.

We hadn't lost as many of our number who had been with Angus, but I had to fight not to shed more tears when I saw how few of the people I knew from my imprisonment returned with them. Vivian and Na'man were not among them.

There might have been other places where they were hidden, someplace I hadn't seen, but I knew Max too well to be hopeful we'd find any other survivors.

Angus led us out, some of the vampires carrying the weakest and injured back to the cars, and the rest making sure the scared senseless ones didn't run off. I wasn't sure how much time had passed, but the shielding the magi had summoned was gone when we made it outside.

Moments after we hit the snow-covered lawn, the guy who kept sprouting bits of hair had shapeshifted into some kind of big cat and darted away from the rest of the group. Not to leave us, but to get some distance. I guessed it might be because the overwhelming scent of blood and fear from the clump of now screaming, panicking humans was tweaking his instincts to hunt and kill. Without my night vision, I couldn't tell if it was a puma or jaguar or what, but he was looking to me, Angus, and Soo-Jin for direction.

It took more time than I wanted to think about to calm people down. The Were had to lie down in the snow and let one of the vampires pat his head—though the cat lifted his lip to show just a bit of fang to express his disdain—for them to believe he wasn't about to maul anybody.

The robe-clad former slaves had no fur of their own, let alone coats or shoes to protect them from the cold. They huddled together, some still crying, but none voicing a word of complaint.

Freedom probably tasted as sweet to them as it had to me when I had fled this madhouse. A bit of momentary physical discomfort paled in comparison to the prospect of spending the rest of their lives in servitude. Well, unless they thought we were taking them from one bad situation to a worse one. If that was the case then the lack of bitching on their end could be due to being afraid of being eaten.

Then Kimberly pulled a surprise out of her hat I wasn't expecting. Though shaky and pale, she still had some spark left. With a gesture, and a look of fierce concentration focused on each inadequately dressed human in turn, she did something that brought looks of wonder to their faces and stopped their shivering.

I wasn't sure what she had done until she turned to the elf. He frowned and shook his head, his dark hair sliding like silk around his face and brushing his shoulders. His voice was just as buttery smooth and enchanting as Royce's, and I'll admit I might have sidled a few steps closer just to hear him better. "I have no need of your illusions, mage."

Illusion. She made those people feel warm. They'd still get frostbite if they were out here too long, but it was one hell of a kindness to take the time and effort to block out the bite of cold on their feet and icy wind chilling their skin. Probably went a long way toward making them realize we weren't here to deliver them to a worse fate than they'd already suffered. It appeared to be more effective proof that nobody here intended to take a chomp out of them, too.

Despite my initial misgivings about Kimberly, I was coming to like the girl.

The magi who had been maintaining the shield were waiting for us by the wall, shivering and clustered together for warmth. Even though they had smudges under their eyes and some were exhausted enough to lean against each other for support, they all appeared to be unharmed and relieved to see us. Most of them viewed Gideon with naked curiosity and maybe a bit of fear once they noticed him limping along at my side.

Soo-Jin shifted back into her human form, giving no sign of discomfort from cold or the stares she was getting, first for the change, then for being buck naked in the snow. There was an intricate tattoo on her back of what she looked like as her other self, similar to one of the paintings I had seen in her house. She dug an extra set of clothes out of a duffel bag in the backseat, dressed like she had all the time in the world, then donned a pair of sparkly pink Adidas sneakers and got behind the wheel.

Mental note: Figure out how to introduce this woman to a new color scheme.

Fitting everyone into the cars was a challenge, but we managed, albeit with a few people sitting on laps or riding in the beds of the SUVs. Nobody wanted to be anywhere near Gideon, so he ended up riding with me, Angus, and Soo-Jin, with the big cat sprawled in the flatbed of the pickup. Now that the Were was close enough, I could see by the glow of the headlights from one of the other cars that his cat-form was a cougar, all tawny fur and sleek lines. He stayed low in the bed of the truck so no random passerby might see him, but I doubted it would be a comfortable ride.

My first encounter with an honest-to-God Were-cat, and I was too tired and hurting too much to give a shit.

Angus said nothing during the interminable ride, but the way he watched the necromancer made it clear that if he so much as twitched in a way the Highlander didn't like, he would suffer for it. Gideon had deep circles under his eyes and kept uncharacteristically quiet, but he stayed awake and behaved himself the whole way.

We went back to Soo-Jin's place. Our little caravan made it back with plenty of time to spare before sunrise, but exhaustion drove everyone—vampires included—to seek quick showers and a place to collapse.

After everyone was settled in and showered, some of the vampires went around to each of the rescued humans, using black enchants to put them to sleep. Considering how scared and lost most of them looked, for once I didn't think that was such a bad idea. Judging by all the hollow eyes and shaking limbs, they might never have gotten a good night's rest otherwise. That, or they might have made attempts to run off on their own, much like I had after snapping out of the blood-fueled haze I had been in after being bound to Max and Royce. The enchants would keep them in a dreamless state, free of nightmares, if only for tonight.

I wished I could have said the same for myself.

None of the vampires or magi would abide having Gideon stay near them, and Soo-Jin was still worried Fane would try to make a move even though Iana had cured me. After getting everyone else settled, she led me and Gideon into her bedroom—but she drew the line at letting the big cat padding after us inside. He made a grumbling, growling-type sound of complaint before curling up in the hallway right outside the door. That settled, she made me shower first, then Gideon, lending us both some bathrobes before she took her own turn.

As soon as she stepped out, a big towel wrapped around her slim frame and a smaller one scrubbing the remaining moisture from her hair, she paused in the doorway and her nose wrinkled in disgust.

She made Gideon take a second shower before she'd let him sleep in her room with us. On his way in, I got a good gander at the bottom of his toned, bare ass hanging out of the too-short, fuzzy pink bathrobe Soo-Jin had given him.

Once he came back out, she also made him spritz himself with half a bottle of jasmine-scented perfume. Then she lit some candles and incense. The mixture of cloying scents made it hard to breathe, but it was better than the rot-and-chemical odors still wafting from the necromancer. How he lived with that constant stench was beyond me.

He must have been exhausted, because he didn't have any snide comments for either of us and seemed perfectly content to curl up on the carpeted floor with nothing but the robe and a pillow.

His green eyes, dull and heavy-lidded, tracked me around the room as I tugged one of the blankets out of the closet for him. He mumbled thanks as I draped it over him, but he didn't close his eyes until I was in bed and under the covers. Having him staring at me like that was worrisome. He'd proven one too many times how clever and vicious he was capable of being, so I had no interest in letting him trick or use me again. Whatever was on his mind, it meant I would have to be on my toes until he was out of my life.

Once it was clear he was passed out, Soo-Jin pulled out a pair of fuzzy handcuffs from a drawer beside her bed and cuffed one of his hands to the foot of a large teak armoire. Probably a good idea since there was no telling what he might do if he woke up during the day and decided that having the vampires running around uncontrolled wasn't good for his health. That, or if he got it into his head to take off and maybe bring Sara along for the ride.

No doubt, even if he was (sort of) on our side now, he was going to prove to be a tremendous amount of trouble.

Soo-Jin turned off the lights and crawled into bed next to me, breathing out an exhausted sigh as she sprawled on her stomach. By dim candlelight, I could see she was staring at me with her eyes narrowed to slits. First Gideon, then her. They were both getting on my nerves and making it difficult to relax.

"Something on your mind?" I asked, keeping my voice soft.

A slow, lazy smile curved her lips. She kept her voice down, too, neither of us wanting to wake Gideon. "You didn't run from me when you saw me feed. You took off on your own to go after Max. You stand up for the necromancer despite who he is and what he's done. The more I see of you, the more I understand why Rhathos and so many others like him are attracted to you."

With a huff, I looked away, not wanting to hear it. It was a sentiment I had heard from Others before, if not in the same words.

"I admire your bravery. Take care who you waste it on and how you exercise it, or you may not survive our world." She paused, then rolled to put her back to me. Something about her tone changed. I wasn't sure if it was warning or sorrow in her voice. "Your choices have led you to a very hard road. You'll be tempted upon your return to take a stand against him in a matter that will seem cruel and heartless to you. Don't. For your sake, and that of everyone involved, accept that there is nothing you can do."

She didn't say anything else, and I didn't ask what she meant.

If I had been any less wiped out and she had been any less cagey, I might have asked for further details. I had the feeling she didn't want to be the one to tell me what was coming. Prying it out of her would be too much damned work. With all the other crap already heaped on my plate, I had zero fucks left to give. Whatever the problem was, I would deal with it when it came.

Chapter Twenty-Nine

Getting back to New York was a freaking *nightmare*. First we had to get out of Max's territory. Due to complications and some kind of bullshit Other protocol that Angus and Soo-Jin didn't care to explain but insisted we needed to follow, Royce had no way of sending us any more resources. All they would tell me is that they didn't want to leave Athena any more clues about his involvement.

That meant we had to drive south over three hundred miles through Illinois and Indiana to cross the invisible bully's line in the sandbox. We couldn't just drive the half an hour or whatever to O'Hare International. Even if whatever Other-related rules that forbade him from helping us weren't deterring Angus and Soo-Jin from taking the easy way out, Royce had no way of providing enough fake IDs or buying off security rapidly enough to get us out of town as fast as we needed.

For some reason, he also couldn't send a plane

into Max's territory without it being tracked back to him. Some combination of Max's payoffs to the local cops plus the Other-related networks in the area made it too much of a risk for him to leave a tangible trail of his involvement. That explained why I didn't know any of the vampires he sent along save for Angus. They weren't part of Royce's bloodline, so any part of themselves they left behind couldn't be traced to him by supernatural means.

Knowing that didn't make the inconvenience of our situation any easier to swallow. Never mind that the guy was dead, Max *still* managed to be a tremendous pain in my ass. Royce insisted that we had to find a private airport in northern Kentucky with loose enough security to bypass pesky things like TSA searches and passenger manifests required by Homeland Security.

Soo-Jin, who had been thoughtful enough to get up early and buy a bunch of sweats for those of us whose clothes had been mangled beyond repair or had none to speak of, came with us as far as the airport. She wished us all luck, and told me to call her now and then.

She also told me to pay her a visit if I was ever back in the neighborhood. I tried not to let too much hysterical laughter slip at the thought, but it was a losing battle. Thank goodness she thought my reaction was funny instead of taking offense.

There was one other thing. Right before she left, she pulled me aside, keeping her voice low and furtive like she didn't want anyone to overhear.

"That boy-child you were so concerned about. The one at the store? He's alive, if a bit more pale than you might remember. He did not recognize me, and had some bandages on one arm. When I asked, he thought he might have slipped on a patch of ice and knocked himself cold when checking on a customer in the parking lot."

So, Max hadn't killed Dustin, just taken a bit of blood and removed his memories of our presence with a black enchant. I was ashamed to admit it, but in all the uproar, I had forgotten about the kid at the convenience store. She did not look too pleased to admit that she had checked on him for me, but the gruff face she put on to tell me the news didn't hide that she was relieved, too.

"Thank you, Soo-Jin."

She gave me a terse nod, turning away. I put a hand on her arm to keep her from rushing off.

"Really," I said, repeating myself with a bit more force. "*Thank you.* Like I told you before—you're kinder than you know."

Her eyes flashed orange as she gave me a fierce, fang-filled grin. "You're welcome. But if you tell anyone I've gone soft, I'll eat that boy's heart."

That startled a nervous laugh out of me. Mostly since I wasn't totally sure she was kidding. Her smile widened, and she shifted to take one of my hands in both of hers, bowing deep over it as she shook it.

"Take care, Shiarra Waynest. I'll remember the gift you've given me."

And with that, she pulled away, stalking off at a

rapid pace—too quickly for me to call out for her to stop and explain what she meant by that.

I put her weird behavior behind me and concentrated on more immediate problems. A slew of gray hairs were my reward for figuring out how to get a gaggle of hungry vampires, half a dozen bitchy magi, one grumpy necromancer, a stuck-up elf, a Were-cat with abandonment issues, and a pile of humans who thought they were being taken for the ride as in-flight snacks, to survive a three hundred-plus-mile road trip and then fit them all in one plane without incident.

The plane was cushy but far too cramped with so many people in it. I counted it a small miracle that the only problems along the way were a couple of fear-fueled fits from the humans, a brief shouting match between the elf and one of the vampires who was being a tad too attentive to him (read: his jugular), and Luke the Were-puma panic-shifting during takeoff. Oh, and learning the hard way that feeding a necromancer drive-thru fast food does nothing to improve his smell in close, inadequately ventilated quarters.

Seeing as no human *or* immortal bodily fluids stained the furniture or carpeting along the way, I figured that was our best-case scenario, and called it good.

A trio of limousines picked us up on the tarmac of a private airport on Long Island. Smaller and not nearly as crowded or as big of a pain in the ass to navigate as JFK or LaGuardia, I might have appreciated it more if I didn't have a bunch of freaked out people begging me for info about where we were going and what was going to happen to them. Angus hadn't made any mention of Royce's plans, and the vampire had left me to ride with the other humans in the second limo.

It didn't take us long to get where we were going. Once off the expressway, we followed a winding set of streets I had never traveled before. And no wonder. This looked like the kind of neighborhood Sara's parents had considered their natural habitat when they weren't strutting around Wall Street. The country clubs, sprawling properties, and large colonial-style homes peeking between the carefully placed lines of trees, walls, and security gates clued me in that we were somewhere near the North Shore.

Old money oozed from the very foundations of these properties. Though I had been suitably impressed by Royce's offices, clubs, and the apartment building within spitting distance of Central Park, my move-along-before-you-get-the-veneer-dirty sense was tingling. Some of the buildings shared a distinct resemblance to, if not the acreage of, Max's property back in Illinois. When we pulled into the driveway for our destination, I fought down an irrational sense of panic. It didn't look *that* much like my former prison.

The place was much less austere than Max's home. Strategically placed lampposts bordering the driveway drove back the dark and illuminated gorgeous landscaping. The ornamental spruce and holly trees gave the place a touch of warm green even though the maple, apple, and dogwood trees on some of the neighboring properties were nothing but bare, skeletal branches clawing at the star studded sky. The grand, sweeping manor was nowhere near comparable in size to the prison I had left behind. This place was maybe ten to twelve bedrooms, judging from the outside.

By the time the limos reached the island walkway at the top of the circular drive, Royce, Mouse, Clarisse, and Wesley were waiting under the columned gable sheltering the front porch.

I wasn't sure who said it, but someone whispered a few words that did a great job at spreading panic all over again. "We're gonna die."

"No, you're not," I said, harsh enough that the frantic whispers quieted. "Relax, you're in safe hands now. Royce will make sure you all get home in one piece."

They didn't argue, but I could see the disbelief written across a few faces. Shaking my head, I didn't wait for the driver to come around, scooting over to open the door myself and step out. I closed my eyes and took a deep breath of air thick with wood smoke and just a touch of saltwater drifting in from the Long Island Sound. Tension I hadn't noticed until it was gone dissipated with the familiar scents of home.

I didn't have to see to know Royce was approaching. The feel of him, his desire and concern, washed over me in the same way as Max's need to control me. It felt foreign, and maybe a little disconcerting, to have someone else's tender emotions in my headspace, but not entirely unwelcome.

When I opened my eyes again, he was inches away, studying me—not reaching out just yet. To see him there, that black, all-encompassing hunger burning in his eyes, sent a roil of terror so sharply through my midsection that I couldn't breathe around it. Even when his features softened with concern, I was so buried under a wave of panic that when he did touch me, reaching up to brush chill fingertips over my cheek, I almost passed out.

"Oh, my little hunter," he breathed, "I am so sorry."

"Little late for that, don't you think?"

My voice might have come out as an undignified squeak, but he got the hint. I felt the remorse he radiated far more clearly than I could see it reflected in the tightening around his eyes or the frown etching little lines around his mouth. He held out his arms in invitation, and this time I didn't hesitate. It took more effort than I wanted to think about to keep from bursting into tears as I leaned into his embrace. Closing my eyes tight, I buried my fingers in the silky fabric of his shirt and released a shuddering breath.

For the first time in a long time, I felt safe.

He tilted his head to rest his cheek against my temple, nose buried in my hair, breathing in the scent of me. Then withdrew a fraction. It was either the smell of Gideon or from being stuck in the car and then the plane for hours that did it, I was sure.

Embarrassed, I pulled away, clearing my throat and waving my hand at the people coming out of the limo behind me and huddling in a nervous clump together. "They're going to need help getting home."

With a little growl, he tugged me back into him, wrapping his arms around me as he examined the others from over my shoulder. I relaxed into him, trying not to be so fidgety and self-conscious.

"Yes, so Angus told me. I'll take care of it. We have much to discuss—Athena will be coming to meet you once she settles Max's affairs in Chicago. Somehow she found out about your involvement, and she's very curious about the human who felled her eldest progeny. Which reminds me, where is the necromancer?"

"He's over here."

Gideon was eyeing Royce with distrust, standing on his own while the magi were a couple yards away in a pointedly separate group over by the last limo. Even in ill-fitting sweats and cheap sneakers, and his neck covered in a red-spotted bandage, he managed to radiate a dangerous combination of power and confidence: It was in the set of his shoulders, the way he held himself, the intensity of his gaze.

I tilted my head up to see what Royce thought of him, but he'd schooled his features into a neutral expression. The only hint I had to his displeasure was the glimmer of red building in his eyes.

"Gideon. Breaker of the Accord." The necromancer's expression shifted to uneasiness, and he took a half step back as Royce continued. "Not to worry.

I know your motivations for turning on Euphron and what you have done to assist Shiarra to return to me. You are welcome here. However," he continued, his voice taking on a dangerous edge that had me squirming in remembered fear, "if I find you making any attempt at the same actions in my home, against my people, I will have the magi bind you."

"I'll do it myself, if you'll let me," Arnold said.

He and Sara came over to us, his arm around her waist and hers over his shoulder. Her color was better, but she was still leaning on him in a way that told me she wasn't at her best. She gave me a quick, tight smile. Knowing she wasn't still pissed at me filled me with relief and made it easier to relax.

Gideon bowed his head, extending his tattooed hand palm up in a strangely subservient gesture. "Master of New York, I wouldn't presume to offer you or yours any harm. If you will accept my fealty, I will serve you in the same capacity as I did the Master of San Francisco."

Arnold snorted in disbelief. Royce smiled, a predatory grin that showed off his fangs and made Gideon flinch.

"Really, now. And what are you expecting in return?"

Gideon lowered his head just a bit more. "Protection. I know my actions went against the Accord, but it was to save my own life, and I'd do it again in a hot minute. If you can guarantee me safety, I'll do whatever you ask."

"Does that include submitting to a blood bond and releasing Ms. Halloway as your familiar?"

Royce's grip tightened on me as I jerked in his arms, surprised. He kept his gaze locked on Gideon, who grimaced but nodded. "As you wish. Will your blood break the bond to Fabian?"

"Perhaps. How many times have you tasted his blood?"

"Once."

"Then yes," Royce replied. "We'll do a permanent bond. I'll discuss this with you in greater detail once I have the others settled." He turned his attention to Arnold, extending a hand. The mage hesitated but accepted the handshake. "Mr. Moore. My thanks for your assistance. My driver will return you and the other members of your coven to your homes. I'll be in touch about resolving Ms. Halloway's . . . condition tomorrow evening."

Arnold's eyes narrowed. "My pleasure. I'll be waiting for your call."

Sara huffed, tightening her grip on Arnold. "*We'll* be waiting. I'm not staying here."

"As you wish," Royce said, giving Gideon a warning look when it appeared the necromancer was about to object. Gideon's mouth snapped shut and he looked away, unhappy but not about to argue.

Arnold and Sara both waved good-bye to me as they returned to the limo, gesturing the other magi inside. Much as I had hoped they would have stayed here with us for the night, I couldn't blame them for wanting to get the hell away from Royce. Magi and vampires didn't get along at the best of times, and Arnold and Sara deserved some time to reconnect and be alone together.

Royce gestured for the vampires to round everyone up and take them inside. I watched him from under my lashes as he led the way, me at his side, into his home.

Only once we were inside did I start looking around. This place was far more in keeping with the kind of old money I had assumed Royce and the other vampires who answered to him would have to throw around. It didn't feel the same as the apartment building: a little too posh, a little too unlived in, a few too many gilded edges. On the inside, it was more like Fabian's home than I wanted to consider. Like it was more for show, a place to flaunt his wealth and impress other people with wads of cash to blow on homes too big for any one family to need.

Royce must have sensed my discomfort. He leaned in to whisper to me, his lips brushing over my ear in a way that sent a delicious shiver down my spine. "I hate this place, but it's the biggest residential property I have within commuting distance to the city that hasn't been burned to the foundations. I promise you'll find our bed more than adequate and far more comfortable. Think you can tolerate it until I purchase and renovate a new apartment building in Manhattan?"

Our bed. He was talking like he expected me to

live here. Or wherever. With him. The thought simultaneously filled me with dread and desire.

Well. Maybe more desire than anything else when he gave me that look. Mouth dry, I nodded, hoping whatever business he needed to wrap up before he could show me that bed wouldn't take long.

Chapter Thirty

We went to a large room with a few couches and chairs, but not nearly enough seats for everyone. Royce set me in one of the chairs to one side, away from the bulk of the crowd but close enough that he could keep an eye on me. At one point, Analie rushed in, ignoring Royce's look of warning. She shoved a small plate of sugar cookies into my hand, bouncing up and down anxiously on her heels.

"Did you see Gavin? What about Jo-Jo? Did they like the cookies?"

The teenaged werewolf didn't look like much with her mousy brown hair and gawky frame still not quite grown into itself, but the feral glow to her eyes and the strength of her hand on my arm were all the reminder I needed of her Other side. Gritting my teeth so as not to startle her or scare her off with a cry of pain, I set the plate aside and tugged her fingers until she got the hint and loosened her grip.

Once the pressure let up, it was a lot easier to give her a warm, comforting smile.

"They both liked the cookies. Gavin sends his love and Jo-Jo misses you every day." I paused, giving her a moment to collect herself as tears built in her eyes. Poor kid. So far from her friends and family, a semi-willing "guest" of the vampires, she must have been frantic for news of her pack. Even knowing she could turn into a monstrously huge werewolf—one of the Goliath pack, who more than lived up to their name—I couldn't resist giving her the hug she so obviously needed. She managed to keep herself together and not crush me, though, pressed so close, I could feel her suppressed sobs.

She pulled back soon enough, swiping the building moisture from her eyes with the back of a hand. Sniffling, she gave me a watery smile. "Thank you. Thank you so much. They mean the world to me."

I nodded, then grimaced. "Analie, I'm so sorry—they both wrote you letters, but after what happened back there—"

Her face fell, the tragedy written there breaking my heart. I grabbed her hand to give it a squeeze, not surprised to feel a bit of fur under my fingers as the stress was getting the better of her. Royce was making his way over, his intent to boot Analie out written all over his face. I tugged her arm to get her going, speaking in a rush.

"Don't worry, I'll talk to Royce. We'll figure out a way for you to get in touch with them. Go on, we'll powwow on it tomorrow."

Her smile wasn't quite so forced this time. With a determined nod, she bolted, zigzagging through the crowd and disappearing through the door.

By the time all of the humans, vampires, and miscellaneous Others squeezed in, the place was packed. Luke kept twitching and moving around. Patches of fur intermittently popped up on his arms and neck as he searched for space to pace, not finding it. Once Royce reached my side, Analie was long gone, and he did not look amused.

"You should let Clarisse show you upstairs," Royce told me, waving her over from across the room.

I shook my head, scowling at him. "What? After all I've been through with these people, you really want me to leave?"

"I do. I know you well enough to know you will object to what needs to be done."

"What's that supposed to mean?"

Clarisse startled the hell out of me when she snuck up behind me much sooner than expected considering the crowd to hook her arm in mine before I could pull away. Her long, curly black hair was tied out of her pale, freckled face with ribbons that matched her bright green eyes. She grinned up at me, her Shirley Temple dimples doing an excellent job of making her fangs look more like part of a cheap Halloween costume than a genuine threat.

"It means the lad's done something naughty and hasn't figured out a good way of keeping it from ye or explaining it in a way you'll accept yet. Aye?"

Royce's response was as sour as hers was cheery. "Aye. Yes. Shiarra, I'm sorry. This won't be comfortable for you to witness. You should wait in the other room."

He didn't word it as a request. This was it. Whatever he was about to do, this was the thing Soo-Jin had warned me about. I knew it in my gut. I widened my stance, digging my heels in when Clarisse pulled my arm.

"I'll stay here, thanks."

His eyes narrowed, but he nodded to Clarisse, who stopped tugging at me. There was a chill edge to his voice that had never been there before, save for when he threatened me into signing the contract that made me his donor.

"If you insist. Keep any objections to yourself. You may not like it, but what I'm about to do is necessary. If you question me or interfere in any way, Clarisse will remove you."

A bit stung by that, I nodded, vowing to keep my mouth shut. Whatever happened, no matter what he did, I would not suffer the indignity of being railroaded out. He pointed me to a plush, overstuffed chair as he moved into position to address the room.

He cut quite a figure there, flanked by the columns at either side of the wide mouth of a granite fireplace. His tailored button-down shirt outlined the sculpted planes of his chest, and I had to suppress a slew of thoughts about biting those buttons off to get at what was hidden under the silky material.

The bastard had just issued an ultimatum that should have had me wanting to throttle him, not rip his clothes off. Though the ghost of a smile that touched his lips, and my sense of his eyes on me before he cleared his throat for the attention of the others, hinted that he knew exactly where my thoughts had wandered. Maybe—just maybe—he'd even had a hand in directing them there.

I would have a little chat with him about that once we were alone.

Gideon sidled close to where Royce had me sit, folding his arms and surveying the room like he owned it. Luke the Were-cat settled on the other side of me, taking a similar stance. If I hadn't known any better, I might have thought they considered themselves my bodyguards. Clarisse sat on the arm of the chair, holding my hand as she watched Royce.

I spared a glance to the group of people doing their best to fade into the background, failing miserably since many of the vampires were drawn to their fear. Most of the humans looked like they were on the verge of losing their lunches or their sanity. Maybe both. One of them was shaking so badly that a nearby vampire getting jostled grabbed her upper arms to hold her still. She promptly fainted, leaving the vampire holding her limp frame looking stricken and confused, and the closest people shuffling as far away as they could.

Royce cleared his throat a second time, and that was enough to send a hush through the room, everyone giving him their attention.

"My thanks to those of you who assisted in returning my property to me."

Clarisse's hand tightened on mine when I flinched.

The reminder of what Max had made me into—what the rest of vampire society viewed me as—coming from Royce's lips hurt in a way I hadn't anticipated.

His gaze flicked over the unfamiliar faces, studying them briefly before he picked out the elf and Were-puma among them. "I assume you two have clans to be returned to, yes?"

"Yes," the elf said at the same time Luke said, "No, I don't have a pride."

Royce gestured to Wesley. "See to these two, would you?"

He waited until Wesley led the pair out of the room. Once they were gone, leaving only the vampires, humans, and Gideon behind, Royce bowed his head, briefly rubbing the bridge of his nose. He was clearly uncomfortable, but resigned himself to whatever it was he was about to do. His expression was hard, though tinged with regret when he turned his attention to the humans huddled across the room.

"Have any of you been bitten? Scarred? Those of you who bear any physical marks from your time in captivity, come to me."

Clarisse's hand on my shoulder was all that kept me from giving in to the urge to approach and join the group of people shuffling closer to him, drawn like moths to a flame. There were only three who stayed where they were, as well as the girl who had passed out and was still cradled in the vampire's arms. The trio clung to each other, staring in mute horror as Royce spread his arms and nodded to the remaining vampires.

Several of them stepped forward to take those people into their arms, looking deep into their eyes and whispering instructions. I was close enough to overhear a few of them. They were enchanting them into forgetting Max, forgetting their confinement, and urging them to sign contracts and move in with one of these other vampires as soon as possible. If questioned about the source of their scars, they were to say it was from their new vampire masters, received after the contract was signed.

The other three girls were still clinging to each other for safety, though they made no effort to run. Outnumbered and adrift in a room full of Others, the futility of their situation was obvious. One, I noticed, was the girl who had spoken in the language I couldn't place. She may not have understood what anyone was saying, but she could see enough to understand and be afraid.

Sick to my stomach by the implications, I looked back to Royce, who was using his considerable mindfuck powers to call over the remaining three women. They approached together, still afraid, but unable to refuse seeing as they were staring so intently into his eyes.

Once they were close enough, he settled his hands on the cheeks of one, tilting her head up so she couldn't avoid his gaze. Her mouth went slack, eyes glazing over.

"Your name?"

"Brittany. Brittany Reynolds," she whispered.

"And where are you from? Did anyone see you get taken by Max's men?"

"From Iowa. Nobody saw. It was dark."

He asked a few similar, probing questions about who she was and where she was from. Her family. Her friends. How she spent her free time. Things that might have given him hints as to how Max or his cronies had chosen her. Things he could use to fabricate a reason for her disappearance that her friends and family and coworkers would accept— something easier to swallow than "temporary un-availability due to enslavement by vampires."

It was both fascinating and chilling to watch him work. Once he had all the info he needed, including a home address for her parents where she could be safely dropped off, the real work started. His gaze narrowed, and he leaned forward, his fingers tightening just a bit to make little indentations on her temples as his tones shifted from questioning to commanding.

"When I tell you to sleep, you will close your eyes and rest. You will not wake until ordered, and when you do, you won't remember anything about who took you, where you were, or what happened to you. You never saw this place or any of these people. You will stay away from vampires and anyone who works for them from now on. Sleep, Brittany. Forget us. Forget Max. Forget me."

Her eyes drifted shut and she sagged against him. He held her to him, smoothing her hair back from her face. There might have been some remorse there, but aside from a slight twist to his lips I couldn't tell if it bothered him at all that the black enchant he had cast over this woman guaranteed pieces of her mind would be altered forever. He slid his arms under her legs and lifted her up so he could lay her out on a nearby couch.

He then looked to me, taking in my reaction much as he had studied her. I'm not sure what was reflected on my face. Disgust, maybe? Amazement, definitely. And a return of that bone-deep fear I had once held for him, a fear I had conveniently forgotten after we had spent an amazing night together in bed.

It wasn't rational, but for a second—just a second—I had to wonder if the memory of that night and the desire I had felt for him was something he had planted in me, too.

He turned back to the other two girls, repeating the process.

When he discovered one of them did not speak English, he called over Clarisse.

"See if you can figure out where she's from and who we have in town who speaks her language. No outside interpreters. If you can't manage, let me know and I'll see what I can do. Oh, and see to those two. Get Mouse to give you some petty cash to make whatever arrangements are necessary and get them out of here as soon as possible."

Clarisse got to her feet and sauntered over to the dazed-looking woman who was lucky that a language barrier was the only reason she'd dodged a mindfuck bullet. The vampire took her arm and led her out. The other vampires were also drawing the other humans away, probably to their own rooms. Most of the people were looking confused, but a few were licking their lips and clinging to their new vampire hosts in a way that made me awfully uncomfortable. All traces of fear radiating off of them were gone.

That was the worst thing—their choices had been taken from them, all because they'd been made victims of a madman. What bothered me more was that, even though it frightened and disgusted me, I had an inkling of why twisting their thoughts and wiping their memories had been necessary.

"Neat trick," said Gideon, who had been watching these goings-on with avid interest. "Teach it to me sometime?"

"If you become one of us, perhaps," Royce said.

Now *that* was curious. Unless there was some sarcasm in that statement I couldn't detect, I hadn't known magi or their ilk could be turned into vampires.

That new train of thought derailed at the station when I realized Royce was looking down at me again. His black eyes glittered like glass, reflecting none of the thoughts that must have been roiling in his head. With a start, I dropped my gaze and bit my lip, clenching my hands into fists in my lap so he wouldn't see my fingers shaking.

I hadn't given any thought to what kind of position I must have put him in by bringing those people here, or what it would mean for the vampire community if word got out to the mundane world what Max had been doing.

Aside from the obvious—so many innocent lives lost—the problems that Max had caused with his murder sprce in one of Royce's clubs had been numerous and lasting. Even though it had been proven Royce and the vampires of New York had nothing to do with it, they were often blamed for the deaths. Even my name had come up in connection with it a few times. Within weeks, there had been a couple of states that passed emergency bills allowing wholesale hunting of vampires. Last I heard, those laws were being reviewed in the Supreme Court, but many vampires, and even people who dressed too Goth for the tastes of those with a need to take out their fears on any convenient target, had died. I couldn't imagine how much worse things would get if word about Max's activities somehow leaked to the press.

What made me feel sicker yet was the realization that I was thinking more in terms of protecting my friends than to look out for the best interests of Max's other victims. They had not chosen to be part of that slave ring, I was sure. They all must have had friends and families that they would want to return to. But if they signed the contracts, then at some point they *could* return to their former lives—albeit with some changes—and no one would be the wiser as to what had been going on.

No one but me and the Others who had been involved in shutting Max's operations down.

That sent a brief pang of alarm through me. Was

Royce going to make me forget, too? I didn't have the charm or Other blood anymore. I had no way to stop him if he wanted to alter my memories. I wouldn't even know if he did it.

My fingers crept to the scar on my hip, and I couldn't help but blanch remembering what Max had told me. *"I'm going to do something to remind you of your place and ensure you never forget the time you spend with me, however long you may live."* Maybe, in some twisted way, Max had known it would come to this. His own sick, perverted version of looking out for me. Even if the specifics were wiped away, I would always have a reminder etched into my skin that I was no better than some prize horse or cattle.

Even worse than that, I was a traitor to my own kind. I did nothing to step in to stop the vampires from wiping the memories of captivity from these peoples' minds. I did nothing to stop them from walking right into another form of slavery. Even if these other vampires were nowhere near as cruel or heartless as Max, these people would never again have a chance at regaining their free will.

Royce had saved these peoples' lives, and mine. Those who could safely go back to their homes and families without risk were being given that option. Only the ones who were unlucky enough to bear scars couldn't be trusted to be released out of the spheres of vampiric influence. Not yet.

Inevitably, if they did go free, someone would see the damage. Question it. Report it. The thought of Royce, or Clarisse, Angus, Ken, Wesley, or any of the other vampires I had met, who had helped or watched over me at one time or another, being hunted or killed for a crime they didn't commit was why I stayed silent.

And that decision would haunt me for the rest of my life.

Chapter Thirty-One

Royce's touch, a light brush of the back of his fingers over my cheek, was surprisingly reassuring. Considering our proximity, he must have picked up on my fears and doubts. The part of me that was still in a semi-panic about having my memories wiped was being buried under the fierce need to be comforted. Of course he would know just what to do to make me feel better.

Not that I would do the stupid thing and look him in the eyes anytime soon, but far be it from me to push the guy away if he was going to kiss away my fears. Considering how I felt like such a shit for sitting back and doing nothing while the vampires used their black enchants to bend those people to their will, anything that might make me feel a little less like the worst person in the world would have been welcome right then.

I reached up to clutch his fingers before he could pull away, needing his skin against mine to have something to focus on other than my own cowardice.

There had to be something I hadn't thought of that could improve the situation for those people. Some better solution than sending them from one cage straight to another. If not for his reassuring touch, I might have given in to the overwhelming urge to fall apart and let my many failures destroy me.

"Try not to worry. Things aren't as dire for them as you think," Royce said, his thumb brushing back and forth along my jaw as I held his knuckles to my cheek.

Voice thick, I pulled back to rub the building moisture from my eyes. "Are you kidding? That was a horrible thing you did to those people. And I just sat here and let it happen."

He knelt down in front of me, his hand staying pressed to my cheek, the other settling on my knee. Though I made an effort to focus on his chin instead of his eyes, I could feel the draw of his gaze pulling at me. Determined not to fall into the same trap as the other girls, I scowled and shut my eyes.

"If you had even a fraction of the experience I have had with such things," he said, "you would wonder at my mercy. Thank your influence for that. Before that unfortunate incident with the sorcerer, I would have taken them as spoils and sold them to the highest bidder to recoup my costs for retrieving what is rightfully mine."

I gasped. My eyes popped open and I pushed his hand away from my face. While I knew he had the capacity to be callous, that was a bit much to hear, particularly on the heels of his latest actions.

Not to mention being reminded of how I had

become contracted to him, about the times he had been under a crazy magic user's influence and tried to kill me, was totally unexpected. He rarely, if ever, brought it up. Neither of us did considering how terrible the circumstances were behind how we met. Until now, it had been nothing but a bad memory that lingered between us like a fart in an elevator; noticed, but politely ignored and unremarked. Using it as a way to make me accept twisting the minds and hearts of innocent people wasn't doing him any favors, that was for sure.

His fingers snaked around my wrist, keeping me from pulling away as he continued.

"Since you had no way of knowing otherwise, perhaps it will ease your conscience to know that the bargain I struck with those other vampires in return for their aid requires these additions to their food supply to be temporary. They are bound by the terms of our agreement to offer the opportunity for the humans to dissolve the contracts and return to their families after a suitable length of time passes for any scarring to be explained away."

My jaw dropped. "Are you serious? Why didn't you say something sooner?"

"I'll admit," he said, a ghost of that familiar, teasing smile returning, "I wanted to see if you could stand by to let me do what was necessary without interfering. You doubted and you disagreed, but you recognized the danger and let me do what needed to be done. Call it a test of sorts."

I hit him as best I could, which hurt like hell since it was the wrist I had sprained in the fight against

Max. He didn't budge, though it did put a crease in his otherwise immaculate shirt. "You asshole!"

"One who saved your life. Perhaps a thank you is in order, hmm?"

"Fine. Thank you, *asshole*."

Gideon gave my shoulder a companionable pat, making me jump. I had forgotten he was there. "Cheer up, buttercup. He's just getting you ready for the lifetimes ahead of hard choices."

Royce gave him a withering look that would have sent me running had I been the one at the receiving end. The necromancer shrugged and leaned his butt against the arm of the chair, invading my personal space and giving no sign that he was picking up the ahem-private-conversation-is-supposed-to-be-private vibes we were giving him.

"Perhaps," the vampire said once it became clear Gideon wasn't getting the hint, his tones silky and dangerous, "you should consider occupying yourself elsewhere until I am ready to deal with you."

Gideon shrugged. "I'm not about to wander around a vampire's den without being introduced to the household first. Your people will either tear me to shreds or force me to defend myself in ways that will get me into trouble. I'll keep my ass planted right here, if you don't mind."

As a born and bred New Yorker, I've honed my skills to a fine art at saying "fuck you" with no more than a look. Gideon ignored my sour expression as he put an arm around my shoulder and turned a pointed look on the vampire. I wrinkled my nose even more when I got a good whiff of him. Ugh, he needed another shower something awful. Airport smells did nothing to improve his natural odor of preservative chemicals with a heaping side of dead things.

Royce frowned, but gave a sharp nod, rising and pulling a slim cell phone from his back pocket. He tapped out a text message, waited a few moments for a reply, and then put the phone back in his pocket. With that, he returned his attention to the necromancer draping himself over me.

"One of my progeny will be along in a moment to show you to a room."

"Great," Gideon replied with a notable lack of enthusiasm. "So when are we going to discuss the terms of my employment? My ex-lover isn't going to be too thrilled with me for my part in killing his sire or running off without a good-bye kiss."

Royce stilled. Though I might have missed it if I hadn't been watching his features so carefully, there was a flicker of something I hadn't expected there.

Sorrow.

It was gone before I could be certain that I had seen it. His tone remained brusque and nonchalant, with a light garnish of irritation on the side. "Max was a fool without vision if he thought he could control someone of your power. I am under no such illusions. Your presence here requires some preparation, so you'll forgive me for taking the time to make the appropriate adjustments to my security before I commit to assigning you a detail or any responsibilities."

Gideon tugged one of my curls, frowning at the

vampire as he directed his question to me. "Does he always talk like that?"

"When he doesn't want to make a promise he can't keep, yeah," I replied.

"Or he thinks he can't trust who he's dealing with," another cheerful voice added. Gideon and I both twisted around to see Ken sauntering our way, his blond hair slicked back and his pinstripe suit immaculately pressed. "Hope I'm not interrupting."

Royce shook his head, reaching out to stop Ken before he could shake the necromancer's offered hand. "Careful, now. Ken, this is Gideon. Gideon, this is Ken Alcantra, one of my progeny and the managing director of my nightclubs."

Ken's bright blue eyes widened, then briefly flickered with a red light. Whether from excitement or fear, I couldn't tell. "The necromancer? I'll be damned."

Gideon withdrew the hand he'd offered, slumping against me like he'd meant to do it all along. I scowled at him and poked him in the chest, but he didn't take the hint.

"Ken, since you're at loose ends until the clubs are restored, I'd like for you to show Gideon around and make him feel welcome."

"Are you sure that's . . ." Ken trailed off, and this time I was sure it was fear that did it. He knew the danger Gideon represented to him, but he also had to know that finishing that sentence could end very badly for him.

Gideon batted his lashes, doing a spectacular job

of failing to appear innocent. "I promise I won't misbehave. Not unless you want me to."

Royce lifted a hand to rub his eyes. Mine had rolled so far that I could see the back of my skull.

Ken, on the other hand, flashed his fangs. "I'm not afraid of you. Touch me and I'll finish whatever someone else started on your neck there."

"Nice. Real nice. Hey, masturbating is supposed to relieve stress, so how about you go fuck yourself and come back when you feel better? Give me the grand tour when you aren't about to piss yourself."

"Ken, Gideon," Royce cut in, voice sharp, "that's enough. This is my home, and you will be civil."

A bit of red brought some color into the blond vampire's paper-white skin, right at the height of his razor-sharp cheekbones. Huh. Who knew vampires could blush?

"Right. Sorry."

Gideon rose, giving my shoulder another pat before offering his hand—the one without the tattoo—to Ken. "I'm sorry, too. Sometimes I let my mouth run. Let's start over, shall we?"

Though reluctant, at Royce's nod, Ken accepted and shook Gideon's hand. The set of his shoulders eased once it became clear the necromancer wasn't doing it in an effort to bespell him.

Before Ken could lead him away, Royce spoke up. "There is one other matter that needs to be attended to before you go."

Gideon tilted his head as he was addressed, a flicker of fear passing through the necromancer's eyes when he saw the intensity of the older vampire's gaze. "You can't twist my thoughts like those sheeple."

"No, I can't. Not that I have any desire to do such a thing. But you did agree to be bound."

The necromancer took an involuntary step back, hunching his shoulders and bowing his head. It was odd, but just then it struck me how very young he looked, like a scared and lonely teenager. I had thought he must have been ageless, like the vampires, but maybe he was younger than I thought and hid his lack of experience behind bravado. Whatever pangs of concern I might have had for him didn't matter. I didn't trust him to behave himself without someone *making* him do it, so I wasn't about to interfere. The bond and Royce's influence were probably the only reason he was going to let Sara go.

"When the bond is set, it will free you from your ties to Fabian. As long as you uphold your end of the bargain, you have my word I will keep you safe."

Gideon took a shaky breath to steady himself, then lifted his gaze. With a visible effort, he lowered his arms to his side and squared his shoulders, nodding as he forced himself to put on a brave face. He chose his fate. Circumstances might have brought him to a terrible place, but he was strong—stronger than I had been when in his shoes—and Royce would never be so cruel to him as he had been to Sara.

Remembering what he had done to her made it a lot easier to ignore any lingering apprehension I might have harbored for his safety and well-being.

Royce lifted his free hand to his mouth, using a fang to slash a crimson streak on his thumb. He then held the small wound out to Gideon.

The necromancer leaned in to lick the thin line of blood, doing his best not to touch any more of Royce than he had to. He grimaced as he swallowed, then made a gagging noise, swiping his mouth with the back of his hand.

"I'll never get used to that."

Royce chuckled in a way that made my skin crawl. "Give it time. You'll develop a taste for it soon enough."

Already the blood was visibly at work in Gideon, his eyes taking on a feverish glow that had nothing to do with his inner spark. He sidled closer, studying the vampire with the kind of lustful, appraising gaze that made my muscles twitch with the desire to put myself between them.

Jealous? Me? Perish the thought.

Royce laughed again, a bit more heartily this time, before turning to scoop me up into his arms. Though Gideon hardly seemed to notice that the vampire wasn't paying him any mind, still staring fixedly at Royce's face like he could will the vampire's attention on himself, I gave a little shriek at the unexpectedness of being picked up. He buried his nose against my throat, breathing deep, making me squirm and pull at his hair to make him stop.

He did pull back, though his puzzled expression threw me for a loop. Whatever might have been bothering him, he didn't say anything about it, instead returning his attention to the necromancer eagerly awaiting a command.

"It would please me greatly for you to take on the task of guarding Ms. Waynest when I am unavailable to do it myself. Will you do that for me?"

Gideon nodded, still staring at Royce without blinking. It was reaching the point of creepy with a side of stalkerish. I vividly remembered how that blood-fueled obsession felt, so I didn't hold it against him, but it still made me feel better to slide a possessive arm around Royce's neck. Ken, on the other hand, was watching all this with some trepidation. He was probably wondering if Royce's blood would keep the necromancer from doing anything rash, like turning the younger vampire into a puppet at some inopportune moment.

"Good. Ken will get you a meal and direct you to a place to sleep. Let him know what supplies you'll need to remove the familiar bond from Ms. Halloway tomorrow, and get some rest."

Though Gideon made no effort to hide his disappointment, he did as he was told. Shoulders slumped, he kept half an eye on Royce as Ken led him to the door that everyone else had left out of earlier. And walked into the frame.

I flinched on Gideon's behalf, even though he barely seemed to notice, adjusting his course and slinking out of the room in Ken's wake. Poor bastard. For the couple of days that followed, he'd be pining for Royce's next command something awful, finding as many excuses as he could to put himself in the presence of the vampire. Hoping for a look, a touch, a word of praise—anything that acknowledged his existence and gave him a reason for living.

He may not have deserved it, but in that moment, he had my pity.

Chapter Thirty-Two

Royce's lips grazed my temple, a cold breath raising the tiny hairs on the back of my neck. "Now that we're alone, care to explain how you managed to cure the infection in your blood?"

I frowned up at him. "Really? That's the first thing you want to ask me about?"

"Far from it, but at the moment I consider it the most pressing issue."

He grinned, wide and deliberate, so there was no way I could miss the extended fangs inches from my neck. Suppressing a shiver, I huffed and poked his chest. "Mister, you are about two seconds away from being banished to the couch. Or me banishing myself there, since this is your house," I amended. "Or where you're staying. Whatever."

"Really? You don't want to spend a single night with me to catch up for all that time we were apart?"

"Well, when you put it that way . . ."

With another laugh, he started walking toward a hallway I hadn't noticed at the far end of the room, carrying me with him. "I thought so. Now, care to answer my question? You smell . . . different. Like you did when I first met you. It's been teasing at me all night but I didn't want to bring it up in front of the others. Tell me—what happened?"

That sobered me. I bowed my head, not wanting to look at him while I talked about this. "You remember the Other I told you about? The collared one? She healed me. In exchange, I made a promise to return something of hers to someone she called the Sleeper."

"The Sleeper? Did she give it any other name?"

I shook my head. "No. I know it's a woman. Or female, whatever it is. If you don't know where I can find her, maybe Arnold will."

Royce said nothing, considering this for a time as he navigated the twists and turns of the hallway. At the end of it, he typed a code into a keypad, and a heavy oak door swung open, revealing a stairwell going down. It gave me a bit of vertigo as he carried me down the stairs, so I shut my eyes, suppressing what I knew was a completely irrational worry about being dropped, and a deeper anxiety about being trapped.

Once we reached the bottom, I cracked open an eye, then both, taking in the splendor. It was like a hotel suite. A really posh, nicely appointed, underground hotel suite. There were no windows, but the huge TV hanging on one wall and artwork strategically placed elsewhere made it easy to forget. Unlike upstairs, the furniture here was overstuffed, plush and inviting. Still tasteful, still expensive, but more for everyday use than simple looks.

Being underground again sent a fearful pang through me, but these circumstances were different. So very different. If only my screaming instincts believed that.

Perhaps sensing my growing apprehension, Royce stopped, waiting until I looked up at him to speak. His voice was low, soothing, and he must have been messing with my head because the urge to fight my way out of his arms to flee faded far too quickly. "You are safe. No one can reach you here."

"You really need to stop that," I scolded, though there wasn't any heat to it.

He nodded, but it didn't stop him from exerting enough control over me to keep me from giving in to the looming panic attack. The worry was still there, but it had lost its substance, like I was separated from it by a great distance. Once he reached his bedroom, he set me down, hands settling on my waist as he leaned in to press a light kiss to my forehead.

"I'll try to contain myself. And I'm sorry to ask, but I want to make sure the infection is gone and see what else may have changed. I know you trusted Iana, but I would like to be certain. May I?"

Another pang of terror gave me a jolt, but if it meant being sure, I would let him do whatever was necessary. Closing my eyes tight, I nodded.

He drew me close, lips brushing over my cheek until he reached my own, settling into a slow, sensuous kiss that did a great job of taking my mind off what was coming. Clutching his shoulders, I leaned into him, doing my best to forget every last iota of regret and fear and shame that had been haunting me these last few weeks. One of his hands settled at my lower back, the other rubbing lightly up and down my spine.

Once the worst of the tension eased out of my shoulders, he pulled back just a bit, whispering against my lips. "Just a taste. Relax."

He dipped his head to reach my neck, and I shivered at the delicious stroke of his tongue over my pulse point, pressing closer to him. Though I should have been afraid, even though I knew what he was about to do, my knees still turned to jelly as hot desire burned through my veins.

He nipped my throat, and after a light pinch, the toe-curling pleasure of his bite washed over me. It didn't last very long, though my interest in tearing his clothes off skyrocketed in the brief time he sucked my blood. Every swipe of his tongue, every stroke of his fingers, every minute bit of pressure he put on my skin, all made my need to drag him to the bed grow nigh unbearable.

A cold, shuddering breath against my hypersensitive throat dragged a moan out of me.

"You," he said, voice thick with desire, "are a modern miracle. The infection is gone. Your blood is clean. And I'll be damned if you don't taste delicious. Better than I remember."

"Alec," I panted against his skin, grabbing a fistful of his shirt and dragging him closer, "shut the fuck up and kiss me."

His laugh rumbled in his chest, vibrating against my skin as he obliged me. He canted his head to one side and his lips slanted over mine, possessive and tasting of salty copper. As my arms slid around his neck, his hands cupped my ass, pulling me up until I was forced to wrap my legs around his waist for balance.

He carried me to the bedroom, easing me down to my feet again. Once I let him go—however reluctantly—he pulled back so he could start taking off my clothes.

A touch of fright returned, but it didn't last long. Once the fabric was in a pile, forgotten by the side of the bed, he reached for my wrist to place my hand on the buttons near his shirt collar. I got the idea quick enough, returning the favor with shaking fingers.

Then a better idea struck, one I'd had earlier, and I inched forward. Gripping his shirt, I pulled him a bit closer and leaned in to bite the buttons off, one by one, working my way down. A pleased growl and his hands buried in my hair made it clear that he liked my plan. Very much.

The moment the last one was gone, he growled out a husky command.

"On the bed. Now."

The deep rumble of his voice slid over my skin like a touch, making me shiver. I hurried over, feeling his eyes on me as I swung my legs up and sank into the feather-soft mattress. It was a little unexpected after my last experience in his bed—or, more accurately, his hard-as-a-rock futon—but not unappreciated.

He was still undressing, taking his time. Shrugging out of the gaping, buttonless shirt, he tossed it onto the growing pile on the floor, soon followed by his pants and boxers. When I met his gaze from across the room, I didn't flinch from the embers of red in the depths of his eyes, hinting at the animal hunger inside. Once the last piece of clothing was gone, discarded and forgotten in a pile on the floor, he stalked over to me, magnificently naked.

Like me, he was flawed, his skin crisscrossed with scars. On me, it was a train wreck. On him, it was a brutal reminder of the savage life he had lived, first as a slave, then later forced to become a soldier in the army Alexander the Great led on to conquer Greece, Egypt, and the Persian Empire. There was something primal and sexy about those marks from failed attempts on his life etched all over his body. Dangerous. Hinting at the contained violence he was capable of unleashing.

He pulled me to him in a quick, demanding kiss, fingers tangling in my hair to hold me in place. Not that I would have pulled away, but the possessiveness of it sent a brief pang of anxiety through me. It was more remembered brutality from Max rather than fear of Royce, but he must have sensed something. He withdrew, eyes narrowing as he looked me over, head to toe. A few cuts, a few bruises, and, oh, let us not forget the shiny new scar from the brand on my hip.

With one hand buried in the curls on my head,

he slid a fingertip from the other hand over the brand, tracing the pattern there as the red in his eyes grew. There was a hint of fang behind his words, though his voice remained steady.

"Lifetimes would not be enough time for me to express how sorry I am. If I had any inkling—"

I put a fingertip to his lips, cutting him off. "Don't. This was Max's doing. Not yours."

His teeth grazed my skin, lightly nipping the digit I'd shushed him with. "I should never have sent you away."

"Regrets won't change it, Alec. It's done. He's dead. I'm not going anywhere."

Those seeking lips and teeth grazed my skin, working their way along my shoulder and collarbone, finding the familiar spot that nearly made me come off the bed. Panting, I lay back as he crept over me, slow and deliberate, refamiliarizing himself with all the places that made me burn for him. It would have been terrifying if it wasn't so damned sexy.

As much as I wanted to forget about Max, my desire waxed and waned as flashes of memories of where the psycho fucker had touched and bruised and scarred me popped into my head every time Royce inadvertently brushed against the marks left behind. Which was unspeakably frustrating considering how badly I needed to forget and how much I wanted to live in the moment.

With a low sigh, Royce stopped what he was doing and adjusted his position. Once he was situated on his elbows above me, for the first time, I noticed the lines of sorrow and regret etched in his face. I placed a hand lightly against his cheek, my thumb stroking the crinkles by his eyes.

"Alec, I'm sorry, too," I said, cutting him off before he could speak. Both of his brows shot up, some of the concern fading. "If it wasn't for a bunch of stupid, terrible decisions on my part, none of this would have happened. I'm sorry you're always cleaning up after my messes. I'm sorry I'm a god-damn nutcase, and that you have to put up with me. I wish I could just box up all my crazy and be a normal person and stop worrying all the damned time—but if I'm not worrying you're going to eat me, then I'm worrying you're going to mess with my head, or do something vampirey and evil, or wake up and realize that I'm nothing special. Even when I want to rip your clothes off—"

He leaned in, swallowing my ranty protests with a kiss. He kept it up until I stopped mumbling against his lips, then withdrew just enough to make sure he had my full attention.

"Shiarra, as much as I would like you to go on about that part involving ripping off my clothes, I don't want to hear any more of this business about me doing something to hurt or abandon you. Yes, sending you away was a terrible idea, but I wanted you safe from the White Hats, from the police, and from the war and the werewolves destroying my property. Not to mention a very selfish part of me hoped that the vampire blood in your veins would burn away the Were while you were away from the Sunstrikers' influence."

I squirmed a bit to get out from beneath him, moving closer to the headboard so I could grab a pillow to hug to my chest. He frowned, but didn't try to stop me, only edging closer so he could settle in the pillows beside me.

"I'm sorry," I said again. "I know we've been over this before, but my head is like a goddamn hamster wheel, spinning around the same crap over and over again. After what I just went through, it's even harder to let it go."

He set a hand on my upper thigh, lightly running his fingertips over my skin. His gaze stayed firmly focused on where his hand rested rather than looking me in the eye.

"Your worry is perfectly understandable. Had you not been taken by Max, it would still be forgivable for you to suffer some trepidation considering how little you know of me or my motivations."

That said, he tilted his head, studying my face as his hand on my leg stilled. The intensity of his depthless black gaze was a bit unnerving, truth be told.

"I want to be worthy of your trust. I want to earn it. You have no idea how pathetic I felt, sending you away, missing you and worrying that you wouldn't want to come back to me. Being afraid that you wouldn't miss me, too. Me, the Master of New York, pining like a fool," he said, with a bitter, self-deprecating laugh. "All these years spent building a kingdom around a reputation for being the most ruthless, unfeeling, vicious monster in the country, and all it took to rip away that mask was a scared little girl—a frightened mortal who is braver than she'll ever admit to herself or anyone else— reminding me of the value of freedom and mercy."

He slid his hand into mine, pulling it to his lips so he could brush a kiss over my knuckles. Speechless, I watched his actions, but didn't move, trying to process what he had to say.

"If you need more time, you need only say the word. You have tamed the savage beast, little hunter. I am yours to command."

Chapter Thirty-Three

I thought about it, considering the power that admission gave me over him.

"You know, I'm tired of being scared. I want to trust you. I don't want to be afraid of you. Not even a little bit. And I'll be damned if I'll let my fears or memories of someone else ruin my life. I guess what I'm getting at is just . . . be patient with me for a little bit longer while I get my shit together. Please."

He laughed, patting my leg. "So eloquent. Yes, I can be patient for you. Would you rather sleep alone tonight? I'll understand if you need more time."

I sat up straighter, clutching the pillow tighter as my gaze wandered over his sprawled, naked frame, lingering a bit too long at the unmistakable evidence of his arousal. He was all coiled grace and muscle, ready to spring into action if I gave him the word. Yet he was perfectly willing to leash that desire, just for me, to wait as long as I needed to get myself together. It wasn't fair to make him wait. Not to him, and not to me.

I wanted him. I wanted him so badly I ached. And I wasn't going to let the ghost of phobias past stop me from having him.

"Alec," I said, tossing the pillow aside so I could crawl on top of him, with a lot less grace than the vampire, "we're starting over. Right now. Right this minute. We're making this better. *I'm* making this better. I'm having my happily ever after, damn it, and if you stop me, so help me God, I will . . . I'll . . . I don't know what I'll do, but it won't be pretty."

This time, his laughter was a bit more hearty, and maybe a bit relieved. He rolled onto his back, his hands settling at my waist as he grinned up at me. "As my lady commands. By all means, have your way with me."

Last time we'd spent the night together, he had made it a point to get to know every part of me. Exploring every inch of my body, learning exactly where to touch me to make me into a quivering mess. Now, it was my turn.

I ran a finger down his chest, tracing the curvature of every scar, bone, and muscle, familiarizing myself with his skin. His own hands slid down to my ass, kneading lightly, but otherwise doing nothing to distract me from the task at hand. I got the idea he knew what I wanted.

He hissed softly when I leaned down and traced the same paths with my tongue. His grip on me tightened when I bit his nipple, my fingers tweaking the other, mimicking the light pinch of my teeth. His skin was cool and satiny under my touch, intriguing rather than putting me off.

"Naughty," he whispered, and I grinned, glancing up to waggle my brows at him. His laugh faded into a groan as I ground my hips against him to let him know he wasn't the only one turned on right now.

Inching my way down his body, I kissed and licked and nipped my way along the trail of dark hair leading to the juncture of his thighs. His fingers slid up my sides and along my ribs to tangle in my hair, and I'll admit I took a bit too much enjoyment being the one with the power this time around. This close, his scent, musky and male, made it easy to sink into the moment and forget about all the things that had me worried before.

Even an ancient vampire could only take so much. As his growl took on a deeper edge, his absent shifting growing impatient with the feel of my breath on the most sensitive of skin, I took him into my mouth. Like velvet ice, cool and slick against my tongue. His back arched, just a bit, the low sound he made filling me with a delicious warmth at knowing that I was the one responsible for dragging that reaction out of him.

Judging by the rhythmic way his fingers tightened by my scalp, he was enjoying the hell out of this. When I tilted my head just a bit so I could catch a glimpse of his face, the hint of vermillion in his eyes and carnal twist of his lips, exposing his fangs, sent a thrill down my spine.

When the muscles in his abdomen began to tighten, I gasped as I found myself on my back, him looming over me, no freaking clue how it had happened. He must have moved like lightning, shoving me into the bedding. His ragged—and entirely unnecessary—breathing told me better than anything else that I hadn't lost my touch.

"That," he said, breathless and lisping very slightly around fangs, "was delightful, but unless you wish to risk being bound again, best not to finish that way."

Once my heart worked its way out of my throat and back down in my chest where it belonged, I wrinkled my nose as the meaning of his words hit me. "Okay, ew. Talk about a mood killer."

He ducked his head between my neck and shoulder, nibbling at the skin there before his lips drifted up to whisper in my ear. "I'll just have to do something about that, won't I?"

I poked at his chest. "My turn, remember? Roll your ass over."

That gave him pause. He pulled back, probably checking to see if I meant it. With a growing smile, he did as I demanded, remaining obediently still as I moved to straddle him again.

Pausing before doing anything else, I frowned down at him. "Should you be wearing a condom? Am I going to—"

"No, sweet. It's only an issue if you swallow any fluids. An enzyme in your saliva keeps the virus from breaking down before it gets into the bloodstream.

Though if it worries you, I suppose I can send someone out to pick some up—"

"No! No, that's fine." My turn to cut him off. This was a subject I did not want to explore, now, or maybe ever. Cripes, I couldn't imagine the embarrassment of facing Mouse or Clarisse or whoever he would send out on that little errand. Besides, I trusted his word. If it were really a problem, then chances were after the last few times we'd had sex, I would have been permanently bound already. With a shrug, I shoved all those weird thoughts to the back of my mind, reached for him, and grinned. "Well then. Let's get this party started."

I took my time, enjoying the sensation of taking him in at my own pace. With my hands braced on his chest, I set the rhythm, the two of us moving together as instinct took over. It was slow and sweet and sensuous, everything I had hoped. Even when his fingers slid over the brand, adjusting the angle of my hips, it barely registered.

Though he had agreed it was my turn to run the show, he did slide a hand between us to help me reach my peak before he hit his. A shiver of pleasure had me throwing my head back, taking to a sensuous grind against him. There was nothing quite so intoxicating as the feel of him reaching the height of his pleasure beneath me, the way his muscles flexed and jerked, and the vibration of his pleased growl under my fingertips.

We didn't stop there, though our pace slowed, taking our time to revel in the feel of each other.

I'm not sure how long we spent entwined like that, touching, tasting, exploring each other in every way. It was sweet and glorious, a heady taste of the sensuality I had missed without the fear and pressure of being trapped beneath him. Maybe not as adrenaline-fueled as our last encounter, but it felt a hell of a lot better not to have that constant doubting voice in the back of my mind the whole time.

Once we both reached satiation for the third or fourth time, I collapsed over him, laughing at the mock-growl he gave me for stopping.

"I need a breather," I told him, rolling a bit to settle in the crook of his arm.

He leaned in to kiss my temple. "As you wish. I'll be ready for round two whenever you are."

"Jeez," I managed between snorting giggles, "I thought you could read my mind. I'm exhausted. Human stamina, not vampire, remember?"

"Despite appearances," he said, tone dry, "I am neither perfect nor psychic, and that kind of cavalier abuse of the bond isn't in my plans for you. Love is a powerful thing, but it does not change people into what you wish they would be."

I tilted my head up, staring at him. He cocked a brow, questioning.

He looked so damned *casual*. One arm behind his head, the other splayed against his bare chest, sheets rumpled and pillows strewn around like some surreal form of art. The unliving statue of an ancient Grecian god, deigning to meddle in mortal affairs.

I hadn't had the chance—or, being honest with myself, been brave enough—to ask him directly before now. The one time I had tried, he had used the blood bond to send me slinking back to Chaz without giving me a real answer to my fumbling, ham-handed attempt to get him to come clean about his feelings about me.

"Tell me, Royce. Please, no dancing around it. Do you love me? Really?"

He didn't hesitate. "Unconditionally. No one has fascinated me the way you do. All those contradictions, all those damaged pieces, all the running and the hiding—the chase told me a great deal about you I don't think you see. All those little things that add up to someone reckless and foolish and brave. Courageous and true to her friends. Beautiful in a way that this society rarely appreciates."

I swiped my palms over my eyes, sweeping away the building moisture there. "Brave? I don't know where you get that idea. I'm always running, reacting without thinking, hurting my friends, hurting myself—"

"Enough," he said, tone so sharp I was drawn out of my growing funk enough to look at him in surprise. "This is far too familiar ground. You hold yourself responsible for too much and cling to your flaws, real and imagined. Enough with the blame. Enough with feeling sorry for yourself. Give yourself some respect. You won't get it from anyone else until you do. You can waste years trying—but you will never find that magical 'good enough' until you find it in yourself to stand up and accept who you are without reservation or apology."

I had nothing to say to that. It stung how right he was.

The hurt was mostly realizing that one of the reasons I had fought so hard to face up to what I had become was that it meant letting go of my fear of Others. Of vampires. Acknowledging that my feelings for Royce went beyond that heady mix of horror and lust.

Well, not horror. Not anymore. Even if he still did things that scared me, what made me sweat and plastered my tongue to the roof of my mouth was the thought of letting go of all the excuses that shielded me from accepting that I wasn't the same person I used to be. That I might have more than just pantsfeelings for a blood-drinking creature of the night. That I was more than human, but still had my humanity.

He was quiet, watching me, probably waiting for the significance of what he said to sink in. Once I looked up from my hands and back to him, he continued, voice soft. Like he thought he might scare me back into being introspective and victimized, ready to find another excuse not to be in the moment if he wasn't careful.

I was done with that, but I wanted to hear what he had to say before I told him so.

"Most people, when they think of destruction, automatically assume it involves violence. Explosions, fire, and waste. You? The path of self-destruction you've been taking is a long road, a gradual wasting away, coming on silent cat's feet. You doubt yourself. Your humanity. Your ability to cope. You haven't taken note of what's been available to you or the opportunities you've let slip away because of this quiet path you've been walking.

"You will die if you continue on that road. Not because of me. Because you can't stop yourself from burning out, becoming a shell of who you are and who you could be. Don't do it to yourself, Shiarra. You're not a monster. No more than I am."

Says the vampire who's been around since before the coming of Christ. Somehow, I managed to bite my tongue long enough to keep from saying that out loud and came up with something a little less snarky.

"I hate how right you are. You always are. I'm not sure if I should be pissed at you for saying it or at myself for needing to hear it."

He gave me a close-lipped smile, and for once there wasn't anything sly about it. "Either way, it's better to be angry than resigned or afraid. It means you're getting stronger. Finding yourself instead of giving in." He leaned in, cupping my cheeks and kissing my brow. "I want you to live. No shame, no regrets, no blame. No more fear."

"No promises," I said, voice thick.

No. No promises. But from that point forward, I would do my best to be the greatest person I knew how to be. To find that thread of self-respect I used to hold so dear, to be brave and thoughtful and worthy of the words he used to describe me. To stop worrying so much about what he *might* do versus what he'd proved himself to be. A friend. I owed it to him. To Sara. To my family. All the people who loved me, even if they didn't accept me. Most of all, I owed it to myself.

It took a lot of hard knocks for the lesson to sink in. Sometimes being brave means letting go.

GREAT BOOKS,
GREAT SAVINGS!

When You Visit Our Website:
www.kensingtonbooks.com
You Can Save Money Off The Retail Price
Of Any Book You Purchase!

- **All Your Favorite Kensington Authors**
- **New Releases & Timeless Classics**
- **Overnight Shipping Available**
- **eBooks Available For Many Titles**
- **All Major Credit Cards Accepted**

Visit Us Today To Start Saving!
www.kensingtonbooks.com

All Orders Are Subject To Availability.
Shipping and Handling Charges Apply.
Offers and Prices Subject To Change Without Notice.

3 1133 06993 7276